"Hush," Chama said to Mary Elizabeth, his lips brushing her own to halt her flow of words and calm her. "You must sleep now."

But perversely, his lips against hers did not have the soothing reaction he'd intended. Instead, her pulse quickened. They were so close that she could see every detail of his face, even the small scar above his full, sensuous lips where he'd been wounded in a fight the year after she'd been taken captive. For some reason she felt the strangest desire to press her lips to his.

She lifted her face and kissed him gently. Excitement flowed through her, her heart beating wildly. She knew she should stop experimenting; but her curiosity was far from satisfied, and he seemed a willing partner.

When his lips left hers and roamed downward, they left a trail of fire across her neck, along her shoulder. . . . Her mind was a spinning whirlpool of desire, and she had no thought to object. She wanted more of the pleasure he was creating and gave no thought to tomorrow. She only knew that she wanted this man. More than anything in the world.

FIERY ROMANCE

CALIFORNIA CARESS (2771, $3.75)
by Rebecca Sinclair

Hope Bennett was determined to save her brother's life. And if that meant paying notorious gunslinger Drake Frazier to take his place in a fight, she'd barter her last gold nugget. But Hope soon discovered she'd have to give the handsome rattlesnake more than riches if she wanted his help. His improper demands infuriated her; even as she luxuriated in the tantalizing heat of his embrace, she refused to yield to her desires.

ARIZONA CAPTIVE (2718, $3.75)
by Laree Bryant

Logan Powers had always taken his role as a lady-killer very seriously and no woman was going to change that. Not even the breathtakingly beautiful Callie Nolan with her luxuriant black hair and startling blue eyes. Logan might have considered a lusty romp with her but it was apparent she was a lady, through and through. Hard as he tried, Logan couldn't resist wanting to take her warm slender body in his arms and hold her close to his heart forever.

DECEPTION'S EMBRACE (2720, $3.75)
by Jeanne Hansen

Terrified heiress Katrina Montgomery fled Memphis with what little she could carry and headed west, hiding in a freight car. By the time she reached Kansas City, she was feeling almost safe . . . until the handsomest man she'd ever seen entered the car and swept her into his embrace. She didn't know who he was or why he refused to let her go, but when she gazed into his eyes, she somehow knew she could trust him with her life . . . and her heart.

Available wherever paperbacks are sold, or order direct from the Publisher. Send cover price plus 50¢ per copy for mailing and handling to Zebra Books, Dept. 3132, 475 Park Avenue South, New York, N.Y. 10016. Residents of New York, New Jersey and Pennsylvania must include sales tax. DO NOT SEND CASH.

APACHE CAPTIVE
Betty Brooks

ZEBRA BOOKS
KENSINGTON PUBLISHING CORP.

ZEBRA BOOKS

are published by

Kensington Publishing Corp.
475 Park Avenue South
New York, NY 10016

Copyright © 1990 by Betty Brooks

First printing: September, 1990

Printed in the United States of America

This book is dedicated to Carrie Oletha Brooks.

Chapter One

Spring, 1838
Bent's Fort, Colorado Territory

The pounding of hooves jerked Mary Elizabeth awake.

Fear turned her body cold, and she swallowed around the swelling lump of panic clogging her throat as the sound of hoofbeats drew closer until finally they stopped outside the cabin at Bent's Fort.

The quick thud of boot heels against the plank floor told her that William Bent had also heard the visitor. Mary Elizabeth heard the grating of wood on wood as the bar slid back, then the groan of the front door opening. A moment later came the sound of male voices, barely distinguishable to her ears.

" . . . here," Bent was saying, "but I can't rightly do that . . . refuge . . . white woman."

The rapid beat of her heart escalated to the sound of a thousand drums in her ears as she listened intently, trying to identify the other voice.

7

But suddenly there was no need. Without warning, the bedroom door was flung open. Her eyes widened in terror as she stared at the man who filled the doorway.

"Chama!" she gasped, jerking upright in the bed.

He was taller than the average Apache, built like a wrestler, and yet, despite his size, he moved noiselessly across the room. The unrelenting quality in his features told her to expect no quarter from him as he held her gaze with glittering black eyes.

Holding the quilt tightly against her shoulders, she scrabbled against the far wall, trying to put as much distance between herself and the savage as possible.

She sensed that nothing in the room escaped his notice; even though his gaze never wavered from hers, he seemed aware of every detail of his surroundings.

A shudder of apprehension quivered through her body as he leaned over the bed, gripped her wrist with fingers of steel and slowly pulled her toward him.

Her eyes darted back and forth, searching frantically for help, but her vision was filled by the warrior and the bear claw necklace he wore against his massive chest. She struck out at him with her free hand but found it caught and held tight. He pulled her close against him, making her aware that the only thing separating them was the thin covering of her quilt and the buckskin breeches that encased his lean male hips.

Becoming aware of a movement behind him, her gaze flickered to the man who had followed the Indian into the room. For a moment hope flared to life, then just as quickly died, for she knew the trader, William Bent, was only one man. Even if he wanted to, he couldn't stop Chama.

Reluctantly, her gaze returned to the warrior.

"Soo . . ." he said harshly, drawing out the word. "You thought to escape me, to shame me in front of my people."

Although Mary Elizabeth was terrified, quaking inwardly, she made a visible effort to control her trembling. She would not let him see how frightened she was.

She wouldn't!

Her temples throbbed, and she closed her eyes against the pain, then quickly opened them again, realizing she was less vulnerable that way.

Swallowing convulsively, she steeled herself to hold his gaze and forced a steadiness she did not feel into her voice. "I will not return with you," she whispered in the Apache tongue.

His fingers tightened ruthlessly, and his voice was a menacing rumble when he spoke. "You will do as I say. Put on your clothing and make ready to travel."

Mary Elizabeth was conscious of her nakedness beneath the quilt she still clutched with fingers that had gone numb with dread. When she failed to move, Chama swiveled his head around and looked at William Bent. "Leave us," he ordered.

"No," Mary Elizabeth protested, falling back to her native tongue. Her eyes pleaded with Bent. "Don't leave me alone with him, please."

William Bent, whose name she'd heard even before she'd been taken by the Indians, was a man caught between two worlds. Married to a Cheyenne woman, he spoke most of the Indian tongues. He was judged a fair man, by the Indians as well as the whites. And even though she'd heard he respected the red man's beliefs,

9

surely he couldn't leave a woman of his own race in the hands of the Indians.

Bent studied her with a serious expression. "Chama said you belong to him. Is he speaking true? Did he pay the bride-price?"

"What if he did? It doesn't mean nothin'."

"It does to him," the man said. "He said you killed one of 'em. That true?"

In answer, she dropped her gaze to the floor.

"Guess that means you did," he said. "Guess everythin' he said is true. Shoulda known. Never known an Apache to lie." He fell silent for a long moment, then, uttering a heavy sigh, he said, "You go with him, miss. He's gonna try to help you."

"No!" she protested, struggling wildly against the man who held her captive. "You don't know him. Don't make me go!"

William Bent's gaze was full of pity. "You can't stay here," he said. "This is the first place they'll look for you. Your only chance is to go with him."

His words effectively stopped her struggles. Realizing he was right, helpless tears welled up into her eyes, threatening to overflow. *Stop it!* Mary Elizabeth silently told herself. *Tears won't do no good. You gotta keep your wits about you and wait for the right time.* Blinking rapidly to dry the moisture in her eyes, she watched Bent leave the room.

When the door closed behind Bent, Chama released her and picked up the deerskin dress that lay across the back of a chair. With a flick of the wrist, he tossed the garment on the bed.

"Put it on," he growled.

She looked at the dress, then up at him. Did he

10

mean to stay in the room while she dressed? "Wait outside," she muttered.

Something flared in his jet-black eyes. Leaning over the bed, he wrenched the quilt from her nerveless fingers and exposed her nakedness to his gaze.

Despair mingled with feelings of shame as she shrank away from him, her cheeks flushing brightly against her pale skin.

"You are a stupid girl," he said, yanking the dress from her and pulling it over her head. "Did you think to kill one of my tribesmen and escape punishment?"

"What will they do to me?" she asked.

"You will die if they find you."

She drew in a ragged breath. It was only what she had expected. She had lived with the Apaches long enough to know what happened to those who broke their laws.

Suddenly, something he'd said gave her pause.

You will die if they find you, he'd told her.

She looked at him, confusion flickering in her eyes. "You said, *if* they find me. Haven't they already done so?"

"No one knows of your presence here except myself," he muttered. "But the others will come soon. We must be gone before they do."

For a moment Mary Elizabeth wondered why he was helping her escape. Suddenly her eyes narrowed with suspicion. Was he only pretending to help her when, in fact, he was leading her into a trap? He wanted her for himself. She had known that long since. But at the moment, she had worse to fear than the loss of her virginity. She had her life to lose.

Slipping from the bed, she smoothed her dress over

11

her hips; but when she made to rise, dizziness assailed her, and she slumped back down on the mattress.

Images danced behind her eyelids, and she put a hand to the dark bruise on her forehead.

Chama made an impatient sound and knelt to put her moccasins on her feet. Then, half supporting her, he led her from the cabin to where William Bent waited beside two horses. One was a big gray stallion; the other she recognized as Chama's brown mare.

"Don't you be afraid, miss," the older man said. "You'll be okay. Chama gave me his word. It's them others you gotta look out for. Just stay with him and you'll be safe."

Safe. A word she no longer understood. Her gaze dwelt on the man for a long moment; then, resigned to the knowledge that he could not help her, she silently mounted the gray stallion and followed Chama away from the fort.

They traveled for hours, headed toward the distant range of mountains called the Sangre de Cristos while the sun blazed hotly from above. The riding became more difficult as they encountered rough, broken canyon country where mescal and prickly pear thrived among scrub oak and mesquite. They took no time for resting, and Mary Elizabeth, still weak from the blow she'd received on her forehead, swayed in the saddle as the strain from the long ride began to tell on her.

Chama chose that moment to turn toward her. His eyes narrowed on her pale face, and he studied her features intently.

She swallowed hard as nausea swept over her. Raising a trembling hand, she pushed her fingers through the damp tendrils of hair curling wetly around her face. She was so hot . . . so thirsty . . . and she didn't know how much longer she could stay upright in the saddle.

As though he sensed her distress, the warrior pulled his mount up beside hers and offered her the water bag. Silently, she lifted the container to her mouth, allowing only a small amount of the tepid liquid to trickle down her throat before returning the bag to him.

"Where are we going?" she asked.

"To the mountains," he said gruffly.

"We are not going to your people?"

His features seemed to be chiseled in stone, and his voice was emotionless when he spoke. "We can never go back. Not if you are to live." Although his feelings were carefully hidden, she sensed an inward violence, as though a volcano simmered just below the surface of a calm lake where the slightest ripple in the water could cause it to erupt.

"Enough talk," he said, suddenly impatient with the short conversation. "We have a great distance to cover before night."

Mary Elizabeth's mind was in turmoil as they continued their journey. Questions tormented her. He said they were headed for the mountains. Why? She knew she had injured his pride by running away from him. And she knew he was angry over the death of Ten Bears. Was he planning to wreak his own vengeance on her? Or could his desire to possess her be so great that he was willing to become an outcast and live apart from his people for the rest of his life? If the question had been put to her last week, she would have said no. Now she was not so certain.

Night had fallen by the time they reached the foothills of the mountains. Mary Elizabeth felt grateful when the warrior pulled up his mount and informed her they would camp for the night.

She was aware of Chama's eyes on her as she skinned and cleaned the rabbit he had killed. Then, after skewering and placing the carcass over a fire, she sat back and watched it cook. The journey had left her exhausted, and she wanted nothing more than to sleep; but the glint in Chama's eyes disturbed her. Did it promise retribution for her escape? She didn't know, knew only that she must stay awake. In sleep she would be totally defenseless.

The meat sizzled, dripping juices on the fire and sending sparks shooting out into the surrounding darkness. Across from her, Chama's face took on a threatening glow in the reflection of the firelight.

When he spoke, his voice startled her. "The woman who heals, the one you call Johanna, left the village with you. What became of her?"

"I don't know," she said. "Johanna was with me when we got to the fort. She went in the cabin ahead of me. There was a man there . . . not William Bent, and Johanna seemed afraid of him. I think he made Johanna go with him."

"You did not see them leave?"

"No. Someone hit me on the back of the head. The next thing I remember is Hawkeye standing over me, demanding to know where his wife, Johanna, was."

"So Hawkeye is alive."

Since it was more a statement than a question,

Mary Elizabeth remained silent and watched Chama from beneath lowered lashes. He paid her little attention, seeming to be lost in his own thought, and that suited her just fine. She needed time to work out a plan, someway to escape from him. Although she wore no bonds, she realized any attempt to escape would be easily stopped.

"The meat has cooked long enough."

At his words, she jerked her head up. She had forgotten about their meal. After removing the meat from the fire, she handed him the greater portion and sat down with her own.

"Where are we going?" she asked.

"I do not know," he said. "I only know that we can never go back. My people must never find you, or they will seek revenge for the death of Ten Bears."

She sucked in a sharp breath, knowing what revenge would be sought. She had had plenty of occasion to see what happened to those who crossed the Apaches, had seen them tortured slowly until death had been welcomed.

"I didn't intend to kill Ten Bears," she said. "It just happened. He tried to stop Johanna and me from leaving."

"As he was instructed," Chama said. "It was by the chief's orders that he was left to guard She-Who-Heals." His eyes returned to the fire. "Ten Bears' woman and children will grieve long for him."

He bit into the chunk of meat, ripping it with his teeth, tearing at it savagely, and Mary Elizabeth shivered as though it were her flesh that he was devouring.

She swallowed hard, pushing down the knot that had formed in her throat. He didn't have to tell her that Ten Bears had a family. She knew it all too well. Hadn't she watched over the children, Meadow Lark and Green Grass? And didn't she already know that fatherless girl children served no purpose in a tribe? Now there would be no one to bring food to the lodge. Ten Bears' widow and daughters would have to depend on the charity of others for their survival.

But she refused to lower her eyes in shame. Instead she lifted her chin and stared at him with glittering blue eyes. "You can't blame me for that!" she snapped. "It was the only way we could leave. You talk about Ten Bears' family . . . well, I had a family too. Before the Apaches killed them!" Despite her efforts at control, her voice wobbled at the mention of her family. "And you think I should care about the people who butchered them and kept me prisoner for four years?"

"You were not a prisoner," he said, ignoring the rest of her tirade. "You were a daughter of the tribe. You were my chosen wife. How is this a prisoner?"

"I didn't want to be adopted into the tribe, and I don't want to be a wife. Especially not yours! You're part of it. Part of them that stole me!"

"I had no part in your capture," he reminded. "You were already at the village when I returned from a hunting trip."

"My sister was there too," she said in a choked voice.

He remained silent.

"Dammit! You have plenty to say for your people. Say something for my sister. Tell me the reason behind what they did to her!"

"We will not speak of it," he said abruptly, tearing another chunk from the rabbit hanging on the spit. "Eat. For it is late and soon we must sleep."

16

She wanted to refuse the food but knew it would be a meaningless and stupid gesture. She must eat in order to keep up her strength. One never knew what tomorrow would bring, and she had to be prepared for whatever came her way.

"Why did you run away?" he asked suddenly.

Her lips tightened into a thin line. After all she'd said, he could still ask that? Her expression was cold as she glared at him. "You know why. I won't be your wife. It's not in my plans to spend the rest of my life with a bunch of savages. My brother Jeb is still alive, and I'm going home to him." Jeb couldn't be dead. She had kept that hope alive for four years, holding on to it during her darkest moments. Sometimes it was all that had kept her going. "Jeb was working the fields when the attack came." Her chin lifted a degree higher. "I know he got away, and I aim to find him."

Chama's face was expressionless as he tossed the remains of the rabbit aside and wiped his hands on his buckskin breeches. "Your brother is dead," he said abruptly.

"No. He's not," she denied, glaring fiercely at him.

"It makes no difference. The bride-price has already been paid and accepted. You will be my wife."

"No!" she hissed. "I will be no wife to a savage. Not ever. If I take a husband, he will be of my own choosing, not some smelly Indian savage with no more brains than a banty rooster in the barnyard."

His dark eyes narrowed into slits. "You would do well to watch your tongue, woman. I have made allowances for your fear, but my patience draws to an end."

Mary Elizabeth opened her mouth to berate him, then thought better of it, realizing she had been courting danger with every insult she flung his way. And she knew the insults had been highly undeserved. It was well known that Chama had a habit of bathing daily whatever the weather. And the part about him having no brains was asinine. Chama was the best tracker the tribe had and the most knowledgeable. Her tirade had only made her feel like a child throwing a tantrum. She found the feeling uncomfortable, one she didn't like at all.

With a mumbled oath, Mary Elizabeth rose to her feet and crossed the clearing to where the needles from a tall pine tree covered the ground with a thick spongy carpet. She was aware of the warrior's gaze as she bent to the ground and raked the pine needles in a thick pile, and goose pimples broke out on her arms.

She had almost decided she had gathered enough needles for a bed when a blanket was tossed down on the mound.

Her head jerked up, and she saw Chama standing over her, a pleased expression on his face. Her eyes widened as her initial fears returned. What did he intend?

"Enough," he said. "The bed should be comfortable." His voice was imperious as he added, "You may prepare your own." Dropping down on the blanket, he looked up at her. "I wouldn't try to run away. You will need me to escape from my people." With that, he rolled himself in his blanket and turned his back on her.

Relief mingled with fury, and she glared at the warrior's back. She'd had no intention of giving the bed to him, but knowing words would be useless and could even result in her sharing it with him, she decided to keep her council. She would wait and bide her time.

But he had another think coming if he thought he had won the battle. The war wasn't over yet. In fact, it had just begun.

Chapter Two

Mary Elizabeth dropped the pail of water and stared in horror at the carnage before her.

There was blood everywhere. It covered Pa, who lay sprawled on the ground, his arms and legs angled awkwardly, a spear driven deep into his chest. His eyes, the same blue as her own, were open and staring . . . staring unseeingly up at the cobalt sky overhead.

And there was blood on Brother Caleb. It ran in bright red rivulets from a cut on his head as he fought silently with a war-painted savage.

And blood streamed from her mother's nose, dripping on her calico dress as she struggled with a savage who carried thirteen-year-old Melissa. Ma . . . who had her mouth open in a silent scream, her curly red hair tumbled loose from the ribbon that usually bound it, her brown eyes wild with anguish and hatred for the savages who had killed her husband and were taking her daughter.

Mary Elizabeth had seen all this before. Many times. But this time would be different. This time she wouldn't stand frozen, watching the scene with horror. This time she would help her mother and sister escape from the savages. She would save *them this time. She forced her limbs into motion, but two painted savages moved to block her path. Hands reached out, holding her captive, and she struggled desperately to free herself, continued to struggle with them . . .*

. . . until she woke abruptly.

Mary Elizabeth's lashes fluttered rapidly, and her breast rose and fell with her quickened breathing. Although beads of sweat coated her forehead, she felt incredibly cold and clutched the blanket tighter against her shivering body. Pushing herself to her elbows, she tried to pull her mind from the past and all its terror, from paint-slashed faces and hag-ridden dreams, knowing insanity lay in that direction.

In the beginning, the nightmare had haunted her every night, but as time had passed, it had come less and less, until she rarely had it anymore. Her conversation with Chama must have been responsible for the nightmare's return.

Chama!

She'd forgotten him!

Her gaze flew across the moonlit glade to the sleeping warrior. He was one of them . . . part of the tribe that had slaughtered her family. And although he had taken no part in the raid, it was only because he had been on a hunting trip with his brother.

If he had returned to the Apache encampment before Melissa died, would he have taken part in her ravishment?

Mary Elizabeth's blue eyes began to glitter. It was past time her sister was avenged.

Her gaze touched on the weapons which lay beside the sleeping warrior, then roamed farther, pausing on the horse hobbled near the patch of new spring grass.

21

The horses first, she told herself. *Just in case something goes wrong.*

Pushing back the blanket, she rose silently to her feet and crept toward the horses. She kept her eyes on the sleeping warrior as she freed the gray stallion and turned her attention to the mare.

Dry leaves rustled as Chama stirred in his bed, and Mary Elizabeth froze, waiting with bated breath for several long moments before her trembling fingers resumed their efforts to free the mare.

When the knot in the rawhide fell loose, she returned to the stallion, intent on leaving the camp as quickly as possible. She didn't see the stone, never knew it was there until her foot accidentally kicked it against a fallen log, resulting in a heavy thud that froze her in her tracks.

Chama was instantly awake. Springing to his feet with his knife in his hand, he swept the clearing with narrrowed eyes. His gaze fell on her and paused. "What are you doing?" he asked.

She swallowed hard, her mind frantically searching for an explanation that would allay his suspicions. Her gaze fell on the water container. "I — I was just going to fill the water bag at the spring," she said. "I d-didn't mean to wake you." Her fingernails left half-round moons in her palms as she waited to see if he would accept her explanation.

Apparently he did, for he turned away and began to roll up his blanket. Mary Elizabeth acted instantly, grabbing the rock and leaping toward the unsuspecting man. Some sixth sense must have alerted him, because his head swiveled toward her just before she struck him. Although he jerked aside at the last instant, he took a glancing blow that split the skin on his forehead and sent warm blood spurting from the wound.

Mary Elizabeth didn't wait around to assess the damage. She realized the advantage she had gained was only slight and ran fleetly to the gray stallion, bounding on its back and winding her trembling fingers through its coarse mane.

"Aa-iii-eee," she screamed, driving the mare before her as she urged the stallion away from the camp toward freedom.

The rhythmic motion of the stallion's steady climb served to lull Mary Elizabeth's mind as she followed a trail that wound through canyons of pines, across dry stream beds and upthrusting ridges on its way deeper into the mountains.

At mid-day, she stopped beside a narrow creek where the water ran swift and clear. Dismounting, she allowed her mount to drink its fill, then moved upstream a few feet where water eddied into small pools. There she knelt to drink.

After quenching her thirst, she cupped her hand, splashed the cooling liquid on her face, then sat back on her haunches and studied her reflection. Her skin was gold-bronzed, and her thick copper hair was confined in a long braid that hung across one shoulder. When she found her brother, would he recognize her? Four years was a long time, especially since the child had become a woman.

A breeze kicked up, blowing silky tendrils of hair around her face, causing the water to ripple and her reflection to waver. At the same moment, the wind wailed mournfully through the pines, seeming to issue a warning, and she shivered with apprehension.

Mary Elizabeth tried to tell herself she was being foolish as she mounted the stallion and went on her way. She had no need to fear. The four years she had spent with the Apaches had been put to good use. She had learned the ways of the forest, and whatever happened, she could take care of herself. Hadn't she outwitted Chama?

Even as the thought came, she wondered if she had really escaped him. She had no doubt he would follow if he was able; for to his way of thinking, she belonged to him, and he would not allow her to escape easily.

Her mount suddenly stopped, claiming Mary Elizabeth's attention. Only then did she realize the trail had become overgrown and was blocked by ivy-twined saplings. She would have to find another way through the forest.

Reining the stallion around, she eyed the verdant growth, searching for another trail. She had begun to think she would have to backtrack when she saw it — a narrow game trail that wound its way beneath a canopy of leaves.

An hour later she broke into a clearing and gazed upward at the sloping forest of pines, aspens, cottonwoods and blue spruce that painted the climbing landscape with a brush of vivid green. Without hesitation she rode toward them, feeling certain that somewhere on the other side of the mountain lay civilization. All she had to do was find her way across it.

Chama's need to find Fire Woman was all-consuming. He had never doubted his feelings for her, feelings that he'd had since the first moment he'd laid eyes on her. Perhaps at that time it had only been a need to protect the young girl who'd stared at him with a mixture of fear and defiance. But as the years had passed and she had matured, the need to possess her — to make her his in every sense — was a fire that burned brightly inside him, a flame that never died. He would give up anything, anyone — even his people — to make her his own.

When he came to the stream, he knelt beside it and studied the tracks she'd left. The sign was clear, seeming almost to mock him. Fire Woman had knelt there to drink from the stream, then had mounted the stallion and resumed her flight, making not the least effort to cover her trail.

Was she so certain she could escape him?

Or perhaps she was underestimating his ability to follow her tracks.

Then another possibility suddenly occurred to him. She might believe she had killed him with the stone. The thought caused his blood to run hot with anger, and his hands knotted into fists, his knuckles showing white. He had become an outcast from his tribe in order to save her life, and she had repaid him by trying to take his life. When he caught up with her, she would pay for her deceit. There was no way she could escape him, and she was a fool if she thought otherwise.

Chama knew his strengths, knew also that running was one of his greatest. He was an Apache warrior who had been trained from childhood as a long-distance runner. He knew how to deal with exhaustion, could cover eighty miles on foot in a twenty-four-hour period if need be, even in the roughest terrain. And he would follow her . . . follow her wherever she went. She would never escape from him. Never.

Fate seemed to be against Mary Elizabeth. By late afternoon the sun had disappeared, and ominous dark gray clouds filled the sky. Although the air had become noticeably colder, she had thought it was because of the higher elevation. Now she realized a storm was on the way, possibly a spring blizzard, and it was imperative that she find some kind of shelter before it struck.

Her breath had become visible in the chill air, and the cold had even begun to penetrate her body when she topped a rise and saw the cliff overhang. Beneath the rocks was a hole, large enough to shelter her. She headed for it and had nearly reached it when she saw the wispy clouds rising in the distance.

Smoke?

Curiosity drove her onward, over another rise. She stared in astonishment at the valley spread out before her. And nearer to hand was a little cabin that nestled beneath a stand of pines.

Hope surged through her breast as she realized the significance of the dwelling and of the smoke curling skyward from a stovepipe in the roof. It meant civilization . . . her own kind. She felt certain the cabin's occupants would help her.

She urged the stallion forward, feeling as though a heavy weight had left her shoulders. As she neared the cabin, a man stepped out the door, a rifle held loosely in the crook of his arm as he watched her approach.

He was a large man, unshaven and wearing buckskin breeches and shirt.

Mary Elizabeth drew the stallion up before the cabin, and the man's close-set eyes traveled over her doeskin-clad form, then narrowed in surprise as they touched on her fiery braids.

He nodded abruptly at her. "Thought you was a Injun fer a minute there. But thet red hair give you away." He spat a long stream of tobacco juice on the ground, then wiped his mouth with the back of his hand. "You travelin' by your lonesome?" At her nod, his eyes went past her and narrowed searchingly on the emptiness behind her before returning to meet her gaze. "What'cha doin' way up here on this mountain?"

The wind gusted, and she shivered with cold. "I escaped from the Apaches," she said. She wanted to dismount but sensed she should wait until invited to do so.

"Apaches around here?" His grip tightened on his rifle.

"No." At least she hoped not. "We was near Bent's Fort. William Bent gave me this horse, and I'm headed for New Mexico Territory. Them Apaches didn't get my brother Jeb. He'll be waitin' for me to come back."

Mary Elizabeth wished the man would hurry and satisfy himself that she meant him no harm. She was tired and cold, and she longed for the warmth to be found within the cabin and the food that she could smell cooking.

As though he was able to read her thoughts, a wide grin split the man's face. "Reckon you're hungry," he said. "Get down off thet horse. I was gonna dish up supper when I heered you comin'."

Gratefully, she slid from the horse.

27

"My name's Jess," he said, reaching for a rope hanging beside the door. "What do they call you?"

"Mary Elizabeth," she said. "My pa was Jake Abernathy." She watched Jess loop the rope over the stallion's head and fasten it to a pole.

"Thet's so he won't stray," Jess said. "I'll see he's took care of after we eat. Them 'paches thet took you kill the rest of your folks?"

She nodded her head. "But not Jeb," she said. "He was in the fields plowin'. He's been waitin' for me to come back." She had to keep repeating the words in order to believe them herself. They had to be true. Jeb must be alive. Anything else was unendurable.

"How long you been livin' with them Injuns?"

"Four years."

"Four years," he repeated. "Musta been hell fer you."

A lump filled her throat, and she swallowed hard. There was no need to speak. This man apparently understood her feelings. She smiled at him. He seemed kind. If she shut her eyes, she might even imagine it was her father speaking to her.

"Go on inside," Jess said. "Warm yourself by the fire. I got some mighty tasty stew on the stove."

Mary Elizabeth stepped into the small cabin and went directly to the stove. Heat radiated out from the iron stove, sending its warmth through her cold body. She seated herself on the stool Jess pushed toward her and allowed her gaze to roam the interior. A rough-hewn table and two benches occupied the center of the room. At first glance she saw no bed, then she realized the two wide planks fastened on the walls were let down at night to afford sleeping space. Her gaze fell on the pile of furs stacked in one corner, and she turned curious eyes on him.

"Are you a trapper?"

"Sure am." came the gruff reply. He nodded toward the pile of furs. "Been a mighty good season fer it too. Beavers and mink aplenty." He set a wooden bowl filled with stew in front of her and laid a spoon beside it. "Now eat up," he said heartily.

"You not having any?" she asked.

"Guess I'll just wait until Jim comes," he said. "He's my partner. Left out early this mornin' to run the trap lines. Reckon he's gonna be mighty hungry when he comes back. Fer more'n food too. But you go ahead and eat hearty. They's plenty more where thet come from. Ol' Jess ain't a bit stingy."

She didn't need any further urging. Picking up her spoon, she began to eat while the trapper sat across from her and studied her features.

"How old are you girl?" he asked abruptly.

"Sixteen," she answered, so intent on the food before her that she didn't notice the glint in his eyes.

"You say you been with them red devils fer four years?"

His close scrutiny was beginning to make her uneasy, but she told herself that naturally he would be curious. Her life with the Indians had made her needlessly suspicious. She would come to no harm here. After all, he was a white man, not a savage Indian.

"Now thets a plumb shame," he muttered. His dark eyes glittered as they studied her delicate features. "Them Injuns don't know how to treat a woman. It takes a white man to know what a woman likes."

She swallowed nervously. She didn't know what he was talking about, but she was beginning to think she would fare better outside. She had seen that same look in the eyes of men before, and it boded no good for the woman who was under view.

She concentrated on the food in front of her, scooping up the last bite and chewing it slowly. Then she looked at the man who watched her so closely.

"It was mighty nice of you to feed me," she said, rising from the table. "An' if you could spare a blanket . . . or one of them furs, I'd see you was paid when I find my brother."

"Now, you ain't figgerin' on leavin' right away," he said. "It's gonna storm out there. You'd likely freeze to death afore mornin' comes. Better you stay here in the cabin with Jim and me."

"That's mighty nice of you," she said, edging toward the door. "But my brother will be expectin' me."

"Thet brother o' your'n has waited four years, ain't he? I reckon if he's still alive he can wait a spell more."

"No," she said. "I gotta go now. I suppose if I keep headin' south —" she broke off as he stepped in front of her, blocking her path to the door.

"You ain't goin' nowhere," he growled, reaching out a hand and grasping her arm with tight fingers. "Jim and me, we ain't seen no woman, red or white, fer over four months now. I reckon you owe us fer thet meal you jist et."

Fear trailed icy fingers down her spine, and her eyes darted back and forth, searching for some means of protection. He yanked her hard against him and ground his mouth against hers.

Oh, God! she silently screamed.

His tongue worked at her mouth, forcing it open, and she bit down hard.

30

Muttering a string of curses, his hold slackened, and she was quick to take advantage, wresting herself from his grip and lunging for the rifle beside the door. Her trembling fingers fastened over the weapon, and she brought it up quickly and swung it like a club, striking him a glancing blow on the side of the head.

He reacted instantly, twisting the rifle from her grasp, and her mind registered the clatter of the weapon against the table even as he struck her a hard blow that sent her sprawling across the room. She landed with a heavy thud against the far wall, where she lay breathless, her senses reeling.

Then his heavy body was covering her own, pinning her beneath him. Hysteria fluttered in her throat as his head lowered, hovering inches above her. God! She wanted to cry and curse and babble out her fear, but she wouldn't give in to her hysteria. She wouldn't give in to her cowardly instincts. Instead, she opened her mouth and clamped her teeth together on the lobe of the trapper's ear.

He screamed out in pain as the coppery taste of blood filled her mouth. His fingers dug into her arms, and he shoved at her, trying to free himself.

Panic gave her strength, and she clenched her teeth, holding on to his ear while flailing out with her fists, striking his nose and face as she twisted and turned her head until she felt his flesh tear.

He let out a string of curses and yanked back his head, and Mary Elizabeth spat out the piece of flesh. Then, bringing up her knee, she struck him a devastating blow that left him moaning with pain while she leapt to her feet and made for the door.

But he wasn't done. His hand snaked out, and his

31

fingers wrapped around her ankle, pulling her up shortly beside the stove. She kicked out and connected with his shin, but his grip didn't loosen as she struggled to free herself.

When Mary Elizabeth's gaze found the coffeepot left warming on the back of the stove, she didn't hesitate. She sent the scalding liquid splashing over him.

With a roar of rage, he yanked on her ankle, sending a bolt of pain shooting through her leg even as she tumbled off balance and landed on the floor.

She lay in a heap, breathing heavily, as the trapper scrambled to his feet and stood before her, menace in every line of his body.

Mary Elizabeth could hardly believe this was happening to her. She had always thought all she had to do was find people of her own race and they would help her. But the man before her was every bit as savage as the Apaches.

Her frantic eyes darted to the closed door. Although it was only a few feet away, it might just as well have been a mile. Her gaze returned to the man who had stopped before her, and her muscles bunched as she waited for his next attack.

"You're gonna be sorry, bitch. By the time I get through with you, you're gonna wish you was dead."

She held his gaze, watching for the flicker that would give away his move. But when it came, she waited a moment too long. He lunged and made a grab for her, his fingers fastening in the neck of her dress. She tried to scrabble away, but he held on tightly while he grabbed her with the other hand and pulled her upright and then toward him.

She opened her mouth and screamed loudly, flailing

out with her arms and legs, pounding at him with her fists.

Suddenly there was a loud crash, and the door burst open.

Chapter Three

Chama's ebony gaze never moved from the trapper who dared to lay hands on his woman. He was aware of everything in the room, had noted every minute detail as he burst through the door, and the trapper's fate had been sealed by the torn dress and the crimson streak of blood trickling from a cut on Mary Elizabeth's mouth.

As for Jess, he remained motionless, his right hand raised threateningly above the bruised, trembling, white-faced girl, seeming to be captured in that moment of time when the warrior burst through the door, knife in hand.

The Apache's jaw thrust forward as hatred surged through him; a low growl of rage boiled up from deep inside, shattering the silence within the small cabin and sounding more deadly than the fiercest war cry.

"Release her!" Chama demanded, his black eyes glittering. "The woman is mine!"

Jess's gaze darted frantically, then fell on the iron skillet resting on the back of the stove. "Then, take her!" he roared, shoving the girl from him with such violence that she fell and struck her head against the table. Then he made a lunge for the iron skillet.

Chama reacted instantly, leaping across the room, his knife hand sweeping up with deadly intent.

Jess's fingers closed around the skillet and brought it up against Chama's arm, deflecting the blow that would have surely killed him. Instead of penetrating his chest, the knife blade sliced through the meaty portion of his arm, and he howled with pain as crimson beads wept through the cut, bubbling forth to form a vibrant slash that flowed down his arm and dripped through his stubby fingers.

Reaching out, he grasped Chama's wrists with powerful fingers, preventing another sweep of the knife while his frantic gaze searched the cabin for some means of defense against the warrior's wrath. Then he noticed the muzzleloader lying discarded on the floor, and his eyes flared with hope. His muscles tensed as he bunched them for the burst of strength that swept the warrior aside for the one moment it took him to leap for the weapon.

The trapper's knees struck the hard wooden floor with a heavy thud, and an expression of pain crossed his features as his fingers wrapped around the barrel of the rifle and swung the butt up toward the savage warrior.

But Chama wasn't to be so easily foiled. One glance at Mary Elizabeth's crumpled figure, and fresh rage surged forth in the form of an upward kick that sent the rifle clattering against the far wall and the trapper scuttling across the room, trying to put as much distance as possible between himself and the savage Apache. Undaunted, the warrior followed the trapper, intent on killing the man who had dared to lay hands on his woman.

The trapper's gaze found the open door, but Chama, correctly interpreting the other man's look, stood his ground, barring the trapper's path to the narrow opening that meant freedom.

"Now you will die like the dog you are!" Chama growled, his fingers tightening around the knife as he raised it toward the other man.

Jess retreated, his eyes narrowed on the warrior threatening him. The back of his knees struck a wooden stool. The grating of the heavy wood across the hard floor mingled with the harsh sound of their breathing as the trapper stepped around the obstruction and continued to back away from the fierce warrior.

Suddenly the man's gaze fell on the wooden stool. He reacted quickly, reaching out, and before Chama realized his intention, he had sent the wooden missile sailing across the room toward the warrior. Although Chama jerked aside, the stool connected with the side of his head, sending his senses reeling and leaving him momentarily stunned.

The trapper was quick to take advantage. Picking up the stool again, he brought it crashing down on Chama's knife hand. The blow numbed the warrior's fingers; he lost his grip on the knife, and it fell to the floor with a clatter.

As the trapper reached for the weapon, Chama recovered his senses and leapt to regain the knife. The two men collided on the floor and rolled across the room, coming to a stop against the far wall with the trapper on top of the warrior. The man's dark eyes glinted with triumph; his fingers closed around the Indian's throat, tightening, as he attempted to squeeze the breath from the warrior.

A crimson haze began to form around Chama, and his eyes darted around the room, searching for some kind of weapon to use against the larger man. The warrior's gaze fell on Mary Elizabeth, lying still on the floor, her fiery hair spread around her white face.

Did she still live?

The blood on her face served as a reminder to Chama of the fate she would suffer if he failed to kill the white trapper. Desperation lent him strength as his fingers clasped the other man's wrists and applied pressure, causing the trapper to concentrate on the pain. Then, using his last ounce of strength, he brought up his knee in a quick jerk and dealt the white man a savage blow that loosed his hands from the warrior's neck. Jess howled with pain and clutched his lower body.

Amidst the red haze of pain that clouded his vision, the warrior's fingers found the knife, and even while he drew in heavy gasps of breath, he positioned the weapon before him, pushed himself to his knees and sent the sharp blade deep into the trapper's chest.

Chama's breath came in painful gasps as he pulled the blade out and sent it plunging downward again. Again and again, he drove the blade into the other man's flesh, continuing to stab the trapper, barely aware of the spreading crimson stain that spurted from the wounds he inflicted until he was too exhausted to raise the knife again and slumped wearily on the floor, his breath rasping heavily in his swollen throat.

* * *

Mary Elizabeth's eyelashes fluttered as consciousness slowly returned. Something hard was digging into her back, and she rolled on to her side and groaned as hot pain stabbed at her temples.

Shifting her body, she groaned again, feeling as though every inch of her flesh were one large bruise.

Cautiously, she opened her eyes and stared up at the logs above her. Her eyes widened. Where was she? Certainly not in Three Toes' wickiup, the place where she'd spent the last four years.

Becoming aware of a harsh rasping sound beside her, she turned her head to locate the source of the noise. Her eyes widened as her gaze fell on the warrior who lay beside her.

Chama!

Her brow knitted with confusion. What had happened to her? Was Chama responsible for her bruised condition? Her silent question remained unanswered. Feeling completely puzzled, she studied the bright crimson flowing slowly from a cut on the warrior's face.

Had she inflicted his wounds?

Chama seemed totally unaware of her presence as he lay with eyes closed, body motionless except for the rise and fall of his chest as he breathed in and out.

Mary Elizabeth's puzzled gaze then traveled past the warrior, found the body of the trapper and fixed on the bloodstain on the front of his shirt. Suddenly, her memory returned, striking with the force of a hard blow.

The trapper had lured her into his cabin and attacked her. Chama had saved her life, and in doing so had killed the other man. Now he lay in an ever-widening pool of blood.

Shuddering, she looked at Chama again. Her stomach muscles tightened, and a curious feeling of regret surged through her as she raised herself on her elbows and stared down at him.

Was he mortally wounded?

As though in answer to her unspoken question, his dark eyes opened, and his gaze locked with hers.

She breathed in a harsh gasp that settled like a lump in her chest before it escaped with a rushing sigh. "How bad're you hurt?" she asked in a hoarse whisper.

His eyes glittered brightly, boring into hers. "The injury is nothing," he said. "You cannot escape me so easily. Have you not learned that?" He continued to stare at her, his ebony gaze probing deeply, as though to search out her innermost secrets.

Lowering her eyes, she said, "I owe you my thanks. He would have killed me."

"He wished more than your life," he said, pushing himself to a sitting position.

"I know," Mary Elizabeth admitted. "I imagined he would help me since we belong to the same race."

Chama's expression stretched into a bleak, tight-lipped smile as he rose slowly to his feet. "I offered you no harm," he said, "yet you sought to kill me and fled."

Guilt stabbed through her when he swayed unsteadily. She tried hard to summon up her anger against him . . . but couldn't. He was right. He'd done nothing to her, and she had caused him injury.

"Sit down," she said, her eyes on the bruises circling his neck. "I'll tend your wounds."

Although her words seemed to surprise him, he sat down on a stool beside the table.

The sun had long since set, and the shadows had lengthened, making it hard to see inside the cabin. Mary Elizabeth lit the lamp and, after placing it on the table, searched out linen to clean his wounds. The water in the tea kettle at the back of the stove was hot, and she poured some in a pan, placing it on the table. Then she wet her cloth and cleaned his wounds. "You are lucky," she said. "The wounds do not need stitches."

A howling in the distance caused her to jerk her head up. Her eyes met the warrior's. "Was that a wolf?" she asked.

"It was not the cry of a wolf," he told her. "It was a dog."

Her eyes went to the dead trapper. "Jess has a partner," she said. "He's been running trap lines."

It seemed they were of the same mind, for the warrior began to gather up his weapons while she reached for the musketloader and began a search for the powder and balls. A loud barking nearer to hand told her the intruders were coming closer, and her fingers fumbled as she poured black powder into the barrel and tamped it down. By the time the door swung open, she had braced herself against the table with the rifle while Chama had taken up position to the side.

The trapper was big, his buckskins stretched across his massive chest. His face was covered by dark hair, and his bulbous nose was reddened by the cold. Apparently the day had been good, for he held several pelts in one hand. The dog, a German shepherd, took one look at the girl holding the loaded gun, and a low growl erupted from its throat. "Easy," the trapper said. "She ain't meanin' us no harm. Ain't thet right, girl?"

"That depends on you," she said. "We had to kill

40

your partner."

His eyes flicked away from her, traveling around the room. Only then did he see the warrior, for the door had hidden him from view. He sucked in a harsh breath, and his body tensed. For a moment it seemed he would spring at the other man, but instead, his gaze moved to his fallen partner.

"Guess if you killed him you had a good reason. He never was no good. Figgered I'd have to kill him myself one of these days." He cleared his throat. "Why don't you set that rifle down, girl. I ain't gonna do you hurt. But I been out runnin' traps since early morn, an' I was sure lookin' forward to some hot food an' a warm fire when I got back here."

Indecision weighed heavily on her, and the man was quick to take advantage.

"I don't know what you an' the Indian're doin' here, but I'm willin' to share the place with you." He took a step, and the warrior's body tensed. The trapper stopped immediately, his gaze locked with the warrior's.

"Let him alone," she said in the Apache tongue. "He said he won't hurt us."

"I know what the white dog said," Chama growled in kind. "But I do not believe his words. Like all white men, he speaks with a forked tongue. It is better to kill him now. Then we do not have to worry about him."

"No," she said grimly. "That's the way of savages. Not my people."

"What's he sayin'?" the trapper asked.

"He wants to kill you," she answered.

The trapper's face was expressionless. "Reckon I'm gonna have to fight him?"

"No," she said. "Close the door. The cabin is getting colder." She shot a warning glance at Chama, wondering how he would react. Would she have to shoot him? Could she do it? She didn't know. He'd saved her life, but she still could not allow him to kill one of her people — not when they were not being threatened.

"Let's get ol' Jess outta here," the trapper said, moving across the room to bend over the dead body. "I cain't enjoy my supper with 'im layin' there like that." He took one of the man's arms and frowned. "Tell that Injun friend of you'rn to help me get 'im outside."

For some reason she didn't tell the trapper that Chama understood English — perhaps because she didn't quite trust him. "You heard him," she told Chama in the Apache tongue. When the warrior remained unresponsive, she turned back to the trapper. "He's not going to help you," she said, reverting to English. "But I don't mind doing it." She started toward the trapper and the dead man, but Chama reached out a hand, gripped her arm and pulled her back. "He's not going to let me help either," she stated. "Guess you'll have to do it by your lonesome."

The trapper's lips tightened, but he pulled the body across the floor and out the door. For a moment he seemed to hesitate, glancing out into the darkness, but as though aware of the watching warrior, he came back inside and shut the door. Although the German shepherd had remained motionless, its eyes had followed the trapper's every move.

"The dog belongs outside," Chama said in the Apache tongue.

"No," she denied, answering him in the same language. Reaching out, she stroked the dog's head.

42

"White men do not treat their dogs as the Apaches do. The dog stays in the cabin." The animal seemed to know they were talking about it. It licked her hand, then crossed to the stove and lay down on its stomach, but its eyes remained firmly fixed on them.

"You like my dog," the trapper said. "He ain't worth much 'cept for company. Are you Dawg?" He gestured toward the benches. "Seat yourself, girl, and help yourself to some food."

"I've already eaten," she said. "But I expect Chama's hungry." She waved the warrior toward a stool, and he sat down across from the white man, his eyes never leaving the trapper while Mary Elizabeth dished up two bowls of stew and placed them before the men.

"Take a seat anyways," the man said. "My name's Jim Coltrane. I hail from Missouri. What's yours and what're you doin' with the Injun?"

Perhaps because she still didn't quite trust the trapper, she chose not to reveal her relationship to the warrior. "I'm Mary Elizabeth Abernathy," she returned. "And Chama—" she looked at the warrior, then quickly away— "he's helping me find my way home."

"And where's that?" he asked.

"In the mountains a few miles from Taos."

"Well, you're headed that way," he said. "But you'll have to wait out the storm."

Mary Elizabeth nodded. "I know and counted myself lucky when I saw the smoke from your cabin— until your partner attacked me." Deciding enough had been said on the subject, her eyes went to the dog. "That's a mighty fine looking animal," she said. "What's his name?"

"Don't have no name," Jim said, his gaze going to

the German shepherd. "I just call him Dawg."

Taking a chunk of meat from the pot, she held it out toward the animal. "Are you hungry, Dawg?" she asked softly.

The dog lifted its head and whined softly. She moved slowly toward it and offered it the meat. Dawg took it gingerly from her hand and swallowed it down, then looked hopefully at her again. It was only then she noticed how thin the dog was, and she frowned. "Has he been sick?" she asked the trapper, smoothing her palm over the dog's rib cage.

"Not so's I'd notice," the man said.

Still frowning, she dished up a bowl of the warm stew and carried it to the animal.

"Hey," the trapper objected. "He don't need all that."

"He's hungry," she said. "Haven't you been feeding him?"

"Dawg's my business," the man growled, but he subsided when he saw the way the warrior was watching him . . . as though waiting for him to make a wrong move.

Mary Elizabeth watched as the dog ate the bowl of stew, cleaning the dish of every last bit. Then it licked her hand. She smiled and patted the animal on the head.

"Spoilin' 'im is what you're doing," Jim muttered. "Dawg don't need much to keep 'im goin'."

She paid him no attention, but sat beside the animal and stroked its head.

Finished with his meal, the trapper pushed his bowl aside and moved casually across the room. When he neared the rifle, Chama was on his feet immediately, his body tense and watchful.

"You better not touch the rifle," she said, her hand still stroking the dog. "Chama won't like it."

"Thought I'd clean it," the man said.

Mary Elizabeth lifted her head and met the trapper's gaze. "Don't touch it," she repeated.

The trapper frowned. "I need to go outside. Does he have a problem with that?"

"Do you?" she asked Chama, switching to the Apache tongue.

The warrior's dark eyes glittered. "The man is evil," he said, speaking in kind. "It would be better to kill him now."

She lifted her chin and glared defiantly at him. "No," she said. "Not unless he offers us harm."

For a moment she thought the warrior would refuse to listen. His mouth was thinned into a grim line, his jaw jutting forward, but with a low growl, he subsided. Coltrane, realizing he would be allowed to leave the dwelling, opened the door and went out into the snow.

Mary Elizabeth continued her stroking, and the dog continued to watch her. Only moments had passed when the dog's head came up to stare at the door. It opened abruptly, and she looked at the buckskin-clad man who filled the doorway. Her eyes widened as she noted the rifle he held, the barrel of which was pointed at the warrior.

She sucked in a sharp breath, and the man grinned. "Didn't know I had my rifle in the sled, did you?" he asked. "Now I'm callin' the shots." His lips lifted into a snarl, and his eyes narrowed into slits as he kept his gaze on the Apache warrior. "Stand back, girl, if'n you don't wanta get hurt," he growled. "They ain't nothin' gonna stop me from killin' that redskin."

"Listen to me," she snapped. "I said he's not to blame. Jess was trying to kill me."

The German shepherd's body tensed at her tone, and its gaze moved from the girl, to the trapper, then back to the girl again.

Coltrane's lips curled into a grin. "Reckon he had a good reason." His eyes glinted. "Now me, reckon I got some other ideas about you. But they'll wait 'til the redskin is dead. Won't be long from now. 'Cause I ain't in the habit of missin' what I shoot at."

Chama's hand touched hers warningly, and she met his gaze briefly. There was a waiting quality in his eyes, and she knew the warrior had something in mind, knew as well that Coltrane had misjudged the warrior's strength. It was a grave mistake. He would not find Chama so easy to kill. She was ready for the move when Chama pushed her aside and sprang at the other man. She landed with a heavy thud against the floor as an explosion blasted her ears, cracking like thunder, drowning out every other sound while the smolder of burning gun powder hung heavily in the air.

A low growl beside Mary Elizabeth warned her the dog was nearby, but her muscles refused to function as she lay breathless, watching the two men locked in combat. Another growl sent fear surging through her, but instead of attacking her, the German shepherd had taken a protective stance beside her, watching the two men with unwavering eyes.

She had little time to wonder at the dog's actions, for a second shot, followed by a heavy crash, caught her attention. Chama stood over the fallen trapper with a smoking rifle in his hand. He had obviously used Jess's weapon to kill his partner.

The warrior turned to look at her, and it was then she saw the blood seeping from a wound on his chest. He swayed unsteadily; then his knees buckled beneath him, and he fell to the floor.

Chapter Four

Mary Elizabeth's heart gave a lurch as she hurried to Chama's side and examined the wound. It was hard to tell much about it because of the blood that flowed steadily from the hole. Her gaze went to his pale face, and she found his eyes on her.

"Now you can . . . escape me," he whispered unsteadily.

Realizing the truth in his words, she felt as though she'd been kicked in the stomach. How could she even contemplate leaving him in such a condition? He had saved her life. Not just once, but three times. If he hadn't come for her at Bent's Fort, the Apaches would have caught her. And her fate at their hands would not have been pleasant.

No. I can't leave him.

"I'm not going anywhere yet," she murmured. "Leastways 'till you're fixed up." Becoming aware of the dog standing beside her, she turned to it and pointed toward the stove. "Go lie down," she said.

The German shepherd obeyed instantly, returning to its place beside the fire. She wondered why Dawg had offered no help to the trapper, but immediately answered her own question. Coltrane had not seemed affectionate toward the animal, perhaps had even mistreated it. She had offered the creature food and kindness and had won its loyalty.

Realizing she must hurry, she put the dog from her mind and gathered up some linen. It didn't look very clean, but she had nothing else with which to staunch the flow of blood.

Although Chama's eyes were closed, he opened them as she cleansed the wound. The hole was big, and she was certain the ball was still inside his chest. She met the warrior's eyes. "I'll have to dig the bullet out," she said.

He made no response, and she began to collect what she needed. His knife came first; the blade was narrow, two-edged and razor sharp, with a point like a needle. A bottle of whiskey was next; and a flannel shirt that she tore into strips. When she returned to the warrior, she was ready.

Suppressing a shudder, she examined the wound closely, finding the flesh black and swollen. Her stomach rolled as her fingers pulled the ragged edges apart. Her brow furrowed with worry as she saw the thick, red rivulets of blood oozing from the hole.

Realizing there was no time to waste, Mary Elizabeth poured whiskey over the knife blade, then handed the bottle to Chama. "Drink it," she ordered.

His face was expressionless, his gaze never wavering from her face as he took a hefty swallow. He made no sound when she pushed the tip of the blade into the hole and began to probe the wound.

"You can scream if you want," she said, knowing all

49

the time he wouldn't, for no warrior of worth would show weakness in the face of pain.

Probing deeper with the tip of the knife, she winced in sympathy as she looked up and saw his eyes closed, droplets of sweat beading his forehead and upper lip. Why should the thought of causing him further pain make her stomach muscles clench? Why should she care how much she hurt him? Hadn't she withstood beatings from his people after each attempt at escape? She should be rejoicing in his pain.

The beatings inflicted on you were not of his doing, a silent voice whispered. And she knew she could not argue with that. Wiping up the blood that was flowing freely now, she pushed the tip of the blade deeper into the wound, searching for the lead that must be removed. Forcing her mind away from what she was doing, she deliberately dredged up the memory of the last foiled attempt at escape from the Apaches. She'd been gone for two days before they caught up to her, hungry and thirsting for water. They'd strung her up by the wrists between two poles and beat her until she lost consciousness. When she had regained her senses, her hands were unbound and Chama held a drinking gourd to her parched lips. She'd been told later there'd been words between Three Toes, her owner, and Chama, and an offer of marriage had been made . . . and refused.

Mary Elizabeth's puzzled gaze moved to his face. The warrior was so fierce and violent . . . and yet, so tender and gentle with her. Why? And why had she forgotten his kindness to her? she wondered.

You've carried your anger against the whole tribe like a banner, a silent voice accused. *Perhaps you deliberately refused to recognize Chama's actions as a kindness.*

Returning her attention to the wound, she probed deeper, feeling the tip of the knife hit something solid. Only moments later she breathed a sigh of relief and held the bullet aloft. But she knew she wasn't finished yet.

After staunching the wound with rags, she added wood to the fire, glancing briefly at the dog which watched her every move. When the flames were roaring, she lifted the top off the wood stove and passed the knife blade through the flames, then she returned to the warrior.

"You know what I have to do," she said.

He nodded silently, his eyes still closed. Swallowing hard, she placed the knife blade on the wound, quelling the sickness in her stomach as the stench of burning flesh assailed her nostrils. Chama's body arched suddenly, then went limp.

Mary Elizabeth's knees felt weak as she went about the business of cleansing and binding the wound. When she was finished, she wiped a thin layer of perspiration from his face and covered the warrior with a blanket. Then, heaving a deep sigh, she swiped her coppery hair back with a trembling hand.

Only then did she look at Jim Coltrane's dead body.

A howling in the distance sent shivers down Mary Elizabeth's spine, and she wondered, not for the first time, if she'd been foolish to come out into the night.

Ominous gray clouds filled the sky, completely obliterating most of the stars, but they thinned out around the moon, encircling the silvery orb with a curious ghostlike haze.

A screech sounded close at hand, and Mary Elizabeth started. But it was only an owl, giving his poignant cry as he hunted among the trees.

"Should've brought the dog," she grumbled. "Leastways he'd of been some company."

But it was too late now. She must stick by her decision to leave the animal to guard the warrior while she went about her grisly chore. She knew the temperature had fallen considerably — she was cold, her breath visible in the chill air — but she plodded on, tugging at the reins of her reluctant mount, forcing it to hurry along the path with its gruesome load.

A sudden gust of wind sent a light scattering of snow off some low hanging branches and into her eyes, serving as a reminder that she had no time to lose. There was not the slightest doubt in her mind that a blizzard was on the way, and if she was caught in the open, there would be little chance for survival.

Mary Elizabeth had nearly reached the cliff before she saw it. Her steps quickened, and her gaze swept the area beneath the overhang, narrowing on the hole she had spied earlier. Although both trappers had been heavy-set, the cave looked large enough to suit her purpose. She would leave the bodies there and block the entrance with rocks.

Dropping the reins, she moved to her mount's side and eyed the dead men. "Should be easier getting you two off the horse than it was putting you on," she muttered, latching her cold fingers around an ankle and giving a sharp tug. But her efforts to dislodge the corpse were clumsy; the horse shifted restlessly, shying away. "Easy, boy," she soothed. "I don't like it either.

But I don't want to wait out the storm with two dead bodies lying about."

The first trapper, Jess, slid off the horse, landing with a thud on the rocks. The startled horse jerked its head up and, with a frightened whinny, tried to pull away.

"Whoa, boy," she gritted, grabbing the pommel of the saddle. "Settle down, now. This won't take long. We'll soon be through with these two."

Fearing the horse would leave her, she reached for its mane, grasping it with one hand and twining her fingers through the coarse hair while she pulled at the other trapper. His body had stiffened and seemed to be stuck across the horse's back.

Speaking softly to the skittish animal, she stroked its long neck, then gave it a soothing pat. She knew it was going to take both hands to free the trapper. Reaching up, she grasped him around the hips and gave a hard tug, feeling rewarded as his body moved slightly. Another tug sent the trapper sliding to the ground to land with a thud beside his partner.

The action proved more than the horse could take. The smell of death was all around it. Rolling its eyes at her, the animal reared up and pawed at the air with its hooves. Crashing down against the rock, the stallion spun around and took flight.

"Get back here, you damned flea-bitten nag!" she raged.

But she might as well have been raging at the storm for all the good it did. The horse kept running, its tail held high as it raced with the wind against its back.

Mary Elizabeth knew it would be useless trying to catch the animal. Another burst of frigid wind reminded her she was running out of time, and she bent and tugged at Jess's legs, pulling him toward the cave.

"Should of left you for the coyotes," she muttered. "Now I've gone and lost my horse."

The body seemed to weigh a ton as she pushed and shoved until it was in the hole. "One down and one to go." Her teeth had begun to chatter, and she wasn't certain if it was from the cold or fear.

When both bodies were in the cave, she began to pile rocks at the entrance. She was only half through when the sound of a growl from behind made her spin around.

Chills raced up her spine, and the hair stood on end at the base of her neck. Facing her was a huge black bear, standing upright on its hind legs. And it was obvious the animal considered the cave its own property. Icy fear twisted around her heart, and it gave a lurch, then began to flutter like a thousand blackbirds taking wing. Her mind whirled frantically; she was afraid to move, and yet, just as afraid to remain where she was.

The bear made the decision for her. Lifting up a heavy paw, it took a swipe at her.

Mary Elizabeth sprang sideways, barely escaping a blow that would have rendered her senseless. Abandoning the trappers, she ran for her life.

With a roar of rage, the bear fell on all fours and chased after the girl who had dared intrude on its domain.

Thud, thud, thud! The heavy beat of her heart thundered loudly in her ears.

He's going to catch me! He's going to catch me!

The words thrummed through her brain, over and over again, as she ran with all her might. Blood pumped through her veins, throbbing in her ears as she sought to escape certain death should the carnivore catch her.

She could hear the bear crashing through the brush as she ran fleetly through the forest, intent on reaching the safety of the cabin as quickly as she could. She tripped over a fallen log and went sprawling on the ground, but she wasted no time in regaining her feet and racing toward the light she could see in the distance.

Thud, thud, thud. Her heart seemed intent on bursting with the efforts she expended to stay ahead of the bear.

God! Will I never get there?

As though sensing it was about to lose its prey, the black bear gave a mighty roar behind her. And then her fingers were on the door, and she opened it wide and dashed through, slamming the heavy wood behind her and pushing the plank that secured the door in place.

Trembling with fear and exhaustion, she slid down the door and onto the floor and waited.

Silence.

She lay there, panting with fear and exhaustion, until a wet tongue on her face brought her head up. The dog stood watching over her anxiously. Its eyes traveled from her to the door and back again as though to reassure her she was safe within the walls of the cabin.

She tried to still her trembling as she waited for the bear to attempt to penetrate the barrier that stood between it and its prey. But there was only silence — not a sound to substantiate her utter terror of what lay outside.

Apparently the bear had given up the chase and gone about its business. She uttered a sigh of relief and slowly relaxed. Then her gaze fell on Chama. Now that the danger was over, she must see to the warrior.

He lay unmoving, his blanket-covered form positioned where she had left it. For a moment she feared he was dead, and the thought tore at her insides. She went to the warrior, falling on her knees beside him. Placing her thumb against his throat, she felt a faint pulse beat, and relief flowed through her.

When she examined his wound, she found the edges were puffy and white, and she was almost certain he was running a fever. She would have to get him off the cold floor and onto the bed.

At that moment he groaned, opened his eyes and looked at her. "You did not run away," he whispered, his dark eyes probing her features.

She swallowed, caught by his ebony gaze. "I couldn't," she said, her throat feeling strangely thick. "It wouldn't be right for me to just let you die. Not after you saved my life the way you did."

Unable to hold his gaze, she looked at the window. The wind had strengthened, and huge snowflakes were now falling at an alarming speed. The storm that had been threatening was upon them.

"The storm is here," she said briskly, turning back to him. "We need to get you off the floor. You'll catch your death of cold lying there."

Rising, she crossed the room and unhooked the bed from the wall. Although the plank was narrow, there was ample room for a big man to sleep in comfort. She pushed at the mattress, surprised to find it soft and springy.

"You're in luck," she told him. "You get to sleep on a feather bed." Her brow knitted with worry. "Now all we have to do is get you on it."

"I am not helpless," he said, shoving himself to his elbows. "I do not need help."

She hurried across to him, determined to be there if she was needed. Sweat broke out on his forehead at the effort he expended, but although he was undoubtedly shaky, he reached the bed without falling.

"I wish we had some of the medicine leaves that Yellow Moon uses for sores," she said. "The trappers didn't have much in the way of healing potions."

After covering him with a blanket, she started to move away, but before she could, his hand whipped out and his fingers snaked around her wrist.

"Stay with me," he said, his voice a husky whisper.

She was aware of the strength and warmth of his flesh against her own, and something—some intangible *something* in his voice—started her heart racing. Her gaze locked with his, and she swallowed hard. "You need to sleep," she whispered huskily.

"Stay with me," he said again. Her pulse skittered alarmingly as he pulled her closer to the bed. The back of her knees struck the bed frame, and she sank down on the mattress.

"Did I hurt you?" she asked, averting her eyes from his mesmerizing gaze.

"No," he said. She was aware that he was still watching her. "You will stay with me?"

It seemed to be of the utmost importance to him, and she found herself nodding her head. "Yes," she agreed. "I'll stay."

She heard him utter a sigh and could feel him relax almost instantly. Why did it matter so much to him? she wondered. But her mind was too weary to dwell on it long. The strain of the last few days was beginning to tell on Mary Elizabeth. She was bone-weary in mind as well as body. The silence in the cabin was absolute, and the wind moaned softly outside. Slowly, her tension began to drain away, her muscles began to unknot and her eyelids grew heavy. A quick glance at Chama told her he was sleeping peacefully, but when she tried to loosen his hold on her, his fingers tightened as though he would hold her prisoner.

Mary Elizabeth, finding herself unwilling to wake him, maneuvered herself around until she was leaning against the wall . . . and only moments later she was sound asleep.

Chapter Five

Chama had no way of knowing what time it was when he woke, but a glance toward the window told him it was still dark outside. His gaze moved to the flickering lamp. The fuel was almost gone. And the fire must have died down, because a chill had fallen over the room, and the woman beside him looked cramped and cold.

His dark eyes dwelt on her face. In sleep, she looked as helpless as a child, but he had reason to know her looks were deceiving. If her life with the Apaches had taught her nothing else, at least it had taught her how to survive.

The nearness of her gave him comfort.

Her hair had come loose and tumbled around her shoulders like a fiery cloud. Unable to help himself, he reached out and stroked his hand down the silky length of it.

Since he'd returned from his hunting trip four years ago and found her at the village, bruised and grief-stricken over the loss of her family — and the more recent violation of her sister — he'd felt a tenderness for

59

her that he'd tried to reject. Such feelings were useless and served only to make him vulnerable: something that a warrior should never be—not if he were to survive.

When she shivered suddenly, he frowned, realizing he must make room for her in the warmth of the bed, else she would fall ill.

Feeling incredibly weak, he summoned every ounce of strength he possessed and scooted closer to where she leaned against the wall, ignoring the pain that shot through him with the movement. The pain was a small thing beside the importance of keeping Fire Woman warm.

Across the room the dog whined, lifting its head to look at Chama, but the warrior ignored the animal as he put a hand on the girl's shoulder and gently shook her awake.

"What is it?" she mumbled, her dark lashes lifting to reveal sleep-dazed eyes.

"You are getting cold," he murmured. "Lie down beside me and share my blanket."

Without a word she moved her legs onto the bed and stretched out beside him. Another pain stabbed at him as he pulled her close against him and worked the blanket over her. One glance at the window told him the snow was coming down fast. Soon they would be snowed in. Just Fire Woman and himself. The thought caused him to feel contentment, and his lips curved into a smile. He sighed, closed his eyes, and moments later was fast asleep.

Mary Elizabeth's nose was cold when she woke, but

her body was enveloped in a cocoon of delicious warmth. Her lashes lifted slowly, and she stared up at the rough-cut logs that made up the roof. For a moment she felt disoriented, but when she turned her head and saw the warrior beside her, her sleep-fogged brain cleared.

She was in the trappers' cabin, and Chama had been wounded. But what was she doing in bed with him? Her gaze went to the stove. The fire had gone out some time in the night, and she must have crawled in bed with the warrior to keep warm.

A rosey blush stained her cheeks, and she eased away from him. She would be so humiliated if he woke and found her sharing his bed. The floor was cold when she rose from the bed and hurried to build a fire.

After putting a goodly supply of kindling in the stove, she set it aflame with some flint. When she had a fire blazing, she pulled a stool up beside the stove to warm her shivering body.

The German shepherd rose and came to her. Putting its head in her lap, it looked up at her and whined softly.

"What is it, boy?" she whispered, scratching behind the dog's ear. "Are you hungry?"

As though answering her question, the dog crossed the room and stood waiting beside the door. "You want outside?" she asked. The German shepherd wagged its tail and watched her until she lifted the bar on the door and opened it a crack. Then the dog darted through the door and out into the snow.

Mary Elizabeth was easing the door closed when a sharp bark warned her the dog was ready to come back inside. "Hurry up, then," she muttered, opening the door wider.

When the dog was inside the cabin again and the door was closed, she returned to her place by the fire. As the room became warmer, she began to think of her stomach and wondered how the trappers were fixed for supplies. It took only moments to discover a small amount of coffee, a can of sugar, flour and dry beans. There was enough foodstuffs to get them through several weeks without hunting fresh meat. Another unexplored tin caught her eye, and she took it off the shelf and peered inside.

Rags.

Now, why would someone stuff rags in a tin can? She put the lid back on and was replacing the tin on the shelf when she paused, frowning at the can.

Rags? It made no sense.

Opening the can, she pulled out the rags and drew in a sharp breath staring at the gold-colored rocks.

It's not gold. It can't be. Can it?

Picking out a small rock, she peered at it. She'd never seen gold before. How would she know for certain what it was? Suddenly she remembered seeing a miner bite a gold nugget and thought it was worth a try. A moment later she stared at the teeth marks she had left in the gold rock.

It *was* gold!

Where had the trappers found it?

Elation filled her as she dropped the nugget in the can and hid it with the rags. After replacing the lid, she looked for a hiding place, then decided perhaps the miners had found the best place after all. Who would think to search on the shelf among the foodstuffs?

A smile played around her lips as she turned her

thoughts toward a meal.

When she found the coffeepot still contained some of yesterday's coffee grounds, she added more water and a small amount of fresh coffee, knowing she could stretch it that way.

The coffee was boiling on the stove when she began to worry about Chama. He hadn't moved at all since she'd woken. Worry knit her brow as she crossed the room to the bed. Was his breathing too fast and shallow? Had he developed a fever from his wound?

Leaning over the bed, she placed her palm on his forehead, drawing in a sharp breath as his eyes flew open.

"Are—are you all right?" she asked, her blue eyes locking with his dark gaze.

"I will live," he said, gazing at her somberly.

Realizing suddenly that she was still leaning over him, she drew away. "I've made some coffee. Would you like a cup?"

"It would be good," he said. "Has the snow stopped falling yet?"

"No. But it doesn't seem as heavy as before." She found two tin cups and washed them out before filling them with coffee, setting one on the back of the stove and bringing the other to Chama.

He pushed himself to his elbows and sipped the strong brew and then eased himself back on the bed. She watched him, wondering if he knew she had slept on the bed beside him. She hoped he didn't.

"I need to check your wound," she said, proceeding to do so. "It looks good. No more bleeding. Perhaps it is healing."

When she found a can of maple syrup, she was

63

elated. They had pancakes for breakfast, and she noticed with satisfaction that Chama seemed to enjoy his enormously.

"That's the first time in four years I've had pancakes with maple syrup," she said, forking the last bite into her mouth.

"The pancakes were very good," he said. His gaze turned to the window. "It has stopped snowing."

She crossed to the window and stared through the pane. The world outside was white, a winter wonderland, reminding her of a time when she lived with her parents. She gazed at the snow-laden trees, her face reflective as she remembered another cabin and another time, unaware of the dark eyes that watched her.

"Of what do you think?"

The voice startled her, and she turned to find Chama's dark gaze on her face, probing, as though he would reveal her innermost secrets.

"I was thinking of my family," she answered quietly.

"Of Three Toes and Pale Moon?" he inquired.

"No," she answered quietly. "Not about them. They were never my family. Just my keepers. I was thinking about Ma and Pa. And Brother Clem and Brother Jeb." She lowered her eyes to hide the momentary flash of pain. "And I was thinking of my sister, Melissa."

Mary Elizabeth's blue eyes were filled with sadness as they locked with his for a long moment. How could she explain the depth of her feelings for her family to him . . . a savage? And why should she even try?

Her gaze moved back to the window — to the snow-laden trees outside — while her mind traveled back in time. "The last Christmas we had together it snowed like this. Ma made Melissa and me new dresses. Me-

64

lissa's was yellow and mine was blue. Ma said they were for the New Year's celebration in the settlement. But we couldn't wait to wear them. We begged Ma to let us wear the dresses on Christmas day, and she finally said we could if we wouldn't get them dirty. Melissa looked like a sunflower in her yellow dress. Both of us tried hard do keep the dresses clean, and we did—until she sent us to fetch wood off the porch." Her gaze turned to Chama. "That was usually Brother Jeb's job, but the boys were off hunting, and the woodbox was nearly empty." She looked outside again. "There was a lot of snow outside. Just like today. Melissa followed me outside and waited until my arms were loaded with wood, then she let me have it with a big snowball." Her lips twitched in memory. "There was nothing for me to do but throw one back at her. So I threw the wood down, but one of the logs ripped the skirt of my dress. I knew there'd be trouble, and it made me angry with Melissa. We started fighting in earnest, throwing the snowballs as hard as we could, forgetting everything else until Pa come to the door and made us stop. We never could stay mad at each other very long, and Melissa helped me carry the wood inside. I remember I was worried about my torn dress and what Ma would say. But the worrying was for nothing, because she didn't see it."

"Why?" he questioned.

"She'd been feeling poorly, and Pa had sent her to their bedroom to rest."

"Did she not see the dress later?"

"No. She didn't. Pa saw the ripped dress, and he told me to take it off. I was worried. Thought he was about to belt me for ruining it." She smiled in remembrance. "You can imagine my surprise when Pa opened the sewing box and commenced to mend my torn skirt."

She fell silent as her mind replayed the scene. With Pa sitting in Ma's rocker, his head bent over his work as his big fingers worked at making tiny stitches that remarkably escaped the notice of Ma's eagle eyes.

"Was your pa a man of strength?"

Chama's voice pulled her back to the present. "Yes," she said. "He was the strongest man I've ever known. And the gentlest." Her eyes measured the warrior's length, just over six feet. "He was bigger than you," she said, and held her hands apart. "He could best any man in the settlement, and yet most knew he was the first to give help where it was needed."

A memory of her father as she had last seen him filtered into her mind, and she quickly shut it out, knowing it did no good to remember.

"It is strange to think of a strong warrior doing women's work."

"Not so strange," she commented. "Pa loved Ma, and he didn't want her upset. She had been sick most of that winter. For a while we feared she had lung fever. But come spring she began to pull out of it."

She sipped her coffee and continued to stare at the white starkness outside. Her voice was soft as she commenced speaking again, relating how they had spent their holidays together, the family dinners her mother had made.

"Ma made the best hot cross buns," she said. "And she knew how to make a pot of red beans that was out of this world. Nobody could cook like Ma." In her mind's eye, Mary Elizabeth could see her mother standing at the stove with her face flushed with heat, her fiery hair curling in tendrils around her face.

"Tell me about the celebration you call Christmas." came the voice of Chama. "Your face changes when you speak of it."

"We always had a big Christmas tree. Pa would call us together, and we would go out in the woods to find it. The last year we were together he let me choose the tree. He chopped it down, and we drug it to the porch." Her lips twitched. "That's when we found it was too big to fit through the door. Pa had to cut about three feet off the bottom to make it fit."

"You wanted the tree in your dwelling?"

"Yes. It's a custom of my people. We stood it in one corner of the parlor and decorated it with popcorn balls and candles and ribbons—red and green ribbons made into little bows—and we made paper chains and hung them around the tree."

Even now she could see the tree standing in all its glory. "Ma had an angel with bright gold hair that belonged to her ma before her, and big as I was, Pa still had to lift me up so I could reach the highest branch on the tree." Her head lifted as she remembered how the angel's halo had touched the ceiling. "I'll never forget how I felt, standing with the others, looking at the angel on the topmost branch."

A shadow crossed his face as he watched her, and he swallowed hard. "What is the cause of the celebration?" he asked huskily.

"We celebrate the birth of Jesus Christ, the son of God," she said.

"Tell me more of this celebration," he said.

And so she talked, never noticing how much time

was passing until the room began to grow chill and Chama's eyelids began to close. When she realized he had fallen asleep, she fell silent and crossed the room to tuck the covers firmly around him.

She felt an overwhelming tenderness for the warrior as she bent over his sleeping form, but she quickly shrugged it away. She could not afford such feelings. She would have to be careful and keep her distance from this man — this Apache warrior — who was able to affect her in such a manner. She owed the warrior a debt. But she would repay it, and then she would continue her journey homeward. With that thought firmly planted in her mind, she began to prepare the dried red beans for their evening meal.

Chapter Six

Chama slept most of the day, waking for a short time in the afternoon to drink some soup, then promptly falling asleep again. But Mary Elizabeth was far from bored. With the German shepherd beside her, she explored the contents of the small cabin.

The mouth-watering aroma of red beans filled the cabin when the warrior woke late that evening. He seemed remarkably well for someone who'd been so recently shot.

Mary Elizabeth felt exasperated when Chama insisted on joining her at the table.

"You have to be careful," she said. "Otherwise that bullet hole will start bleeding again."

"I am all right," he insisted, seating himself at the table and heaping his plate with biscuits and red beans. "Talk to me," he ordered imperiously. "I wish to hear more about your pa."

She looked startled. "Why?"

"Perhaps I wish to understand him," he said. "He was a man who did the work of a woman, yet you say he was stronger than most men. Was he not afraid others would see him doing such foolish work?"

"No," she said. "It wouldn't have mattered to Pa. He cared nothing for the opinion of others. He often said there was no act too small or unworthy if it brought happiness to his loved ones."

"The Apache people would consider such a man a weakling."

"Don't you dare call my pa weak!" she snapped, her eyes glittering with anger. "He was more of a man than you could ever be."

Anger sparked in his eyes. "Your tongue is sharp, woman," he growled. "It may yet prove to be your downfall."

She paled instantly. He had said those same words to her just before she escaped from the Apaches. And the words had brought to mind the same picture then as she saw now: a white woman, mute, her tongue cut out, making horrible sounds with tears running down her face.

He reached across the table to take her hand, and she shrank away from him. "What have I said?" he asked. "Why do you look at me in such fear?"

She swallowed hard, refusing to meet his eyes, but he would have none of it. He rose and came around the table to her. Lifting her chin in the palm of his hand, he said, "Tell me, Fire Woman. Why do you shrink from me?"

"You said . . . my tongue would prove to be my downfall."

"And such words make you fear me?"

Her gaze met his searchingly. Did she dare tell him why she was afraid? If he didn't already have such thoughts in his head, wouldn't speaking of it put them

70

there?

"Come, little one," he coaxed. "Tell me what causes you such fear."

"There was a white woman in the village when I first was taken there . . ."

He waited silently for her to continue.

". . . she didn't have a tongue."

Heaving a sigh, he pulled her against his chest and stroked her hair. "My thoughtless words have caused you much anguish, haven't they?"

She could hardly believe the tenderness she heard in his voice.

"I am sorry, little one," he said. "I would never do such a thing . . . never do anything to cause you harm. Please believe me."

She pulled back and looked up at him. "You said those same words, about my tongue, when we were on the march to Bent's Fort. You didn't mean them then either?"

"No," he said emphatically. "I was angered." His dark eyes probed hers. "Was that the reason you ran away?"

She nodded. "Part of it. I was afraid of what you would do."

"Because of my thoughtless words a man is dead. And we are now outcasts from my tribe."

She bent her head. "Perhaps they would take you back. You had nothing to do with any of it."

"To go back without you is not my desire," he said. "We will stay together."

"But we can't!" she burst out. "When the pass is clear, I'll be going home."

He put her from him. "We will speak more of your destination later," he said firmly. "Now tell me more of

71

your white-eyes family."

They talked until darkness was long since past; then Mary Elizabeth checked his wound once more and told him it was healing well. After securing the bandage around his shoulder again, she banked the fire and let the dog out for a short run.

When the German shepherd returned, she stifled a yawn. She was tired and sleepy, but she looked nervously at the bed.

"Do not worry," Chama said, seeming to guess her thoughts. "Come to bed. You will come to no harm from me. But I will sleep much better with you beside me."

Mary Elizabeth frowned and started to protest, but when she saw the drained look on his face and realized he had pushed himself beyond his limits, she knew he was speaking the truth. He could present no danger to her, even had he wanted to. And it was obvious that he needed to rest. If she needed to check on him during the night, it would be much easier with her lying beside him.

So she blew the lamp out and allowed herself to be coaxed into the bed. She lay beside him a long while, her body stiff with tension. But as time passed and the warrior's even breathing told her he was asleep, she began to unwind; the tension slowly drained . . . away . . .

The next few days passed swiftly. They talked during the day and slept soundly at night. And all the time Chama's wound was healing. By the fourth day, the sun came out and the snow began to melt. Chama proved to be restless that day, and Mary Elizabeth put it down to the fact that he was feeling confined in the cabin. To keep him occupied, she began to ask him questions about his parents.

"My mother died when I was a young boy," he said. "My father took her sister to his wickiup, and she saw to our needs. When I was ten summers, my father was killed in a battle, and my mother's sister went to another's wickiup. The warrior she went to had no use for a young boy."

She looked at him, aghast. "Where did you go?"

"Nowhere."

"I mean . . . who took care of you?"

His face was expressionless. "I took care of myself. I would not go where I was not wanted."

She swallowed, feeling tears clog her throat. *A ten-year-old boy. On his own.*

"But the villagers . . . they seemed to admire you. Did none of them offer you help?"

His mouth thinned. "I did not need help," he said grimly. "But when I was ten summers, I did not live with that tribe. I was with the Comanches. Two summers after my father died, I contracted the white man's disease."

"Small pox?"

"Yes. For the good of the tribe, I was left behind. I survived the disease, and before the snows fell, Chief White Cloud found me. He allowed me to join his tribe."

Although his voice was emotionless, she realized how much it had cost him to leave the Apaches. Why had he done it?, *To save your life,* said a silent voice from within. *But why?*

She was still worrying the question over in her mind when darkness fell.

Realizing the fire must be banked for the night, Mary Elizabeth crossed to the stove and covered the live coals with ashes. Her gaze fell on the woodbox.

"We need wood," she said. "There may be another storm tonight."

"There is a plentiful supply beside the cabin," Chama said, his attention on the knife he was sharpening.

The dog followed her outside, and although it seemed restless, she paid the animal no attention, intent on selecting the best wood for the stove. But when the German shepherd made a dash across the clearing, stopping short of a grove of pines and barking furiously, she dropped the wood she'd gathered and went to investigate.

At first she saw nothing except a darker shadow among the many shadows in the forest — until, with a loud roar that sent fear surging through her, the bear dropped to all fours and charged.

The scream died in her throat as she turned to run, stumbled, and fell sprawling in a puddle of melted snow. The bear let out a loud roar, and she scrambled backward, leaping to her feet and running for the cabin, with the dog keeping pace beside her.

The cabin seemed to be an eternity away while her heart thudded loudly in her breast . . . and then her hand was on the door latch, yanking at it, fumbling in her haste to get it open. She didn't even realize she was sobbing in her terror as she yanked open the door and dashed inside with Dawg at her heels.

Fear, stark and vivid, glittered in her eyes. "It's the

bear!" she cried wildly. "Shut the door!"

Another roar, closer at hand, had Chama whirling to the door, slamming it shut and plunging the bar home. When the heavy wood was safely barred against the carnivore, the warrior took Mary Elizabeth's trembling body in his arms, holding her tightly against him, pressing her head into the curve of his neck. He held her thus until her trembling stopped, and then he began to unfasten her dress.

"You are wet," he said. "We must get this off."

She offered no protest, too exhausted and confused by her close call. When the dress fell free of her body, he wrapped a blanket around her quivering form and led her to the bed. When he tried to release his hand, her fingers tightened. "Stay with me," she said.

"I will. But first I must put out the light."

She lay shivering within the blanket until he returned; then he gathered her into his arms and pulled her against him. His hand softly stroked through her silky hair.

She pressed herself against him, finding reassurance in his strength, and her clinging hands slid around his neck, her fingers winding through the hairs at his nape as she unconsciously caressed him.

She felt the muscles beneath her fingers tense, and his body seemed to harden against her own; but her mind was still filled with the bear.

"Why should the bear attack me?" she asked.

"Perhaps he is wounded," he said. "When the sun lights the morning sky, I will hunt for him. You need fear him no longer."

"I'm sorry," she whispered. "I shouldn't have been so cowardly."

"Hush," he soothed, his lips brushing her own to halt the flow of words. "You were no coward. It is only prudent to flee from a bear. Now you must put it from your mind and go to sleep."

But perversely, his lips against hers did not have the soothing reaction he'd intended. Instead, her pulse quickened. They were so close that she could see every detail of his face, even the small scar above his full, sensuous lips, where he'd been wounded in a fight the year after she'd been taken captive. For some reason she felt the strangest desire to press her lips to his.

No sooner did the thought cross her mind than she lifted her face and kissed him gently. She had often seen her mother kiss her father, but she was astonished at the warrior's reaction. A muscle tightened in his jaw, and his eyes seemed to smolder with an inner fire. His lower body hardened, and his fingers tightened, then relaxed against her waist.

She looked up at him, wide-eyed. *What a curious reaction.* She wet her lips with the tip of her pink tongue, knowing she wanted to kiss him again.

And really, there was no reason why she shouldn't, was there? She was considered a grown woman, and yet she had never been properly kissed. Deciding to remedy the situation immediately, she closed her eyes, pursed her lips and pressed them against his again. But this time he showed no reaction.

Disappointment swept over her.

Doesn't he like my kisses?

Perhaps she wasn't doing it right.

Taking a deep breath, she snaked out her tongue, intending to wet her dry lips; but he had leaned closer, and his mouth brushed softly against hers.

A jolt of excitement went through her as she tasted the slightly salty flavor of his flesh. With her mouth partially opened, she traced the outline of his lips with her tongue and heard his sharp intake of breath.

What a curious reaction.

Excitement flowed through Mary Elizabeth, her heart beating wildly. She knew she should stop experimenting, but her curiosity was far from satisfied. And he seemed a willing partner. Perhaps this would be her only chance to discover what kissing was all about.

Emboldened, she put her arms behind his head and pressed her mouth to his harder, but she didn't get the same feeling as she'd had when she'd traced his lips with her tongue. Eager for more of the same, she opened her mouth slightly, and so did he. His tongue entered her mouth, probing the moistness within, and she shuddered at the feeling he was arousing, a feeling that she wanted to prolong.

When the blanket slipped down and his hand found the curve of her breast, she was lost. Her heart was thudding fast as she arched toward him, moaning with pleasure. His lips soon left hers and roamed downward, leaving a trail of fire across her neck and her shoulder; then his mouth was on the taut peak of her breast, pulling at it with his teeth while his hand roamed farther downward until it reached the apex of her desire.

Her mind was a spinning whirlpool of desire, and she had no thought to object. She wanted more of the pleasure he was creating and gave no thought to tomorrow. She only knew that she wanted this man — more than anything in the world.

When he moved away from her, she moaned a protest, but it was only moments before he joined her again. Then he lay on her, his naked body fitted against hers. His lips found her neck, and he nipped at the sensitive cord there.

She became aware of the throbbing hardness at her thighs, but was unsure of what it meant. She was moaning with pleasure, wanting something that she could put no name to. But it was a shock when he rose above her and plunged downward.

Pain stabbed through her, and she gasped, a shiver of panic surging through her. She uttered a small cry, but it was quickly swallowed by his lips on hers. Her body was stiff, protesting, but he made no move, lying completely still for several moments, allowing her to get used to his body within hers. And then something happened. She felt a movement deep inside her, and a slow, languorous yearning began somewhere in her lower body. When he started to move slowly, she moved with him, urging him to thrust faster, twisting and writhing beneath him, her pulse pounding. Fire raced through her being until he was plunging deeper and faster, harder and deeper, raising her upward toward some far distant peak until they were soaring . . . soaring among the clouds with the eagles.

Chapter Seven

The early morning sun streamed through the window of the small cabin, highlighting the girl who moved briskly about preparing the morning meal, transforming the masses of silky hair tumbling unrestrained about her shoulders into a fiery cloud.

Chama, seated at the table, lifted the steaming cup to his mouth and sipped cautiously. His dark gaze was puzzled as he watched Mary Elizabeth. In the morning light, her skin looked pearly white, smooth as the finest satin, but her back was straight, her body rigid as steel.

He hadn't been prepared for the abrupt change in her mood when he woke this morning to find her curled in the crook of his arm, her cheek pillowed against his shoulder.

She had wakened slowly, her eyes lighting with a smile when she'd first seen him. But the smile had quickly died as realization set in. Her eyes had darkened to navy, and she had lowered her lashes to hide them, but not fast enough to keep him from knowing her feelings.

Mary Elizabeth had been angry, and he knew without being told the reason for the anger that had her scrambling off the bed and scuttling across the room for her clothing. The dawn of a new day had brought rationality and the memory of her goal. Was she afraid of what she'd allowed to happen? Afraid . . . and perhaps ashamed?

The thought caused him pain. Why did she continue to resist him so? Although the memory of her warm curves and the clean scent of her hair tormented him, his face remained expressionless.

Lifting his cup to his mouth, Chama drained the contents and waited a long moment for her to notice. When her back remained firmly turned against him, he spoke.

"My cup is empty."

If possible, her back became even more rigid. Slowly, she turned around and smiled sweetly at him. "Then fill it," she said. "As you can see, I'm busy." With that, she turned around again and began to stir the pot more vigorously.

Chama frowned. She was obviously trying to anger him, for she knew a warrior did not wait upon himself. She had taken refuge from her feelings behind a mask of anger, but he refused to fuel it. Instead, he rose from the table and crossed to the stove. While pouring a fresh cup of coffee, he took a peek in the pot she was still stirring so briskly.

Beans.

Puzzled, his gaze went to the shelf behind the stove. The bucket of maple syrup was still there. Why was she giving him leftover beans when she had been providing delicious pancakes each morning for their breakfast?

Suddenly, comprehension dawned, and his lips twitched. She was apparently prepared to go to great lengths to make him angry. When her gaze lifted and met his, she seemed to be daring him to comment on her choice of food. For a moment their eyes remained locked together, the silence stretching out between them.

She was holding her breath, waiting for his reaction, her hand clenched around the wooden spoon she had been stirring with.

A soft whine broke the silence, and they both looked at the German shepherd. Its head was lifted as it looked anxiously up at them. A smile played around Chama's lips as he stooped to scratch the dog behind one ear before returning to his seat at the table.

Chama's stomach rumbled as he watched Mary Elizabeth reach for a small can on the shelf, dip her hand in and sprinkle something in the pot of beans. What was she doing now? he wondered, watching her stir the pot again. He was hungry and had already resigned himself to eating the beans instead of delicious syrup-covered pancakes.

Seeming to read his thoughts, she lifted the pot off the stove and put it on the table. Taking a clean bowl and spoon from the shelf on the wall, she slammed them down in front of him. Then she stood there, hands on hips, daring him to speak.

"Where is your bowl?" he inquired mildly.

"I'm not hungry!" she snapped.

Reaching for his spoon, he dished up a huge portion of the squashed-up beans. "I am glad you warmed the beans up," he said conversationally. "They were very good last night." He managed to look appreciative as he took his first bite.

Her glittering eyes should have warned him. He forced himself to swallow before he reached for his coffee. What had she done to the beans? His lips tightened as his gaze went to the small can on the wall. It obviously contained salt, and she had sprinkled it liberally on the already salted beans.

He lifted the coffee cup to his lips again and took a long swallow. Then he looked at the bowl of beans. Why had he filled the bowl so full? Aware that she was still watching, he forced himself to spoon another mouthful of beans into his mouth.

"This is good," he said, quelling a grimace. "You really should eat with me."

A frown crossed her brow, and she looked at the pot of beans, obviously wondering if perhaps she hadn't succeeded in her attempt to ruin them. Then her lips twisted bitterly. "I'm not hungry," she mumbled.

Thwarted in her attempt to make him angry, she poured herself a cup of hot coffee and crossed to the window, staring out at the melting snow.

"How long will it be before the pass is clear?" she asked. Before he could answer, she muttered, "God! I hate this mess!" Chama remained silent and sipped at his coffee. Suddenly, she spun around and glared at him. "Don't you have anything to say at all?" she questioned. "You've hardly spoken a word all morning."

"There was no need," he rejoined quietly. "Words would only have made things more difficult."

"What does that mean?" she snapped.

He sighed heavily and put down his cup. "Why are you so angry?" he asked, his gaze locking onto hers.

She opened her mouth, then quickly closed it again. "I'm going out," she muttered. After putting her cup on the table, she crossed to the door and opened it. Instantly, the dog was beside her, eager for a run outside.

Chama made no move to stop her. He knew the pass would still be closed. It would be days, perhaps weeks, before the snow melted enough to allow them to leave. She obviously needed some time alone to sort out her feelings, and perhaps if he allowed her the time, she would return in a better frame of mind.

Meanwhile, he had things to do.

Swallowing the last of his coffee, he rose and gathered his weapons together.

It was a good day to hunt bear.

At first the German shepherd seemed content to follow behind Mary Elizabeth, but after an hour had passed, it began to roam. Walking briskly along, she heard the croaking of frogs before she saw the stream. As they neared the sparkling water, Dawg routed a raccoon that had left its hole in a tree to hunt the frogs, but Mary Elizabeth paid little attention to the wandering dog. As she walked, she had grown calmer, and her anger had slowly evaporated, leaving her feeling foolish over her actions.

And with good reason.

She had done her best to start a fight with the warrior. He had asked her why she was angry, and she hadn't known how to answer him. Not because she didn't know. Because she did. She was angry because she had allowed him to make love to her.

Allowed him? a silent voice asked. *You started it. If you hadn't been so curious, it never would have happened.*

She gritted her teeth. Hindsight did no good, but she would have to watch herself in the future. Bending down, she cupped her hands and scooped up some of the cold water and brought it to her lips.

Then, keeping in mind the bear at the northern end of the mountain wall, she turned south, following the stream which ran along the valley floor. With her gaze on a distant peak, she continued to walk. Her breathing became labored as the trail wound upward. She rounded a stand of trees and stopped abruptly. Before her was the gaping entrance to a tunnel. It had been dug into the mountain and shored up with timbers.

Why would someone go to all the trouble of digging a hole through the rocky shale?

Mary Elizabeth's gaze fell on the rock and debris piled in front of the tunnel, and something clicked in her mind. She was standing before an abandoned mine. Was it possible the gold in the cabin had come from here? Her eyes glittered with excitement. Could there be any gold left in the mine?

Perhaps she could dig the gold out if there was any left. She examined the timbers. They looked sturdy enough. There should be no danger if she went inside. She substituted action for thought and stepped into the shadowy entrance, wrinkling her nose as musty air assailed her nostrils.

When her eyes had adjusted to the shadows, she moved farther inside. She had only gone a few feet when she saw the streaks of gold color. Her heart beat faster as excitement surged through her. She could dig some of the gold out. Why had the mine been abandoned? she wondered, moving deeper into the shaft.

When another streak of color caught her eyes, she moved closer. Upon finding it was another vein of gold, she searched for something to dig with. While examining a heavy piece of metal, elation swept through her as she realized it was a pickaxe. But it had become wedged beneath one of the poles. If she could shove the pole aside and pull out the pickaxe, she would be able to dig for the gold. It was certainly worth a try.

Bending over, she braced her shoulder against the pole and shoved with all her might. She felt it give . . . just as a heavy rumbling sounded somewhere above. She looked up in horror as the roof collapsed in on her.

Chama moved silently through the forest, listening for movement on the leaf-covered ground. His thoughts had been on Mary Elizabeth and their problems all the while he searched. It was well past midday before he caught a glimpse of a dark shape ahead and knew he had found the bear.

The animal trotted through the woods, moving slowly upwind, its lumbering gait lacking grace, though it moved easily through the forest considering its weight of three hundred pounds. As though sensing Chama's presence, the black beast stopped and moved its head from side to side; then it sniffed the ground. When the bear found no cause for its uneasiness there, it lifted its head and raised its nose to read the air for scents carried on the wind.

Finally, as though satisfied there was no danger, the bear continued on its way.

Chama moved cautiously, surveying the shrubs and

trees as he walked. He watched the bear climb over a ridge and hurried along, knowing he dare not lose sight of the animal. But when he topped the ridge, he stared in consternation. There was no bear. The animal had completely disappeared.

In the distance he could hear the sound of running water and turned his steps in that direction. Perhaps he would find the bear there. Suddenly he heard a growl echoing through the woods . . . and in one agonizing moment the forest exploded in a bundle of growling teeth. The black beast was coming through the underbrush, straight toward him!

Chama pulled an arrow from his quiver, strung it in his bow and let it fly. The bear stopped, stunned momentarily by the quivering arrow stuck in its neck, then charged again.

Sending another shot winging toward the black beast, Chama watched the arrow penetrate the thick black fur of the bear's chest. The bear stopped and reared up on its hind legs, paws lifted to the sky, its neck hairs puffed in a fighting posture. Letting out a mighty roar, the bear dropped to all fours again and rushed toward the warrior.

Chama had time for only one more arrow. It struck the bear through the eye as one slashing paw raked the warrior's shoulder, tearing into the flesh and driving him sprawling to the ground. The warrior lay there, senses reeling, conscious of the heavy mass of black fur pinning him to the ground and knowing that his life-blood was slowly ebbing away.

Mary Elizabeth tried to keep her fragile calm as she

inched her way through the blackness, across rocks and fallen earth. Fine particles of crushed debris filled her lungs and irritated her throat. She had no way of knowing how long she'd been crawling through the darkness; it could have been hours or days. The mass of rubble seemed to go on forever, and she sensed her air supply was dwindling. Perhaps she should lie still so that it would last longer. And maybe . . . just maybe . . . Chama would come to her rescue.

But that was a ridiculous idea. He didn't know where she was, so how could he rescue her? She had left the cabin in a huff. Now she would probably never see him again. She would probably die here in this hole, and someday, sometime in the future, some miner would find her bones.

She began to shake as the fearful image built in her mind and cold sweat broke out on her forehead. "No," she cried, forcing false courage into her voice. "I won't die here. I have to get out. I have to!"

She moved forward again, scrambling frantically over the debris, ignoring the pain in her hands and knees. She would find a way out. She must! When her head bumped against something above, she cried out with pain. With palm forward, she put her hand out and encountered rock — and realized the roof was slanting toward the floor. Her narrow passage was becoming even narrower.

Was the way completely blocked?

Panic choked her, and her body felt chilled. God! She'd never get out! Never see Chama again! She felt stricken with remorse. She would never be able to apologize to Chama for being so horrid to him. And she had been. If she hadn't given in to her foolish anger, she would be safe at the cabin now, not trapped in a hole in the ground with no way to get out.

Tears streamed down her face, and she wiped at them with her palm, chiding herself for her cowardice. "Get hold of yourself!" she commanded, taking comfort in the sound of her voice. "Tears won't help."

She made herself take deep breaths, fighting down the useless panic. As her heartbeat slowed, she became more aware of her surroundings—rubble, shale, fallen rocks—and that the area around her left shoulder felt cooler than the rest. She put out her hand and began to feel in front of her shoulder. When she encountered rock, she worked her way down until she touched emptiness. She measured the distance with her hand, feeling disappointment surge through her. The hole was too small. It would do her no good.

Suddenly her heart gave a jolt! She felt air. Cool fresh air! And it was coming from the hole! It must be a tunnel. Lowering her head, she peered into the hole. Was it her imagination or could she see a tiny pinpoint of light in the distance? Could it be the way out? And if it was, could she possibly squeeze her body through the tunnel?

God! If only it were bigger.

She inched her way forward, her shoulders catching against the rocks. Realizing this was the widest part of her body, she pushed her elbows close together and tried to enter the opening. If she could just maneuver around . . . "Like . . . uh . . . this!" she exclaimed triumphantly as she felt her torso slide into the tunnel.

Panic like she'd never known welled in her throat, gnawing away at her. Suppose she got stuck in here? "Oh, you ninny," she chided herself. "You couldn't be any worse off than you are now." Her mind was a crazy mixture of hope and fear as she crawled forward. With her forehead scraping against solid rock, she came to an abrupt stop, tears of frustration gushing into her eyes. But she refused to give in to them. Setting her jaw, she lowered her head and squirmed forward, wriggling through the long tunnel like a snake, using the muscles of her butt and back to propel herself along with help from elbows and hands, her mind focused on the real or imagined pinpoint of light at the other end.

Chapter Eight

A warm wetness brushed against Chama's ear, immediately followed by a sensation of cold air. Again he felt the moist warmth and again the coolness. The process was repeated over and over again. First the moist warmth, stroking? Then the cold air. Moist warmth, cold air.

Chama heard a muffled groan, realized the sound was his own and opened his eyes . . . to darkness.

Night?

How long had he slept?

His mind seemed slow, barely able to function as he worried over the problem. He didn't know how much time had passed before he became conscious of a heavy, smothering warmth, only that when he did, his nostrils twitched at the same moment as the stench of bear assailed his senses.

Bear?

He tried hard to concentrate, but his brain was sluggish. Sleep hovered just beyond the mist. Peaceful . . . sleep . . .

Suddenly he sucked in a sharp breath. His ear felt

cold, wet. Hadn't it been moistly warm before?

Yes, he decided, trying to shake off the lethargy that still surrounded him. He stirred, tried to move, and realized at the same moment that he was unable to do so. Something heavy pinned him down.

Heavy? Pinning me to the ground?

Stench of bear?

Something is wrong!

Wake up! an inner voice screamed. *Wake up!*

An anxious whine penetrated the whirling vortex that was his mind. It was immediately followed by the moist warm stroking against his ear . . . then the rush of cold air.

He concentrated on the whine, trying to penetrate the mists surrounding his memory.

Dawg!

The German shepherd was whining and licking his ear!

A door seemed to open in his mind, allowing him access to his memories, and Chama recalled his fight with the bear, as well as the arrow he'd sent through the bear's eye just before he'd been rendered unconscious. Apparently his aim had been true and the steel arrowhead had found its way to the beast's brain through its eye. Now he was being smothered by the bear's thick fur.

Chama jerked his head toward the whining dog and the narrow slash of light and realized the darkness was an illusion created by the bear's heavy bulk.

In fact, the German shepherd was bathed in sunlight, dirty, its neck hairs tangled with broken bits of twigs and leaves. And it sat with head cocked to one side, its expression undeniably anxious.

"Fetch Fire Woman, Dawg. Go get her!"

Dawg whined, a long drawn-out sound, leaned over and licked Chama's ear, then sat back on its haunches and gazed at the warrior.

"Go, Dawg!" Chama ordered sternly. "Get Fire Woman!"

The German shepherd remained motionless.

Realizing the dog would not leave, Chama pushed at the mighty beast covering him. The bear seemed incredibly heavy, and the warrior muttered curses as he struggled to free himself from the enormous weight. One leg slid out from under the animal, and feeling encouraged, the warrior called on every ounce of strength he possessed to roll the beast away; then he lay still, breathing heavily, trying to gather enough strength to get to his feet.

Dawg trotted over and licked his face. "Get away!" the warrior snapped, feeling angry the animal had proved so worthless.

Dawg understood the tone of his voice, even if it didn't understand the words. It whined softly and backed a few steps away, pausing to watch as Chama pushed himself to a sitting position. Chama felt incredibly light-headed and tried to assess his injuries. Fresh blood seeped slowly from the gash on his shoulder; but his wound would heal, and at least the bear was dead.

Dawg whined, an anxious sound, and Chama scowled at it. "Little good you are," he said grimly. "I could get more help from the squirrels in the trees than from an animal such as you."

Lowering its head, the German shepherd slunk on its belly toward Chama, but the warrior ignored the animal as he rose to his feet. Then he stumbled on trembling legs up the path leading to the cabin.

The dog was up in a flash, bolting around the warrior, blocking the trail.

"Go away, Dawg!" Chama ordered. "Get out of here!"

His words seemed to anger the German shepherd. The dog bared its teeth and growled low in its throat.

Chama frowned. What was the matter with the dog? Was it sick? Keeping a wary eye on the German shepherd, the warrior attempted to pass.

Dawg reacted instantly, snarling ferociously, then barking wildly at the man facing it.

Chama's anger mingled with his sudden fear that the dog might be rabid. "What is the matter with you?" he asked.

Dawg sat back on its haunches, head cocked in a listening posture, its tongue lolled out, panting.

Chama studied the dog for a moment. The German shepherd seemed to be trying to keep the warrior from returning to the cabin. But why?

When he took a cautious step forward, Dawg reacted instantly, lunging ferociously, catching Chama's moccasin between its teeth and nipping the warrior's toes in the process.

Then, as suddenly as the dog had attacked, it released its hold on the warrior's moccasin and, with a wild bark, darted up the trail behind Chama. But the animal went only a few feet before it stopped and looked back anxiously at the warrior. It whined loudly and then barked again. Then it went a few more feet and stopped again, repeating its action.

What was the matter with the dog? It was almost as

though the German shepherd wanted to lead him somewhere. A sense of uneasiness crept over Chama. Something tugged at the corner of his mind, some realization.

Then he knew!

The dog had been with Fire Woman when she'd left the cabin. Why had the German shepherd left her?

Could she be in trouble?

Chama took a step toward the dog, and the animal barked wildly and raced a few feet ahead, then stopped and looked back again.

When Chama kept coming, the dog raced through the underbrush, then sat on its haunches, tongue hanging out, watching anxiously as the warrior made his way around the brush. Chama was certain now. The dog was trying to lead him somewhere. And it had to be to Fire Woman.

His anxiety gave him the strength to continue following behind the dog. At times he thought he could go no farther, but his concern for Fire Woman overcame all else as he and Dawg traveled to the southernmost end of the canyon. When the ground began a slow rise, the dog was still going . . . up over the crest until it disappeared from sight.

But only for a moment. Chama topped the rise and saw the dog stopped before a mound of rubble, pawing at it and whining. At first Chama thought the dog had led him on a wild goose chase, but then he noticed the rock slide was fresh. Timbers lay at an awkward angle, indicating there had been a shored-up mine entrance that had given way.

Realizing Fire Woman must have gone inside and become trapped, Chama began to work at clearing the entrance while the dog sat on its haunches, cocked its head to one side and watched with approval.

Every part of Mary Elizabeth's body felt sore. Her arms were scraped and bleeding, but her raw flesh was not the cause of the tears that crept down her cheeks; the reason for her tears was the blocked passage.

Despite the cold in the narrow tunnel, she felt beads of sweat on her upper lip as icy terror held her in its clammy embrace.

She had been so near to her goal, the light only a few feet away. And then the passage had become impassable, blocked by a rock that was too heavy to move, yet allowed her to see how close she had come to escape.

Chama's muscles strained against the massive boulder as he attempted to roll it away from the entrance but no matter how hard he tried, he couldn't budge it. He would have to find a log, something to put beneath the rock to use for leverage.

Beside him, Dawg's ears lay back and its neck hairs stood straight out. A deep rumble sounded in its chest and turned into a low growl. Chama jerked his head around, saw the German shepherd's gaze fixed on the wooded area nearest them, and wondered if another bear had made its presence known.

His question was answered when Chama saw a tall man clothed in buckskin step from the woods. Even from this distance, the warrior was aware of a dangerous quality about the man, a dark wildness barely held in check, and it had nothing to do with the rifle held in the crook of his arm.

The stranger paused only a moment before starting across the clearing toward the warrior, and although the barrel of his weapon was pointed toward the ground, Chama knew it would be easy to swing it up if the man were so inclined.

"You got somebody caught in thet cave-in?" the stranger asked in English.

"My woman is there," Chama replied in the same language, feeling desperate enough to discount the man's dangerous quality. He needed help badly, and there was no one else to give it.

The stranger peered out from beneath prematurely grayed brows at the warrior before him. His blue eyes dwelt for a moment on the warrior's bloody shoulder and the blood that seeped slowly from the long gash. "The bear back yonder do thet?"

"Yes."

The buckskin-clad man nodded his head abruptly. "Figgered as much. Looked like he caught his foot in a trap. Thing like thet tends to make 'em purty mad. You'd be better off if'n you'd bind thet wound. But since you're set on gettin' your woman out first, we'd best get on with it."

When the stranger laid the gun aside and put his shoulder against the boulder, the warrior hurried to join him. Within moments their combined strengths moved the huge rock aside. But Chama's relief proved to be short-lived.

The boulder had been bracing what was left of the roof, and when the last support was removed, the remainder of the roof collapsed in a heavy rumble.

The two men leapt back simultaneously, barely escaping the shale and rocks collapsing inward. As a cloud of dust settled over Chama, his strength seemed to drain away, and he sank to his knees, feeling an acute sense of loss.

Fire Woman was surely dead, gone from him, and with her departure, she had taken his reason for living. A raw and primitive grief overwhelmed him, and his head sunk downward, his shoulders slumped with despair.

Chama knew, without a doubt, that even if Fire Woman had escaped the first cave-in, she could not have survived the second collapse. The falling roof had quickly extinguished the last spark of hope he'd had to recover her.

He was so deep in his depression, so wrapped up in his memories of the woman who had been his for such a short time, that he was totally unconscious of the stranger beside him. She had been so young to die, so brave and fiesty, and yet, she must have been terrified if she survived the first cave-in.

Guilt weighed heavily on his shoulders. He had not been there to help her, had allowed her to leave the cabin alone. He swallowed hard around the anguish closing his throat.

Slowly he became conscious of a distant barking, but he paid it no mind. The barking drew nearer, trying to pull him out of his thoughts of Fire Woman. He paid no attention until the man beside him stirred and rose to his feet.

"Think thet dog might of found somethin'?" the stranger asked.

Hope surged through Chama, giving him strength,

and he sprang to his feet at the same instant Dawg broke through the brush. When the dog saw Chama, it stopped in its tracks, abruptly faced the other way, then looked over its shoulder at the two men.

Yes, Chama breathed silently. Dawg wanted to lead him somewhere.

Chama barely allowed hmself to think as he hurried toward Dawg. That was all the encouragement the dog needed. The animal ran ahead, racing through the underbrush, then around a curve, keeping close beside the mountain.

As Chama followed the dog's trail, he was vaguely aware of the buckskin-clad stranger hurrying along beside him.

Dawg stopped at the base of a cliff, sniffing at a hole that stood about two feet off the ground. Then the animal lifted its head and uttered a howl, a long, mournful wail that sent chills through the warrior.

Chama fell to his knees beside the dog. A quick examination of the opening sent fury surging through him.

"A rabbit hole!" he exclaimed.

Picking up a rock, he threw it at the dog; but the German shepherd leapt aside, and the missile crashed harmlessly into the brush behind him.

"Hold on!" the stranger said. "Mebbe not." He knelt down and peered into the hole, his brows drawn together in a frown. "I ain't so sure it's a rabbit hole. Could be a way into the mine shaft." He shoved his large hand into the hole, then shook his head and stood up. "Nope. Looks like I was wrong. It ain't no tunnel. Thet hole ain't no more'n three feet deep."

Chama looked at the dog, noticing the way the German shepherd's eyes were fixed on the small opening. Why? Had the dog lost interest in its mistress's plight so quickly? The warrior didn't think so. Dawg was smart. Remarkably so. It was true the animal had led Chama to the rockslide, but when the roof collapsed, it had quickly lost interest. Because it knew they could not free her there? Had it gone to search for Fire Woman's scent elsewhere? Perhaps find another opening into the mountain?

Chama was almost certain of it! The dog refused to leave the opening because its mistress was near.

Pushing past the other man, Chama knelt and peered into the hole. It was small, perhaps the length and width of his arm. Surely it was too small for Fire Woman to be inside.

A bitter cold despair settled around his heart, and he was assailed by a terrible sense of foreboding. She must be beneath the fallen rocks on the other side of the mountain.

In his mind's eye he saw her crumpled lifeless body, but he quickly pushed the image away.

No! Chama thought. *She is not dead. I will not allow her to be dead.*

His legs trembled as he rose unsteadily to his feet. He was wasting time here. He must return to the blocked entrance.

But it seemed Dawg had other ideas. When Chama turned to go, Dawg leapt in front of him, blocking his path and growling fiercely. Chama hesitated, remembering the dog's earlier actions.

Could it be possible?

* * *

Mary Elizabeth stirred as she slowly regained consciousness. Her lashes fluttered, and she opened her eyes.

And wished she hadn't.

For a moment, the feeling of claustrophobia was almost more than she could bear. The blackness was penetrated by a round tunnel of light; the air was thick and heavy. Somewhere in the distance she could hear the sound of falling rock.

Was the end nearing?

Was the rest of the mountain about to collapse on her? God! If that were the case, then why hadn't it collapsed before she regained consciousness? Why did she have to regain her senses, only to face the inevitable?

Suddenly she became aware of another sound. Cocking her head to a listening posture, she strained her ears.

There it was again! A coughing, hacking sound.

Barking?

Her brow creased, her fingernails made half circles in her palm, and she forced herself to take slow, deep, calming breaths.

Think!

Concentrate!

There was something she should remember.

What was it?

A large dog flitted through her memory and was quickly gone. Was she going mad? Was her brain starving for lack of oxygen in this narrow, dark hole that ran deep in the bowels of the mountain?

She didn't know, but was afraid it was so.

The picture of the dog came again. *A German shepherd.* She caught and held the image close, clutching it tightly within her mind.

"Dawg?" she called, but her voice was weak, husky with the grit from the cave-in. She coughed, trying to clear some of the grit from her throat. "Dawg!" she called again.

Dawg began to bark wildly. The animal grabbed Chama's moccasins between its teeth and held on tight, slinging its head from left to right.

"Stop it, Dawg," the warrior said, trying to shake the dog loose.

" 'Pears he don't want you to leave," the stranger said. He looked back at the hole for a moment, then at the dog still worrying at Chama's moccasins.

"Get out of my way, Dawg," Chama said.

The stranger moved toward the darkened hole again, and the dog released Chama's moccasin and trotted after him. The warrior looked after the two, feeling the need to hurry back to the blocked entrance, and yet, afraid to leave in case the dog actually was trying to help him find Mary Elizabeth.

As he'd done before!

Chama watched the stranger kneel beside the hole and cock his head as though listening for something. He frowned and bent closer.

Chama held his breath. Had the stranger heard something?

Dawg began to bark loudly again.

"Hush!" Chama snapped, swiveling his head to stare at the German shepherd. Dawg quieted instantly as the warrior hurried to the hole and knelt beside it.

"Dawg!" The voice was faint, but Chama knew in-

101

stantly it was Fire Woman. He began to dig frantically, and the stranger helped him.

They were both unaware the dog had moved closer to them and settled down on its stomach, its gaze riveted to the dark hole.

Chama's heart raced frantically. He knew without a doubt that Fire Woman was alive. She must be. He would not allow himself to think otherwise. He worked furiously, trying to widen the hole, and the stranger matched him, stone for stone. Occasionally it took their combined strength to move a larger rock, but move it, they did.

Mary Elizabeth was unconscious when they found her, but Chama dared not allow himself to wonder if she lived. He only knew that she must. He fell to his knees beside her.

And then the stranger was pushing him aside, and Chama turned to snarl at him like a mountain lion defending its young.

"Take it easy," the man said. "You're too weak to carry her. I'm just aimin' to do it for you."

Realizing the truth of the other man's words, Chama allowed him to lift the unconscious girl. Then he rose and led the way back to the cabin.

Chapter Nine

Mary Elizabeth was drowning in a sea of blackness, suffo-cating from the lack of oxygen. Far ahead in the distance she could see Chama, but when she cried out, pleading with him to help her, he faded away into the darkness.

"Chama!" she cried aloud. The cry woke her, and she bolted up from the bed, stark, vivid fear glittering in her eyes.

Instantly the warrior was by her side, his arms cir-cling her protectively, drawing her head against his one good shoulder. Mary Elizabeth slid her arms around him, her fingernails digging into his back as she clutched at him convulsively, the memory of her ordeal uppermost in her mind.

"It is over, little one," he whispered against her ear. "You are safe with me." His hand stroked her cheek, soothing away her fear. As her panic began to subside, she became conscious of Dawg's anxious whine and lifted her head to reassure him.

A movement in Mary Elizabeth's peripheral vision caught her eyes, and she turned to see the stranger bending over the blackened pot on the potbellied stove.

Her eyes widened, her nails digging into Chama's back.

"You need not fear the mountain man," Chama murmured. "He helped me dig you out of the rubble."

His words brought back the fear she'd felt in the mine, and she shuddered against him and squeezed her eyes shut tight. But the blackness proved too much, and Mary Elizabeth opened them again, taking comfort in the solid feel of his warm chest against her cheek.

"How did you find me?" she whispered.

"Dawg found you."

Her gaze sought out the German shepherd beside the stove. "Thank God!" she said. "I could have died in there."

"Do not think of it," he said harshly. "And you must promise never again to enter such a place when you are alone."

"Don't worry," she said, barely controlling a shudder. "I could never bring myself to do it. Not after spending most of the day buried beneath that rubble."

She wasn't aware of the shadows darkening the cabin until the flare of a match brought it to her attention. She looked past Chama and saw the mountain man put the match to the wick in the lantern. A moment later the man hung the lantern on a nail hammered into the ceiling for that purpose.

Outside in the growing dusk, the wind moaned through the pine trees, but the silence in the cabin was broken only by the crackle of the fire.

At that moment the stranger turned around and looked at her. His gaze was shrewd, penetrating, and seemed intent on baring her soul.

She lifted her chin, ever so slightly, and stared back at him. Was this white man condemning her for being in the arms of an Indian? Her gaze became hard, blue chips of ice. He had no business looking at her in such a fashion. He knew nothing of her life, nor her circumstances.

His gaze shifted to Chama, and she could have sworn it changed. The look he bestowed on the warrior was so dark and wild, so filled with barely subdued rage, that a shiver of apprehension crept through her.

Her stomach muscles clenched tightly and her voice was small and frightened when she spoke. "What do you want here?"

"You got no call to be afraid," he said gruffly. "I ain't aimin' to cause you hurt."

His words, meant to calm, did nothing of the sort. Perhaps he didn't intend her harm, but she wasn't so certain he felt the same way about Chama.

Pulling her head back from the warrior, she repositioned her lips near his ear and whispered, "How long does he plan on staying here?"

He pulled his head away and looked at her with puzzled eyes. "We have not discussed it," he murmured. "But it would be unkind to turn him away from shelter when he has helped us."

Although she wanted to protest, Mary Elizabeth held her tongue. Perhaps she was reading too much in the stranger's dark glance. Chama wasn't easily fooled by others. Even so, she felt the stranger would bear watching, and if Chama wouldn't do it, then she would.

"Supper's ready," the man said. His words were accompanied by the sound of cutlery clinking against tin plates as he set the table. The two hide-bottomed chairs scraped across the floor as he pushed them up to the table.

Ordering Mary Elizabeth to remain where she was, Chama released her and joined the mountain man, who was filling the plates at the stove. After serving Mary Elizabeth, the warrior seated himself across from the other man.

Keeping a wary eye on the two men, Mary Elizabeth dipped a fork into the stew on her plate and carried it to her mouth. She chewed slowly, her gaze never leaving the stranger.

She wondered who he was and what he was doing there. She didn't realize he was aware of her interest until he looked up and spoke.

"Guess you're wonderin' a mite about me," he said. "My name's Saul Jacobs." His gaze was shrewd as it held hers. "Chama called you Fire Woman. You got another name?"

Chama paused in the act of carrying a bite of food to his mouth. His brows drew into a frown. But Mary Elizabeth saw no reason to keep her identity secret. Perhaps Saul might even know her brother Jeb. The possibility caused her heart to pick up speed.

"My name is Mary Elizabeth Abernathy," she said, her eyes on his face, searching for the slightest flicker of recognition. But there was none. "My brother is Jeb Abernathy," she explained. "Do you know him?"

His blue eyes were penetrating as he shook his dark head. "Nope. Cain't say as I do. He live somewheres aroun' these parts?"

"Yes," she said. "He lives in the mountains north of Taos."

"Well, me not knowin' about him don't mean much. These mountains cover a lot of territory." His voice deepened, his gaze dropping to his plate. "Makes it easy fer them thet wants to hide. Too damned easy."

Hide? Why should Jeb want to hide from her?

Suddenly she realized he wasn't referring to her brother.

Curious, she waited for him to say more, but he gave his attention to the food on his plate. When he had scraped every morsel from it, he pushed back his chair and rose to his feet.

Her body tensed as he picked up his rifle and slid it into the crook of his arm. Slowly, she laid her plate aside, her heart beating loudly in her ears. A quick glance at Chama showed that he was unconcerned by the other man's actions.

"Guess I'll take me a walk," Saul said, reaching for the board that barred the door.

As soon as the door closed behind him, Mary Elizabeth was on her feet and moving across the room.

"I don't trust him," she told Chama in a low voice.

Chama frowned. "Why?"

"I'm not sure," she replied. "But there is something about the way he looks at you . . . something—" she struggled to find words for her feelings—"wild and dangerous. I don't think he likes you."

Chama's lips quirked into a grin. "It does not matter," he said. "There are many men who do not like me."

"He's different," she insisted. "He wants something from us."

Chama seemed unperturbed by her words, but she wasn't going to let it alone. She was going to find out

107

what the man's intentions were. Mary Elizabeth was ready for him when he came back inside.

"What were you doing when you found us?" she asked.

He leaned his rifle beside the door and turned to face her.

"I was hunting a spot to set my traps," he said.

"Then you're a trapper?"

"Sometimes. They's a big market for pelts. And this mountain's a good place for trappin'. Plenty of bear and beaver here to make it worthwhile."

"You said you were a trapper . . . sometimes. When you're not trapping, what do you do?"

Something in the lines of his face, the glint of steel in his eyes, sent a chill through her body, and she suppressed a shudder.

"When I ain't trappin', I'm lookin'," he said.

Chama, realizing something was amiss, rose to his feet and came to stand beside Mary Elizabeth. "You look for the white man's gold?" he asked.

"I done my share of lookin' for gold," Saul said. "But thet ain't what I'm lookin' for now."

"Then tell us," Chama said. "Perhaps we can help."

Saul nodded. His blue eyes were hard as he held the warrior's gaze. "Maybe you can. Fact is, I'm lookin' for my wife. She'd be with the Apaches . . . unless she managed to escape."

At his words, Chama and Mary Elizabeth reacted in opposite ways — the warrior stiffened while Mary Elizabeth felt the tension leaving her body. The reason for the mountain man's anger was obvious now. She had been right when she'd thought it was directed toward Chama. After all, he belonged to the same tribe of Indians who had taken a loved one from Saul.

"Could you describe her?" Mary Elizabeth asked.

He nodded, and his eyes took on a faraway look. "She's got dark hair. An' it's all shiny. Kinda like a raven's wing when the sun's shinin' on it." A shadow crossed his face, and he seemed to have difficulty in swallowing. "She's just a little bit of a thing. Apache life would be mighty hard on 'er."

Was he searching for Johanna? The description certainly fit.

"I escaped from the Apaches with a girl," she said slowly. "She had dark hair and was about my size."

"That must be her!" he growled, reaching out and grasping her upper arms. "It ain't likely they'd be more'n two of you like thet. I knowed she was alive. I knowed it! Where's she at, girl? Where'd she go?" Each word was punctuated by a hard shake, and he seemed unaware of anything in the room but her.

Chama wrapped an arm around Saul's neck and applied enough force to make him release her. Mary Elizabeth was vaguely aware of the German shepherd uttering a low growl of warning and moving toward them, but it was Chama who claimed her attention . . . he who was the most dangerous.

"You will not touch my woman!" Chama warned.

"Mister Jacobs," she said hesitantly. "You better listen to him. He don't like people touchin' me."

Saul's breath came harshly when Chama finally released him. Mary Elizabeth wouldn't have been surprised had the two men engaged in a battle, but the mountain man seemed to be struggling with some inner turmoil.

"He didn't hurt me," she told Chama. "He was anxious and didn't know what he was doing."

Chama remained silent, his stance threatening.

"Sit down," Mary Elizabeth told him. "Both of you. There's no sense in fighting."

"Do not give me orders," Chama said harshly.

"Oh, hush!" Mary Elizabeth snapped. "Can't you see this means a lot to him? And you did say he helped you. It seems to me we owe him."

Chama's lips tightened grimly, but he remained silent.

"Where did Ruth go?" Saul asked, trying to get a grip on his emotions.

"Ruth?"

"Yes. Her name's Ruth."

"I'm sorry," she said gently. "I don't know Ruth. I was talking about a girl named Johanna McFarley."

"But—" his eyes were puzzled—"you said you ran away from the Apaches with Ruth."

"No," she replied. "I didn't say her name. But it wasn't Ruth. It was Johanna."

"Maybe it was Ruth," he insisted. "Maybe she's just usin' a different name."

"Why would she do that?" she asked.

"I don't know," he mumbled. His shoulders sagged, and the fight seemed to go out of him. His fingers trembled as he untied a pouch from the waist of his buckskins and extracted a small, shiny gold object, a locket, Mary Elizabeth realized.

"This's her picture," he said gruffly, holding out the locket. "Would you take a look at it?"

She found herself staring at the likeness of a smiling, dark-haired girl.

"Is thet the girl?" Saul asked unsteadily.

"No." She shook her head. "I'm sorry."

"An' you ain't never seen her before?"

"No. I'm sorry," she said again, swallowing around an obstruction in her throat.

Saul took the locket from her and held it out to Chama. The warrior remained unmoving, refusing to look at the picture.

"Please, Chama," she pleaded. "Just look at the picture."

He turned away from them.

"I'm sorry," she said. "He would feel he was betraying his people."

"What about your people?" he asked gruffly.

"What do you mean?"

"You're just as white as she is, but you're livin' here with him." His eyes glittered with barely contained rage. "Don't you think you're betraying your people by stayin'?"

Chama whirled around. "You go too far, white dog. Take your things and go while you can. You are no longer welcome here."

Saul's eyes blazed blue fire. "It ain't up to you to tell me leave," he said. "I ain't leavin' until the girl says to go. An' if she's got any sense left at all, then she'll come with me."

Mary Elizabeth looked helplessly at the two men, feeling they were hovering on the verge of a fight that could only end when one of them was dead. She must do something to prevent the clash. But what? She could understand the mountain man's feelings, but having lived with the Apaches, she could understand Chama and the loyalty he would naturally feel for his people.

Suddenly she realized there was someone else she hadn't considered: the girl, Ruth, who was being held captive.

"How long has it been since the Apaches took Ruth?" she asked.

The glare faded from Saul's eyes and was replaced by such a depth of pain that Mary Elizabeth could hardly bear it.

"Been nigh on to a year now," Saul replied. "We was travelin' 'long the Red River when them Injuns stole Ruth off thet wagon train."

"But —" her brow wrinkled in thought — "isn't the Red River southeast of here?"

"It is," he said. "But Apaches don't tend to stay long in one place."

She nodded her head, knowing from experience that he was right.

"I heered tell the Apaches hidin' in these mountains had a white captive 'bout Ruth's age. So I come lookin'."

"I wish there was someway I could help," she said. "But I haven't seen her." The next words she spoke were hard, but she realized they had to be said. "You could spend your life searching for Ruth and never find her."

"I ain't never gonna stop lookin'," he said harshly. "It's my fault them Injuns got her."

"Your fault?"

He nodded, his eyes dark with some inner emotion. "Ruth didn't want to leave our farm in Missouri. It was me all along. Thought we'd have a better chance at life if we was somewheres away from all her folks. We joined up with a wagon train headed for Fort Garland.

Didn't never reach it though. Them injuns attacked from behind whilst I was ridin' lookout up front. Time I got back, they was only a few people left alive. Nobody to worry thet Ruth was gone. Just me. I rode away from what was left of thet wagon train to look for her. An' I been lookin' ever since. Don't even know if she's still alive."

Tears welled into Mary Elizabeth's eyes. "Chama," she said. "Please look at the picture. You don't have to help him find her, but it would help him to know if she's alive. Please. We owe it to him. He did help us when we needed it."

The warrior's face was rock hard, but when his eyes met hers, they softened slightly. "I will look," he muttered, taking the locket.

She watched him closely as he studied the picture. "Do you know her?"

He shook his head. "No. But I have heard of a woman with grass-green eyes who was taken from a wagon train at the Red River.

"Thet's her!" Saul snapped. "Ruth's got green eyes! Where is she?"

"I do not know," Chama said. "I have heard of her, and she was alive. I cannot tell you more."

"You know somethin' else," Saul growled. "You ain't tellin' it all."

Mary Elizabeth paid little attention to the two men who had squared off again. Something tugged at her memory, something that was proving to be elusive.

Then she remembered. During the time of the buffalo hunt, she'd heard the women speak of a woman with green eyes who'd been taken captive by the Chiricahua Apaches. The conversation had found a place in

Mary Elizabeth's memory because of the circumstances. Her own bride-price had been under discussion. She and several other women had been bathing in the river when she overheard them talking. Chama had made another offer to Three Toes for her just the night before, and already everyone in the village seemed to know about it. It wasn't the fifty horses offered that generated the talk. It was because the offer had been rejected.

One of the women had laughed and remarked that Three Toes must think Fire Woman was worth more than the woman with the grass-green eyes.

Mary Elizabeth became aware of the men facing each other.

"You have heard enough," Chama growled, his ebony gaze on Saul. "Now leave this place."

"I ain't goin' nowhere until you tell me where Ruth is," Saul said. His hands clenched into fists, and his muscles bunched together as though he wanted nothing more than to kill the man facing him.

Mary Elizabeth stepped between the two men and put a restraining hand on the mountain man's chest. "He won't help you," she said sadly. "But I know the name of the warrior who has her."

"What is it?" Saul snapped.

"His name is Broken Knife. He belongs to the Chiricahua Apache tribe. I have no idea where they are."

"Does he?" Saul looked pointedly at Chama.

"I don't know," she said. "But it makes no difference. He won't tell you."

"Don't matter where he is," Saul said grimly. "I'm gonna find him. Now thet I've finally got a name, I'm gonna find him." His blue eyes had the wild, angered look again, the look that had been tempered by sadness before. Now the sadness had completely disappeared, and only the wildness remained, the look of a man who had been driven to the brink of madness and should be approached only with caution. "Broken Knife!" he muttered. "I'm gonna find him. I'm gonna save you, Ruth. And before I'm through, I'm gonna make Broken Knife wish he was dead."

A thick knot formed in Mary Elizabeth's throat as she watched the mountain man pick up his rifle and cross the room. She knew Chama was angry about her intervention between the two men, angry as well because she had chosen to tell the mountain man what she knew. But she had her loyalties the same as Chama did, and they were not to the Apache people.

Her feelings were mixed as she watched Saul open the door. She wondered what would happen if she ran to him, begged him to take her with him, back to civilization and her people.

But such actions would prove useless. Chama would never let her go without a fight. And somehow, despite the mountain man's size, she didn't think he could win a fight against the warrior, nor was she certain she'd want him to, she realized as Saul stepped out into the night.

And then the door was closing behind the mountain man, leaving her to face the angry warrior within the confines of the one small room of the cabin.

Chapter Ten

A tense silence enveloped the room, brought on by the abrupt departure of the mountain man. Mary Elizabeth clenched her hands until her nails bit into her palms. Her throat was tight, and she swallowed hard as the silence lengthened, spreading around them like the ripples in a pond that continued to grow in ever-widening circles.

She threw a quick glance at Chama and wished she hadn't. As she'd expected, his expression was cold, harsh as a winter storm. She gave an inward shudder, and the tight rein she'd kept on her emotions threatened to give way.

His look was so forbidding, so obviously angered, but how could he have expected her to act in any other manner?

Mary Elizabeth's gaze fell on Dawg, stretched out in its place beside the fire. Although the animal was quiet, she knew that it too, felt the strain. It showed in the way its head was lifted, the way it stared at her, its gaze surprisingly intelligent, until finally, as though it could take the tension no longer, the German shepherd issued a long, drawn out *woooooooof* that began deep in its throat and barely escaped being a howl.

"Quiet, Dawg!" Chama growled harshly.

Although the dog fell silent, its eyes never left its mistress as it rose to its feet, padded across the room and licked sympathetically at her clenched hand.

The dog's obvious affection proved her undoing. The tears she'd managed to keep at bay welled up and fell silently down her face. She swiped an impatient hand at them, but they kept falling, faster and faster, blurring her vision.

"Why do you weep?" Chama demanded.

His harshness stabbed at her, but the tone of his voice succeeded in drying her tears where Dawg's sympathy had not. Her eyes glittered as she swiped at the moisture on her face, shame at her weakness expressing itself in anger.

"Why should I bother trying to explain something that you'd never be able to understand?" she asked, keeping her eyes on the dog. How could she tell him why she was crying when she wasn't really sure herself?

"But the white-eyes would understand?" Chama's voice held barely controlled rage.

Although Mary Elizabeth's lips tightened into a thin line, she still refused to look at him, feeling that if she did, she would be forced into an argument that she had little chance of winning.

"Look at me, Fire Woman," he said. "Do not shut me out of your thoughts."

His use of the name the Apaches had given her loosed her tongue, and her gaze snapped up. She

117

shot him a hostile glare. "My name is Mary Elizabeth!" she cried. "Mary Elizabeth Abernathy! And I will answer to *no* other name!"

The two were so intent on their argument that they were unaware of the German shepherd which left its mistress and padded silently to its place beside the fire again. The animal gave a heavy sigh and laid its head on its front paws. Its ears were laid back against its head, its sorrowful eyes fixed firmly away from the two people who were so intent on their anger.

When Mary Elizabeth renounced her Apache name, Chama's irritation turned to scalding fury. His hands clenched into fists as he watched her. His arm and chest muscles were bunched as though he would leap toward her and silence her tongue. She felt suddenly weak and vulnerable in the face of his terrible anger, and her chin quivered unsteadily, her expression becoming hurt, wounded.

With a muttered oath, he was around the table and pulling her trembling form into his arms.

"L-let me go," she cried, flailing out with her fists against his shoulders.

But her efforts to free herself were puny against his greater strength, and as he continued to hold her firmly against him, she laid her head on his chest and gave way to her tears.

Great sobs shook her slight frame, sobs that continued to grow in proportion until they were rendering her almost breathless. There was such a world of tenderness in Chama's embrace that it proved her undoing.

She cried in compassion for the mountain man

whose love was so great that he might spend the rest of his life in a never-ending search. And she cried for Ruth, who had become a captive of the Apaches.

Then, when she had cried enough tears for the two lovers, she cried for her parents, who had been killed in the prime of their life. And she cried for her brother Clem, who had died trying to protect his family from the Apaches.

She cried for her sister, Melissa, who would have been better off dying with them.

And when her sobs for her lost family finally began to subside, she began to cry in earnest again. Dry, hacking sobs were this time cried for herself, for she realized she was coming to care for the Apache warrior who held her so gently. But she could not allow herself to love him. The two of them were too far apart, from two different worlds that would never meet.

Chama was racked with pain as he held the sobbing girl in his arms. How could her tears affect him so? he wondered. He was supposed to be a strong warrior, and yet, when she cried with such heartbreak, he felt as though his heart was breaking into tiny pieces.

He . . . a warrior whose strength had endured throughout the years, never wavering or faltering.

He . . . a warrior who could stand even the most intense torture without flinching.

How could the tears of this small girl accomplish something his fiercest enemies could not do? How could she make him crumble inside? Why did he feel so helpless in the face of her tears?

What could he do to stop her sobbing?

Unable to think of a way to console her, he lifted her in his arms and carried her to the bed. Then he lay beside her, holding her against him and stroking her silky hair. "Do not weep," he murmured, kissing her wet eyelids and pulling her tighter against his lean, hard body. His hand stroked her back soothingly, and her hands crept around his neck, her fingers twining through his hair.

When he pressed his mouth against her neck, he meant only to soothe; but she turned her face toward him, and their lips met in a long kiss. She gave a shuddering sigh and pressed herself closer to him. The feel of her curves, so warm against his lower body, was almost overwhelming. His body was hardening, becoming almost painful with his wanting.

She pulled away slightly and stared at him with reddened eyes. "Love me," she whispered.

Needing no further urging, his fingers found the fastenings of her garments, and only moments later he cast them aside and removed his own, quickly rejoining her on the bed. Their coming together was swift, the end too soon; then he held her in his arms until her breathing became even and he knew she was fast asleep.

But long before that time he had come to a decision. If Fire Woman's happiness depended on returning to her brother, to what she called civilization, then he would take her there, for her tears had accomplished what her anger could not. He had come to the realization that he would rather lose her than see her filled with such unhappiness. Even though the loss would cause him more pain than he could possibly bear, he would take Fire Woman to the brother who meant so much to her.

When Mary Elizabeth woke, the sun streamed through the window. Her eyes felt gritty as though they had sand in them.

Remembering her tears of the night before, Mary Elizabeth turned her head and let her gaze wander around the room, searching for Chama.

But she searched in vain, for she was alone in the cabin — alone, without even Dawg left behind to keep her company.

Where have Chama and Dawg gone?

Her gaze moved to the door as though she would find the answer to their whereabouts there, but the rough-cut boards held no clue.

Pushing back the covers, she rose from the bed, the memory of her tears staining her cheeks with a bright red flush. She had shamed herself before Chama. Why had she allowed herself to give way to her weakness in such a manner?

Mary Elizabeth's stomach growled, and she forced herself to eat a cold breakfast of dried venison. Afterward, she stepped outside the cabin.

The mid-morning sun felt warm against the bared skin of her arms, and she breathed in the fresh scent of pine.

Where is Chama? a silent voice asked.

She forced her thoughts away from the warrior and focused them instead on the surrounding country-side, realizing there were only a few patches of snow

121

left near the cabin. Her gaze lifted, studying the distant peak. Had the snow melted enough near the pass to allow her to cross the mountaintop?

Her gaze skittered away from the peak, then reluctantly returned. "It's colder up there," she muttered. "The snow will be longer melting." For some reason, the thought caused her to feel relief.

Turning back toward the cabin, her gaze fell on the silent woods nearby. Saul was somewhere in those woods, searching for the woman the Apaches had stolen from him. Mary Elizabeth could not help him, and Chama would not.

"Where *is* Chama?" she asked aloud.

Her only answer was silence.

Her thoughts remained on Chama, an enigma she would never be able to understand. How could he be so tender with her, yet have no feeling for another man's pain? She had lived with the Apaches four long and bitter years, but she would never understand them.

God! Why am I just standing here?

You could go if you wanted, a silent voice said. *He couldn't stop you now.*

Even as she realized she could leave, Mary Elizabeth felt a curious reluctance to do so.

Go! the voice insisted. *Go now! If you don't, you'll lose the chance.*

Mary Elizabeth finally gave in to the silent warning and entered the cabin again, feeling a curious ache around her heart. Although her mind was in turmoil, she tried to concentrate on what she'd need for the journey across the mountains.

Food.

She reached for several hide bags filled with pemmican, dried venison pulverized and mixed with berries and bear grease, and laid them on the table.

Water.

The waterskin was already full. She laid it beside the pemmican bags.

Weapons.

Taking the muzzleloader from the corner of the cabin, she laid it beside the other supplies. Then she searched for the butcher knife, found it on the shelf behind the stove, and added it to the growing pile.

Ammunition.

Powder and shot were added.

Pack.

A quick search revealed a red flannel shirt. She spread it out on the table and dumped the supplies — everything except for the rifle — into the middle of the bundle.

Feeling a sudden need to hurry, she folded the tail of the shirt across the supplies, then tied the arms together. She was on the verge of leaving when she realized she'd forgotten something.

The gold!

She'd need the gold nuggets when she reached civilization.

It was only a matter of moments before the gold had been tied into the bundle and the supplies hoisted over her back. Sliding the rifle into the crook of her arm, she opened the door and stepped outside. A moment later she left the cabin behind.

At first she found the going easy, for only a few patches of snow lay here and there. She tried not to think what Chama would say when he came back and found her gone, but there was no doubt in her mind that he would follow. She knew as well that she could not allow him to stop her. No matter what her feelings were for the warrior, feelings she refused to face in the bright light of day, the drive to find her brother, to return to civilization and to people who thought the way she did, had returned and become all-consuming, a flame that would never die until she reached her goal.

What then? a silent voice asked.

But Mary Elizabeth studiously ignored the question. She had no way of knowing the future, would have to take one day at a time.

She felt almost glad when she encountered the swollen stream. Now she would have to concentrate her efforts on reaching the other side, where a path would lead her over the mountaintop.

She traveled upstream, keeping a sharp eye out for a way across the flooding water. She had traveled about a quarter of a mile when she saw the large rocks rising out of the stream. They looked close enough together to allow her safe passage across.

Crossing proved more difficult and time consuming than she'd imagined but she finally reached the other side and continued on her way, noticing as she did that the air was considerably colder now, making her breath almost visible in the thin mountain air.

When she first saw movement near the pass, she thought it was her imagination, but she had only gone a few more feet when she realized it wasn't.

She stopped . . . and shivered, but her reaction was not caused by the cold. Had Chama been to the pass and was even now returning? What would he say when he saw her? Would it do any good to hide? Her head swiveled, her gaze searching, but there was nowhere to conceal herself. She had no choice except to face him and try to bluff her way out of the situation she found herself in.

He was almost upon her before she realized the man, although undoubtedly an Apache warrior, was *not* Chama. Sensing the danger she faced, she came to an abrupt stop, dropped her bundle of supplies and swung the rifle up. Her heart hammered wildly in her breast as she braced herself and faced the warrior. She was unaware the sun had turned her coppery red hair to flame, unaware as well that the short stout warrior dressed in frayed buckskin was bent on taking her alive.

When he was a distance of ten feet away, he stopped and spoke in the Apache tongue. "Put down your weapon," he said gruffly. "I mean you no harm." Something about his ebony gaze, the way it flared possessively, told her he lied.

"Who are you?" she demanded, speaking in the same language.

The warrior lifted his arm and held his palm forward, the sign of peace. "I am only a traveler," he said. "My name is Broken Knife. My people are the Chiricahua Apaches."

Broken Knife! Instead of reassuring her, the name sent a tremor of alarm through Mary Elizabeth. "Why are you here?" she asked, her gaze never wavering from his.

"I am a traveler," he said again, his face impassive. "Only a warrior in search of his woman."

Ruth! She must have escaped from him. Although elation flowed through Mary Elizabeth, she gave no outward sign of emotion, nor did she relax her grip on the rifle.

His gaze became wary, watchful. "Like you, my woman is a paleface. Perhaps you have seen her." It was more a statement than a question.

"I have seen no one," she said, her finger tightening on the trigger of the rifle. She was tempted to shoot him where he stood, but somehow could not quite bring herself to be so cold-blooded. Although his very presence felt threatening, to kill him would be murder.

"Are you alone?" he asked, his ebony gaze on her doeskin garments.

"No." There was ice in her voice. "I have a companion."

The warrior's gaze went to the rolled-up bundle she'd tossed on the ground. His eyes glittered when they returned to hers, but whatever he was thinking, he gave no outward sign.

"I will go now," he said. "I must continue to search for my woman."

She relaxed slightly as he began to turn away, letting the barrel of the gun drop and expelling a silent breath of relief.

His eyes should have warned her of his intention, but when he seemed to be leaving, she had relaxed her guard. In that instant he spun back, leaping forward, knocking the barrel of the gun aside and wrenching it from her. Then he flung the weapon out into the snow, clamping his fingers around her arm and squeezing tightly.

"Let me go!" she gritted, struggling to free herself

from his grasp.

But it was useless. His fingers wound tightly through her hair, and he wrenched her head backward with a snap. "Where is my woman?" he demanded.

"I haven't seen her!" she cried, struggling furiously with him.

His fingers bit savagely into her arm, and he yanked her head back harder. "You knew she was a white-eyes!" he snarled. "You must have seen her."

"No! I haven't!"

She kicked out at him, managing to connect with his shinbone. With a harsh curse, Broken Knife drew back his hand and struck her a hard blow across the jaw. The force of his blow sent her sprawling on the ground, and she felt a raw pain in her arms and legs as broken twigs bit into her exposed flesh. Her heart beat wildly, her stomach churned and her blood was pounding in her ears. Her blue eyes were wide with fright as she watched the Apache who stood over her, grinning with evil intent.

Mary Elizabeth knew she was in a dangerous situation. Why had she left the protection of the cabin? She had been foolish beyond belief, and she couldn't, for the life of her, figure out how she was going to get herself out of the mess she was in.

But she was determined she wouldn't give in to panic. When Broken Knife made his move, she reacted instantly.

The Indian leaned over, intent on pulling the fallen girl to her feet, but she lashed out with her foot and connected with the soft flesh between his legs.

He grunted with pain, clutched at his lower body

and crumpled to the ground . . . so close beside Mary Elizabeth that she could smell his fetid breath.

She rolled away from him, out of his reach. Then she was up in a flash, running . . . her moccasins making little sound as she thudded over the uneven ground, intent on putting as much distance between them as was possible.

But the time she had gained was precious little. Before she had gone twenty feet, she could hear him behind her, his moccasins crunching over the occasional patches of snow, and Mary Elizabeth knew that she had little hope of outrunning him. Like Chama, Broken Knife was an Apache warrior, trained from childhood for long-distance running.

She felt the impact of his body striking hers, and she fell beneath his weight, not the least bit surprised. She had known there was no way she could escape him, known also that the least she could do was try.

The impact of her body striking the ground stunned her, driving the breath from her lungs. She lay helplessly, the warrior pinning her beneath him as she tried desperately to catch her breath.

Her ears were ringing, and a red haze swirled around Mary Elizabeth, threatening to overcome her. Realizing she was on the point of losing consciousness, she fought the darkness enveloping her.

When she first heard the low growl coming out of the mists surrounding her, Mary Elizabeth thought she'd imagined it . . . until the voice sounded behind them.

"Release the woman!"

Chapter Eleven

Taken completely by surprise, Broken Knife's head jerked around. His eyes widened when he saw the warrior who had spoken . . . and the dog that stood beside him, growling low in its throat, its stance no less menacing.

Whatever else he was, Broken Knife was no fool. His movements were cautious, his gaze never leaving the other man's as he rose to his feet.

"I have no quarrel with you," Broken Knife said. "We are of the same tribe.

Chama's expression gave nothing away as he looked at the girl lying on the ground, taking in her wildly disordered hair, her disarranged garments, before his gaze returned to the man standing before him.

"I have a quarrel with any man who lays hands on my woman," Chama said harshly.

Broken Knife spread his arms wide to show he was weaponless. "I had no way of knowing she belonged to you," he said. "She was alone."

Mary Elizabeth was aware of the tension in the air

surrounding them as the two warriors took each other's measure. Dawg, sensing all was still not well, moved to stand between her and the warrior who had attacked her.

Uwilling to allow for any sign of weakness, Mary Elizabeth rose unsteadily to her feet. Broken Knife's dark eyes left Chama's momentarily, caught by her movement. She gave an inward shudder as she saw the savage glitter in Broken Knife's eyes before he looked away.

Mary Elizabeth was frightened by her narrow escape and took several backward steps, determined to put as much distance as possible between herself and Broken Knife, but Chama, obviously misconstruing her intention, reached out and captured her wrist between hard fingers.

"Stay here," he snapped.

She did, but took up a position that put her slightly behind Chama, feeling much safer with the other warrior facing Chama instead of her.

"This woman is mine," Chama said.

Mary Elizabeth had no mind to object to Chama's words. Being known as Chama's woman put her far above Broken Knife's reach.

"Who are you?" Chama asked the other man.

Broken Knife identified himself and explained he was searching for an escaped white captive. "Have you seen her?" he asked.

"No," Chama said. "I have seen no other woman but mine on this mountain."

Turning from the other warrior, Chama's dark gaze dwelt on Mary Elizabeth. "Why did you leave the cabin?" he asked.

"I wondered if the pass was clear," she said, her voice betraying her nervousness.

Chama glanced pointedly at the bundle of supplies at his feet. How had the pack come to be there? she wondered. When she fled from Broken Knife, she had left the bundle behind. Realizing Chama must have found the supplies, she felt her cheeks flushing scarlet.

"I didn't know how long I would be gone," Mary Elizabeth muttered. She didn't like telling untruths and knew he didn't believe her, but she wanted to put off a confrontation until they were alone.

"We will speak of it later," he said coldly. Turning his attention to Broken Knife, he said, "Did you come across the mountain?"

Broken Knife replied, "I came through the canyon south of here." His eyes glittered savagely. "My woman escaped. I have been searching for her for two sunrises." His fingers curled and uncurled again and Mary Elizabeth knew it would go badly for Ruth if she were caught. If only there were some way she could help the girl, she thought. But how could she possible help Ruth when she couldn't even help herself? It seemed Saul was Ruth's only chance to retain her freedom. Mary Elizabeth knew if the mountain man ever found his wife, he would die before giving her up again.

Becoming aware that Chama had invited Broken Knife back to the cabin to eat with them, she felt anger surge through her. She had no wish to feed the man who would have used her so badly. But she knew the invitation was issued through politeness. Since Chama had told the other man of his prior

131

claim on her, Broken Knife had kept his distance and apparently thought that was enough to satisfy Chama who had no other reason to quarrel with Broken Knife.

But Mary Elizabeth was not so quick to forgive. She threw a heated glance toward Chama. How could he extend an invitation to someone who had treated her in such a manner? But then, what else could she expect from a heathen savage such as he.

Tightening her lips grimly, Mary Elizabeth reached for the flannel-wrapped bundle, tossed it across her shoulder and led the way back to the cabin. She could hear the two men speaking in low tones as they followed along behind her, but paid them little heed. She was too angry, too wrapped up in her own thoughts about her thwarted attempt at escape.

Upon opening the door of the cabin, she found the place in an upheaval. The contents of the cabin looked as though a bear, or some other wild animal, had entered, bent on destruction. The table was turned over; tin plates and cups were strewn on the floor amid the scattered pelts.

She looked at the mess surrounding them, then at the door. "How could a wild animal come inside with the door closed?" she asked.

Although Broken Knife seemed curious as well, he made no comment, and Chama seemed totally unaffected by the upheaval, a state of mind that seemed curious in itself.

Ignoring the chairs, Chama strode across the room to the pile of furs and sat down. Crossing his legs, he invited the other warrior to join him.

She stared at him in astonishment. Didn't he care that something had come into the place and made such a mess?

Suddenly, a thought gave her pause, and she narrowed her eyes on the warrior.

No, she silently argued. *Chama would never do such a thing.*

Not even if he returned and found you gone? argued a silent voice.

No!

But she couldn't dismiss the suspicion so easily. It continued to worry at her mind.

Could he have done it? Did he come home and find the cabin empty and fly into a rage?

With the suspicion came anger, but she forced herself to remain calm as she straightened up the cabin and prepared the food. All the while she listened to the men talking, hoping she could learn more about the girl who had escaped from Broken Knife.

"She is good to look upon," Broken Knife was saying in the Apache tongue. "And worth many horses."

Chama gave no sign that he had ever heard of the girl, and the warrior continued to talk. "I took her from a wagon train where many white-eyes were killed and many scalps taken," he boasted. "I am envied by all the warriors of my tribe."

"Such a prize should be well guarded," Chama commented. "How did she escape?"

"I have no one to watch her while I hunt," Broken Knife said bitterly. "The villagers are jealous of my success and will not help me. When I left the village to hunt fresh meat for my wickiup, I left her bound, but she managed to free herself and run away. It is

133

my belief that she was seen escaping but no one cared to stop her."

Mary Elizabeth listened to the man complain, hoping that Ruth was well and truly out of his hands.

"Perhaps you should sell her," Chama said.

"For a time I thought of doing that," Broken Knife said. "But the other warriors said the price was too high."

"If you find the girl, I might consider buying her from you," Chama said.

Chama's words stabbed at Mary Elizabeth, and her lips twisted bitterly. Why had she thought him so different from the others? she wondered. He was obviously intrigued by Broken Knife's description of Ruth and wanted her for himself.

Don't be petty, a small voice chided. *Think of Ruth. Chama would be kind to her.*

"What would you offer for her?" Broken Knife asked.

"It depends on how she looks," Chama said. "Has she been ill-treated?"

"You know how it is with captives," the other said, his eyes turning to Mary Elizabeth. "Sometimes one must teach them a lesson. I might consider a trade. My woman for yours."

Revulsion ran swift and hot in Mary Elizabeth's breast, and she paused in the act of filling the coffee-pot with water. She would rather be dead than have Broken Knife touch her, but Chama would never let such a thing happen.

Surely he wouldn't.

Her heart pounded in her breast, the blood throbbing in her temples as she waited for Chama's refusal. But it never came.

To her absolute horror, he actually seemed to be considering Broken Knife's offer. The day seemed to grow dark and cold, and the icy hand of fear wrapped itself around her heart.

She hardly dared breathe as she waited for his answer. Finally, he spoke.

"A bird in hand is worth two in the bush," he said.

"Then, perhaps we will speak again of a trade when my bird comes out of the bush."

"Perhaps," Chama said.

Hurt stabbed through Mary Elizabeth, establishing itself in anger. She banged the pot on the stovetop and reached for more wood. Upon finding the woodbox empty, she crossed the room and opened the door.

"Where are you going?" Chama growled.

"To fetch more wood," she snapped, stepping out of the cabin.

And if he tries to stop me, then he can get it himself!

Dawg nearly tripped her in its haste to leave the cabin. While she gathered an armload of wood, the German shepherd made a dash for the bushes.

"Come back here, Dawg!" she ordered in English.

The animal whined and looked her way, but refused to obey. It turned back to the woods, sniffing the ground. Curious, she dropped her load of wood and followed him. When she was about forty feet from the cabin, a girl darted from the cover of the woods and raced toward her.

Although the girl was dressed in the Apache fashion—buckskin skirt that came to midcalf, and shapeless buckskin top with her legs modestly covered by

135

the distinctive high moccasins that pulled above the knees — Mary Elizabeth had no doubt in her mind that she was Ruth.

She was not more than five feet tall, slender, with lustrous, hip-length black hair. And at the moment, she was breathless.

"Thank God!" Ruth breathed. "I've been watching the cabin for the last few minutes, uncertain whether or not I should come out of hiding. I —"

"Go back into the woods," Mary Elizabeth interrupted hurriedly. "Broken Knife is inside the cabin, and you can't let him see you."

Sudden terror filled the girl's large, green eyes, and without another word, she made a dash for the cover of the woods. None too soon, it proved, for Chama's large frame suddenly filled the doorway of the cabin.

"What are you doing?" he called.

She swallowed hard, realizing she must not let him suspect the girl was anywhere nearby, not when he'd been considering a trade between himself and the other warrior.

"Dawg scared up a rabbit," she answered, raising her voice so he could hear. "I didn't want him chasing away from the cabin."

"Leave him there!" he ordered.

"There might be another bear around," she protested

Pretending she was only going to fetch the German shepherd, she walked closer to the brush and grasped the dog around the neck. "Come, Dawg," she said in a loud voice that carried across the clearing. Then, speaking in a husky whisper, she murmured, "You must keep out of sight, Ruth. I'll return as soon as I can."

She had no way of knowing if Ruth heard her words, knew only that she must return to the cabin . . . and the two men who waited for her inside.

The two warriors talked quietly together as she prepared the meal and served them. But as she moved around the cabin doing her chores, her thoughts were far away from the small room and its other occupants. Her thoughts had flown the confines of the cabin to find refuge with the tall mountain man, Saul, who must be, at this very moment, getting farther and farther away from them in his search for his wife, the woman who waited in the bushes outside.

She must find a way to let Ruth know that her husband was searching for her in these mountains. And she must find a way to keep Broken Knife inside the cabin until Ruth had a chance to get far enough away from here.

But how?

Chapter Twelve

Mary Elizabeth was conscious of Broken Knife's gaze following her every move as she went about the cabin doing her chores. She threw herself into a vigorous house cleaning, washing all the pots and utensils she could find.

She sensed Dawg was restless, even before the animal crossed to the door and scratched on it.

"No, Dawg!" she said sharply, pointing back to the stove. "Go lie down."

The German shepherd gave a short woof and scratched on the door again.

"No!" she insisted. "Lie down!"

The dog looked up at her with sad eyes and gave a deep sigh. Then it padded softly across the room and lay down in its place on the floor, put its head on its paws and gazed woefully at the far wall.

"Why do you keep Dawg inside the cabin?" Chama asked.

"There could be another black bear around somewhere," she said, "and I don't want him wandering around getting into trouble."

"The dog is smart enough to stay out of trouble," he said.

"I don't want him out alone," she said sharply; then she turned away from him and grabbed up the broom and began to sweep the floor with unnecessary vigor.

Mary Elizabeth felt as though she had to get out of the cabin, had to get away from the eyes of the two warriors. Her gaze fell on the mattress, and she decided to give it a good shake and hang it out in the fresh air. Perhaps she could get to the forest and find out if Ruth was still there.

Chama made no comment when she threw back the blankets and pulled the mattress off the bed. She could feel his gaze following her as she opened the door.

Dawg was up in an instant, trying to squeeze through the small opening left by the bulk of the mattress filling the door, but was brought up short by her curt tone.

"No, Dawg! Go back!"

The German shepherd whined softly, but it turned around and padded across the room.

Dragging the mattress through the doorway, Mary Elizabeth laid it over a low-hanging limb, picked up a stick of wood and began to beat it, all the while casting furtive glances toward the heavily wooded forest.

Was Ruth still there? Or had she already taken flight?

She was so intent on her thoughts that she didn't hear the door open behind her, didn't know anyone was there until he spoke.

"What interests you about the forest?"

Whirling around, Mary Elizabeth found Chama behind her. "Nothing," she denied, forcing herself to hold

139

his gaze. "Have you finished with your meal?"

"Yes. But Broken Knife would like to be served again."

Her lips twisted wryly as she entered the room ahead of Chama. Broken Knife was still seated cross-legged on the hides. His black gaze fastened on her instantly, sliding boldly down her body. She lifted her chin and glared angrily at him. How could Chama allow him to look at her in such a fashion. Was it possible Chama hadn't even noticed?

Or, perhaps he had noticed but did not care. She moved with stiff dignity as she served Broken Knife again. Finding it almost impossible to avoid the man's eyes, she felt impaled by his almost possessive gaze.

A shiver, barely controlled, crept over Mary Elizabeth. Perhaps she was spending too much time worrying about Ruth when she would do better to consider her own circumstances.

Had Chama and Broken Knife reached some sort of agreement about her?

She had never before considered that Chama might sell her, although why she had not was a mystery to her, because he looked on her as a possession, to be bought and sold whenever he desired.

For a while, she had actually forgotten that.

The memory of his lovemaking surfaced, burning into her mind. She recalled the ecstasy of being held against his strong body, and her lips tingled in remembrance of his touch. He had been gentle and loving then and had left a burning imprint on her.

Mary Elizabeth went to the window and gazed outside, her expression sad, pensive. Last night, in the ecstasy of their lovemaking, she had almost forgotten the difference in their cultures, had almost forgotten her overwhelming need to return to civilization, to her own kind, her brother Jeb, and people who thought the way she did.

She had almost forgotten . . . but not quite.

Even then, had she allowed herself to consider it, she would have known that there could be no future with Chama. Not with a warrior whose tribe was known for its savagery. Never with such a man.

If only she had succeeded in her attempt to escape from him. Now there would be two men to hold her captive.

Although her spirits were low, she knew she fared better than the girl hiding in the woods. From the looks of her, Ruth's strength was nearly spent. She must have food to replenish that strength, and she must be told that Saul was in these very same mountains searching for her.

Mary Elizabeth turned away from the window, and her gaze fell on Dawg lying on the floor beside the pot-bellied stove.

The German shepherd looked up at her as though sensing her unrest.

Across the room, the two men were conversing in low tones, Broken Knife bragging about the raids he had participated in, white-eyes he had killed and scalps he had taken. The warrior was so intent on impressing Chama with his bravery that for the first time, he seemed unaware of Mary Elizabeth's presence.

But not so Chama. Although his gaze was on the other man, Mary Elizabeth sensed he was aware of her every move as she crossed to the stove and put the last two logs inside.

141

She was proved right when she picked up the remaining biscuits and meat left on the table and, motioning for the dog to follow her, opened the door.

"Where are you going?" Chama asked sharply.

Her lips tightened as she faced him. "Dawg is hungry," she said. "Since we need more wood, I thought I would feed him outside. There is no need to dirty the cabin further with crumbs."

His lips twitched, and there was a glint in his eyes. He knew she was referring to the sloppy way Broken Knife had eaten. Chama offered no objection as she stepped outside with the dog. Then girl and dog made straight for the woods, stopping just inside the concealing shrubbery.

"Ruth?" Mary Elizabeth called softly.

Ruth moved so silently she was beside her before Mary Elizabeth heard her.

Mary Elizabeth offered Ruth the food. "I'm sorry I couldn't bring more, but I had to pretend the food was for the dog. They must not suspect you are here."

"How did you know my name?" Ruth asked.

"Saul told me."

Ruth's eyes widened at the mention of the mountain man. "Saul's been here?" she asked.

"Yes," Mary Elizabeth said. "He left yesterday." She put the food in Ruth's hand and closed the girl's fingers over it. "Eat that," she said gently. "I know you must be hungry."

Ruth paid no attention to the food. Instead, tears welled into her eyes and overflowed. "Saul was here," she said despairingly. "God! If only I could have come sooner. Before he left. If only I could have known."

Suddenly her knees gave way, and she crumpled to

142

the ground, pressing her face into her knees in anguish.

Kneeling beside the girl, Mary Elizabeth spoke softly. "Don't give way now," she encouraged. "You've got to be strong. Broken Knife has no idea you're out here, and you'll have to leave while he's inside. You may never get another chance to escape from him."

"You don't understand," the girls sobbed. "You could never understand what I've been through."

"I do understand," Mary Elizabeth countered. "I've been the Apaches' prisoner for four years."

"You're a prisoner? How could you be? I don't see any ropes binding you."

"Not now. But there were before."

"Then, leave with me!"

"I can't. If I don't go back inside soon, they'll come looking for me, and you'll be caught. As for myself, I'm in no danger. Chama promised to take me to my brother as soon as the pass is clear."

"You trust him to do that?"

"He gave me his word."

"What good is the word of an Indian?" the girl sobbed. "God! They're a bunch of savages. I've lived with them for a year now, and there hasn't been a moment that I haven't prayed Saul would find me. All this time I didn't know if he was dead or alive. Not until now. I can't believe he was here. So close to me and I didn't even know it."

"Get hold of yourself!" Mary Elizabeth commanded. "You might still be able to find Saul. He knows Broken Knife had you. I told him that. And somehow, he'll find you, even if Broken Knife captures you again."

Ruth's lips twisted bitterly. "If Broken Knife finds

me, I won't live through the beating he'll inflict. He's a cruel man. Without an ounce of mercy in him. He'll beat me until I'm dead."

"Then don't waste time here," Mary Elizabeth said. "Get up off the ground and run. I may be able to delay them. Broken Knife wants me, and I think Chama is considering a trade. If they come to some sort of agreement, then both of them may hunt you down. If Chama decides to sell me, they may not even search for you."

"Broken Knife will never let me go free," Ruth said bitterly. "Not as long as he lives."

"Don't worry," Mary Elizabeth said. "Saul will find you."

"I can hardly believe he's still searching for me," Ruth said. "It's been over a year."

"You don't stop looking for someone you love."

"He still loves me?" Sadness darkened Ruth's eyes. "How could he? But then, he still doesn't know about—" She swallowed hard, then continued, "Still doesn't know what they did to me."

Mary Elizabeth didn't have to ask what the Apaches had done to the girl, for the memory of Melissa was clear in her mind. "Don't think about it," she advised.

Dawg had been watching them all the time. Now the animal whined softly, and Mary Elizabeth's eyes darted toward the cabin. Chama was standing in the doorway, looking toward the woods.

"Chama's looking for me," she said softly.

"Chama?"

"The warrior who thinks he owns me," Mary Elizabeth said grimly. "I'd better go or he'll get suspicious. As soon as we get inside the cabin, you must leave

144

here. Follow the trail that leads south. That's where Saul went." A quick glance at the cabin told her Chama was headed her way. "He's coming!" she hissed. "I can't talk anymore. Good luck, Ruth."

Ruth whispered her thanks as Mary Elizabeth left the shelter of the woods and hurried toward Chama.

"I wondered if you were trying to run away again," he growled. Taking her by the arm, he led her back toward the cabin. "Where's Dawg?"

It was the first time she realized the dog had not followed them. "He's probably chasing a rabbit again," she said. "You know how he is." She quickly changed the subject. "Is Broken Knife staying the night?"

"I have no wish to share my dwelling with him," he said. "And Broken Knife is not used to being in the white man's cabin. He will fare better in the forest."

"Then, you're not planning on selling me to him?" she asked.

He looked steadily at her. "Surely you did not think I would."

"It sounded as though you were considering it."

"I was angry with you," he said. "When I came back and found you gone, I suspected what happened." Something undefinable glittered in his dark eyes. "Why were you leaving me?"

"You know why," she said. "You've always known I was going home. It's never been a secret."

"You would still leave me? Even after what happened?"

She sucked in a sharp breath. She hadn't expected him to refer to last night. She became conscious of his hands slipping up her arms, ever so slowly, and the stroking of his fingers sent pleasant jolts through her.

145

She could feel her nipples becoming taut beneath the heavy fabric of her dress, and her breath quickened, her heartbeat picking up speed. He continued to stroke her, his touch light and teasing, and he seemed completely aware of what was happening to her.

"Perhaps it is time to send Broken Knife away," he murmured.

His words snapped her back to reality. Broken Knife couldn't leave yet. It was too soon. Ruth must be given a chance to escape from him. "It wouldn't be polite to ask him to leave so soon," she murmured. "He enjoys having an audience to listen to his manly exploits." She could hardly keep the sarcasm from her voice.

The subject of their discussion appeared in the doorway, and she was surprised to see that he was preparing to leave. Realizing she was taking a chance, yet knowing as well that Ruth must have her chance, Mary Elizabeth offered him her widest smile and managed to make her gaze appreciative as she ran it over his chest, then lifted her eyes to hold his gaze.

Chama's grip on her arm tightened, and his nostrils flared with sudden fury. Giving her a shove toward the stack of wood, he ordered her to take some inside. Then he went in the cabin. After only a moment's hesitation, Broken Knife followed him inside.

Mary Elizabeth's arms were nearly full of wood when Dawg returned. The German shepherd looked back toward the forest and whined softly.

"Go inside, Dawg," she ordered. She didn't want the warriors wondering why the dog was interested in the woods. Ruth must be given a chance to escape.

The men were arguing when she entered the cabin with an armload of wood, and she realized Broken

Knife had renewed his offer to purchase her.

"You say you will pay a hundred horses," Chama said. "But you have no horses with you."

"I will have to return to my village to get them," Broken Knife replied.

"It is foolish to want another girl when you already have one."

"That should not concern you," Broken Knife said angrily. "All that should matter to you is the horses I can give."

Mary Elizabeth stood waiting quietly, feeling she had made a grave mistake while trying to allow the other girl time to escape. Was Chama angry enough now to sell her to Broken Knife? Her eyes darted to Chama and away again. One look had been enough. His ebony gaze was hard, cold, his expression forbidding. A sense of doom enveloped her, causing a red haze to swirl around her. She feared she was about to faint and knew she could not allow herself the luxury. She must stay awake and learn her fate. If she passed out, she might wake up to find Chama had left her with the other man. And she had no doubt about her fate if she wound up belonging to Broken Knife.

No doubt at all.

Chapter Thirteen

Chama crossed his arms and leaned back against the wall, his black eyes holding Broken Knife's gaze. "The woman is not for sale."

"You would be foolish to keep her when she favors me," Broken Knife said.

Chama's anger had been simmering just below the surface; now it erupted in scalding fury. "She is not for sale!" he snarled. "And I will discuss it no longer." He looked out the window. Darkness had gathered around the cabin, and the stars were starting to show in the clear, purpling sky. He had been arguing with Broken Knife so long, he'd been unaware of the lateness of the hour.

Chama felt a grim satisfaction when he turned back to Broken Knife. "Even now the sun has set and you would do well to find shelter for the night."

Although Chama knew he was being impolite by refusing to offer the other warrior shelter, he no longer cared. Right now his main concern was to get rid of the man. He'd never had any intention of selling Fire Woman. Such a thing was unthinkable.

And he knew without her telling him that she had no wish to belong to Broken Knife.

But she had smiled at the man as though she *did* favor him. This both puzzled and angered Chama. Because of her actions, Broken Knife would not give up his hope of owning her.

Chama studied Fire Woman. Why did she have to be so pleasing to look upon? Her mass of fiery curls framed a face that was perfect in every detail, and her eyes, normally blue and clear as the sky on a cloudless day, were dark and stormy.

But why?

She was a complete mystery to him. Would he ever understand her?

Broken Knife claimed his attention again.

"If you will not sell the woman, perhaps we could come to some other agreement," Broken Knife suggested.

Chama knew he wasn't going to like Broken Knife's suggestion, didn't even want to hear it. But the man meant to be heard.

"She is nothing but a paleface," Broken Knife said. "I do not need to own her. I will buy her for one night only."

Fire Woman drew in a sharp breath and widened her stormy blue eyes. She was obviously unsettled by Broken Knife's proposal. *Good. It serves her right to be anxious. Let her think about the consequences of her actions.* Had it not been for her encouraging smile, Broken Knife would have accepted Chama's first refusal and left them.

Chama delayed his answer, drawing out the tense moment. The silence in the cabin was absolute as the two waited for his answer. Even Dawg seemed to sense the strain and was made uneasy by it. The animal whimpered, peering out at its master from soulful eyes.

The tension in the cabin increased.

It was Dawg who finally broke the silence. Obviously unable to stand the tension, it whined again and slunk over to Fire Woman, laying its head in her lap.

Mary Elizabeth uttered a sigh of relief when Broken Knife finally left the cabin. She kept her head lowered, aware that Chama was glaring at her. She knew he was angry with her, knew also that her actions had been necessary to allow Ruth time to escape.

She threw a quick glance at Chama and felt impaled by his black eyes, fathomless eyes that resembled pools of liquid ebony. Although he hadn't spoken a word since Broken Knife left, she knew he was angry, could feel it in the very air she was breathing . . . and although she couldn't hold his gaze, neither could she abide the tension that continued to grow heavier with each passing moment.

Suddenly, Chama's voice broke the silence. "I should have sold you to him!" he grated. "Would that have pleased you?"

"Of course not!" she gasped. "I have no wish to belong to any man."

"You belong to me!"

The force of his seething reply set her teeth on edge, and her blue eyes darkened like angry thunderclouds. "I belong to no man." Her fists clenched, and she stomped to the door. "I'm going home."

"Whatever you do is for me to say." He grabbed her shoulder. "I paid a hundred horses for you. Until they are repaid, you are mine." He pushed her toward the bed. "We will speak of this no longer this night. It is time we rest."

Rest? She stumbled over her suddenly leaden feet, and her stomach knotted. *He doesn't have resting in mind.*

Her heart picked up speed, thundering like a herd of buffalos stampeding across the plains. "I have no wish to go to bed with you!" She flung the words at him like stones.

"Nevertheless, you will," he said, and a sudden chill hung on the edge of his words.

Mary Elizabeth swallowed hard, trying to think of some reason to delay the inevitable. But Chama was one step ahead of her. He allowed her no time to think.

His eyes were black with dazzling fury as he blew out the lamp and came toward her in the moonlit shadows. She sucked in a sharp breath, trying to still the dizzying current racing through her. His fingers found the lacings of her doeskin top and began working at them.

She couldn't allow him to make love to her. And yet, she dared not try to resist, not in his present mood.

He pulled the garment over her head and tossed it aside; then he unfastened her skirt and let it drop to the floor.

Stop him! her mind silently screamed.

His breath whispered softly against her ear as his palm slid across her silken belly.

Stop him!

Her breasts surged at the intimacy of his touch and she trembled before him as his hand seared a fiery path across her stomach and down to the apex of her thighs.

Stop him!

His finger entered her moistness, and her knees threatened to buckle beneath her.

No!

Stop him!

She knew she should listen to the inner voice that continued to scream a silent protest, but instead, she remained silent, weak-kneed. He moved his hands away, stripping off his clothing and leading her toward the bed.

Their coming together was swift. He did not even try to woo her first, and hurt stabbed through her — not a physical hurt, she knew, but a mental one.

Mary Elizabeth realized Chama thought she wanted Broken Knife. Now his manly pride was wounded. She realized as well that she could offer no excuse for her actions. She couldn't tell Chama about Ruth. He was an Apache, and his loyalties would have been with his Apache brother, not with the white girl he considered the warrior's possession.

No. She couldn't tell him about the girl, couldn't take the risk that Chama might help Broken Knife find Ruth.

A bird in the hand is worth two in the bush.

Chama's words returned to her, worrying at Mary Elizabeth's mind. What would happen if the bird was no longer in the bush? she wondered. Suppose they were both in hand. Would Chama consider trading her for Ruth? After all, she had not proved a biddable wife.

Tears welled into her eyes, trickling slowly down her face. She could only hope the darkness would keep him from noticing. Mary Elizabeth tried to make herself hate him for what he was doing to her, tried to keep her body stiff, but as his mouth found hers, soft, coaxing, caressing, she felt herself becoming pliant beneath his touch.

Don't give in to him! an inward voice whispered fiercely. But when his hand cupped her breast, it swelled beneath his touch. Her nipple tautened beneath his fingers as he caressed it gently.

Her breath came harshly as his lips left hers and moved over her closed eyelids.

No! her mind screamed. But she paid no attention. Slowly but surely, against her will, her body continued to betray her. When his mouth found hers again, she parted her lips and allowed him entry to the dark moist cavern within. A languorous yearning had begun deep inside her being, a sensual warmth that continued to blossom beneath his ministrations.

As he entered her for the second time and began to move in the age-old rhythm, her fingers tangled in his dark hair, then circled around to the back of his head. Shivers slid down her spine, and her breath quickened; her pulse raced, and she lifted her body to meet each thrust until she was climbing, climbing toward some distant peak . . . unwilling to halt the climb until she was soaring . . . soaring . . . soaring among the clouds with the eagles.

Mary Elizabeth lay in the darkness, her body still tingling from the pleasure Chama had given her. She knew from the sound of his breathing that he had not fallen asleep but lay wakeful beside her. She wanted to reach out and caress him, but was afraid of how her touch would be received.

Tears again filled her eyes, welling over and trickling down her cheeks, wetting her ears and his shoulder where her head still lay.

He drew in a sharp breath. "Do not weep," he said harshly, pulling her into his arms. "I did not mean to hurt you."

Didn't he? Wasn't that the reason he'd made love to her so savagely? The thought brought more tears, and they made her angry. What was the matter with her? she wondered. Why did she break down in tears at his words?

He stroked her hair softly. "Let us forget what happened," he said in a quietly controlled voice. "Let me hold you in my arms tonight, knowing it may well be our last night together."

"What do you mean?" She forced her whispered words to remain steady. And though her heart picked up speed, she lay quietly beside him, giving no hint of her emotions.

Cupping her chin in one of his hands, he tilted her head as though he wanted to read her expression. His eyes glittered strangely when he spoke.

"There is no need to fear," he grated roughly. "I have decided we will leave this place tomorrow. I will see you safely to your destination."

154

Still she didn't understand. "My destination?"

"I will take you to your home. If your brother is still alive, I will return you to him."

She jerked her head away from his fingers, her breathing halted by a sudden lump in her throat. She swallowed hard around the obstruction.

"You're going to take me back? To Brother Jeb?" Her voice was weak, only a quiver away from a sob.

"Yes," he ground out savagely.

Please, God! Why do I hurt so much? Her breathing seemed blocked somewhere in the region of her heart.

It's what you wanted, isn't it? a silent voice demanded. *You wanted to go home. To be among civilized people again. Brother Jeb is there. He's been waiting for you all these years. With Chama guiding you, nothing can stop you from attaining your goal.*

But no matter what her reasoning told her, her heart refused to be denied. How could she leave Chama? How could he show her such happiness existed and then walk away from her?

"Do you have nothing to say?" he grated.

"Wh-what do you—you want me to say?" she stuttered.

His fingers tightened on her shoulder until she cried out with pain, and he relaxed them immediately, muttering an apology. "I thought perhaps you would be grateful to me."

"I—of course I am," she said quickly, brushing at a tear that leaked from the corner of her eye. "It's just that . . . you surprised me. You never—you always—" She stopped when she found herself floundering. What could she say? That his words had

155

sent her spinning? That until today, she'd been convinced he wanted her so badly that he'd never let her go? For some reason she felt betrayed and didn't know why.

"I'll—when we get there, I'll ask Brother Jeb to repay you for your horses." Remembering the family's circumstances four years ago, she added, "I don't know how Jeb is fixed for money. You might have to wait awhile, but—"

"Your brother cannot repay the horses?" Chama asked.

"We didn't have much before—before the attack," she said. "And your people—"

A picture of Ma as she'd last seen her flashed through her mind.

Get away from the memories! a silent voice warned. *Chama is not responsible!*

"I don't know how much he's got," she whispered shakily. "But we'll repay you as soon as we can."

He watched her expression in the moonlight. "You will worry about the bride-price?"

She nodded her head. "Yes," she murmured.

He seemed thoughtful for a moment. "We could delay our trip." When she drew in a sharp breath, he went on hurriedly, "Only until we find more of the yellow stones the white-eyes value so much."

The gold!

Her eyes glittered with excitement until she remembered the cave-in. "We couldn't dig through all that rubble," she said. "It would be impossible."

"There would be no need," he said. "There are many such pebbles to be found in the streambeds."

"A lot of them?"

156

"Yes. I have seen them myself."

"And you would help me find them?"

"I will help you." He waited a long moment, then spoke again. "If you could delay your trip for a few more sunrises, you could take some of the yellow pebbles to your brother."

"It would be foolish not to stay."

Curiously, her heart felt lightened by her decision. She told herself it was only because she would be able to take enough gold with her to help pay for her keep, but her heart knew different. Her heart sang with the promise of a few more days alone with Chama.

Why? she wondered.

Why should she wish for time with him . . . the Apache warrior she had tried so hard to escape?

Chapter Fourteen

The thin, pearly light of a new dawn found Mary Elizabeth beside the swiftly flowing stream. Taking off her moccasins, she stepped into the icy water and stifled a shriek. She'd had no idea the water would be so cold. Leaning over, she used the pan she carried to scoop gravel from the streambed and lift it out of the water. Then she began a rocking motion, sloshing the water out of the pan until only rocks and pebbles remained in the bottom. Her blue eyes were intent on the search, and she was unaware that Chama had joined her in the water until he spoke.

"Perhaps we should wait a few days until the water warms up. It would do no good for you to come down with a chest ailment."

She was tempted to agree with him, but the lure of gold was too strong. When she saw nothing that even resembled the precious metal in the bottom of the pan, she scooped up more of the gravel from the streambed and began the rocking motion again.

Th-there ought to—to be a f-faster way," she stuttered, her voice shaking with cold.

Chama made a growling sound low in his throat. "Foolish woman!" he chided. "Come away from here. Let's return to the warmth of the cabin."

"No!" she protested, steeling herself against the icy cold as she poured out the tray of pebbles and dipped the pan into the gravel again.

She couldn't leave without at least attempting to find some gold. And yet, her feet and legs were almost numb from the cold water.

Mary Elizabeth was sloshing the water back and forth when her numb fingers lost their grip on the metal pan. Quickly, she made a grab for it, but the swift current caught her. The rocks beneath her feet were slick with dark patches of river moss. She lost her balance and flailed out with her arms.

With a muttered oath, Chama reached out, his arm wrapping around her waist. Scooping her up into his arms, he waded to the bank.

"Wh-what are you doing?" she stuttered.

"I'm taking you back to the cabin. The water is much too cold right now."

She looked at him in dismay, and her voice broke miserably. "B-but we were going to pan for gold."

"Never mind," he consoled, as they reached the cabin. "There are yellow nuggets to be found elsewhere."

"There are?"

He nodded his dark head and pushed open the door with his foot, carrying her inside. "We will look for some later."

"Later?" She looked over his shoulder, toward the stream and beyond. "Why don't we look now?"

He laughed. "Because right now I wish to make

love to you."

His words yanked her gaze back to him. "Now?" she asked, wide-eyed and blushing. A small pulse raced in the curve of her throat. "While the sun is shining down?" She'd never heard of such a thing, wasn't even sure it was decent.

The golden light streaming through the door made his skin gleam like a bronzed god's, and the smile that lit his ebony eyes drew her. "While the sun shines down upon us," he agreed, lowering his face until his lips hovered only inches above hers. "You have taught me the way of the white man's kiss, Fire Woman, and I find it very pleasing. At this very moment, I want to press my mouth against yours and taste the honey in your lips."

His words aroused her, and she lifted her face for his kiss; but he didn't accept the invitation. His eyes were dark pools of liquid ebony as he gazed into hers.

"I want to kiss your nose," he said, his voice low and seductive. "And I want to taste the sweetness of the pulse that even now throbs so quickly at the base of your neck."

Mary Elizabeth's breathing had quickened, her body felt boneless as he continued to seduce her with his words, and she knew that if he hadn't been holding her in his arms, she would have collapsed, weak-kneed, on the floor. She had forgotten the time of day, forgotten her shame when he made mention that she'd taught him to kiss.

"I want to strip away your garments," he said huskily. "I want to taste the nectar of your rosy nipples, to hear you moan soft and low in your throat as you beg me to hurry and bring you to completion."

MORE PASSION AND ADVENTURE AWAIT... YOUR TRIP TO A BIG ADVENTUROUS WORLD BEGINS WHEN YOU ACCEPT YOUR FIRST 4 NOVELS ABSOLUTELY *FREE*
(AN $18.00 VALUE)

Accept your Free gift and start to experience more of the passion and adventure you like in a historical romance novel. Each Zebra novel is filled with proud men, spirited women and tempestuous love that you'll remember long after you turn the last page.

Zebra Historical Romances are the finest novels of their kind. They are written by authors who really know how to weave tales of romance and adventure in the historical settings you love. You'll feel like you've actually gone back in time with the thrilling stories that each Zebra novel offers.

GET YOUR FREE GIFT WITH THE START OF YOUR HOME SUBSCRIPTION

Our readers tell us that these books sell out very fast in book stores and often they miss the newest titles. So Zebra has made arrangements for you to receive the four newest novels published each month.

You'll be guaranteed that you'll never miss a title, and home delivery is so convenient. And to show you just how easy it is to get Zebra Historical Romances, we'll send you your first 4 books absolutely FREE! Our gift to you just for trying our home subscription service.

BIG SAVINGS AND FREE HOME DELIVERY

Each month, you'll receive the four newest titles as soon as they are published. You'll probably receive them even before the bookstores do. What's more, you may preview these exciting novels free for 10 days. If you like them as much as we think you will, just pay the low preferred subscriber's price of just $3.75 each. *You'll save $3.00 each month off the publisher's price.* AND, your savings are even greater because there are never any shipping, handling or other hidden charges—FREE Home Delivery. Of course you can return any shipment within 10 days for full credit, no questions asked. There is no minimum number of books you must buy.

4 FREE BOOKS

FREE BOOK CERTIFICATE

4 FREE BOOKS

ZEBRA HOME SUBSCRIPTION SERVICE, INC.

NAME

ADDRESS _____ APT _____

CITY _____ STATE _____ ZIP _____

TELEPHONE
( )

SIGNATURE _____ (if under 18, parent or guardian must sign)

GET
FOUR
FREE
BOOKS

(AN $18.00 VALUE)

ZEBRA HOME SUBSCRIPTION
SERVICE, INC.
P.O. Box 5214
120 BRIGHTON ROAD
CLIFTON, NEW JERSEY 07015-5214

"Stop," she whispered, her voice ragged with emotion. "It's not right for you to be talking this way. Don't say any more."

"Shall I show you, then?"

He waited for her answer, his eyes never leaving hers, sensuous, passionate, holding her mesmerized, knowing that only he would be able to quench the fire he had kindled in her loins. She told herself that she should break away from the spell he had woven around her and knew as well that she didn't have enough willpower to do so.

"Shall I show you?" he repeated. "Shall I?"

Unable to speak, she simply nodded her head.

And he showed her.

Mary Elizabeth's lashes fluttered, and she opened them to see Chama leaning on his elbows, staring down at her with a curious expression in his eyes. Her lips curled into a slow smile.

"We really should go look for the gold," she said.

"There is plenty of time," he replied, lowering his head and brushing her lips with his. "It is much too cold to search the streambeds, and the other place is higher in the mountains. It would take too much energy to climb there now."

"Does that mean you're tired?" she asked.

"Only too tired to climb the mountain," he said. "Not too tired for making love."

She grinned up at him. "You do seem to have a lot of stamina when it comes to that," she agreed.

"Perhaps I wish to store up memories," he muttered, burying his face in her neck.

His words brought a heaviness to her heart that was barely lightened by his caress.

"Chama?" she whispered.

"Yes?"

"What will you do when you leave me?"

He became still. But he did not answer. Somehow, the answer was important. She had to know.

"Chama, tell me. What will you do?" Still he remained silent, and her need to know became stronger. "Will you return to your people?"

"I have said I can never go back there," he said, an underlying harshness in his voice.

She looked up at him, at the harsh lines in his face, and tried to smooth them out with her fingers. "Please don't be angry with me," she pleaded. "Hasn't there been enough fighting between us already?" Her voice was as soft as her touch. Although she felt she understood his anger, she was unwilling to accept it. Instead, she wanted him to understand her and the reason she must return to her brother.

His muscles tightened beneath her fingers, and she thought he was finally going to speak; but she was wrong. He remained silent. She sighed, her breast heaving against his. Her fingers worked their way through his hair to the back of his head, and she laid her head against his chest, her ear above the thumping of his heart.

"Please don't be angry," she repeated, her voice muffled by his chest.

"I am not angry," he murmured softly into her ear. "The feeling I have is far removed from anger."

His breath whispered against her forehead, and his words were followed closely by the touch of his lips

162

brushing lightly against her flesh. Slipping his arm beneath her, he drew her closer against his hard chest.

Mary Elizabeth couldn't help the shudder of relief that escaped her. His words had seemed to unlock a door, and she could feel the tenseness draining from his body. She felt the steady rise and fall of his breathing and curled her hand up against his chest.

"Love me, Chama," she whispered, opening her mouth and placing a wet kiss on his naked flesh.

Tilting her head up with his palm, he lowered his face until his lips were on hers, his breath flowing warmly, mingling with hers. His hand began to move in soft circles against the sensitized flesh of her naked back, sending shivers of excitement throughout her body.

His hands wove through her hair as he deepened the kiss, his tongue circling her mouth gently, awakening a slow-burning flame in the region of her lower body. Beneath the fingers that rested on his chest, she could feel the increased tempo of his heartbeat as her nostrils registered the clean musky fragrance of him.

When his hand found her breast, her nipples hardened. Her breast swelled beneath his touch as his fingers teased the tautened peaks. Mary Elizabeth's pulse raced rapidly, and she pressed her lower body hard against his, eager for him to complete their union.

But he ignored the movement. Instead, his tongue speared the moist cavern of her mouth, plunging deeply, meeting hers in a silent duel of desire. She moaned beneath his mouth, wanting more than he was giving.

His hand left her breast and moved downward, touching her hip and continuing across the flat planes of her stomach until it reached the apex of her desire. And then his finger searched out the most intimate part of her body, entering her moistness, rubbing gently, igniting a fiery passion that flowed outward.

Her heart pounded erratically as she arched against him, moaning loudly beneath his touch, but he stopped the sounds with his mouth, sucking in hard, catching her tongue with a motion that sent thrills of excitement shooting through her. His hand at her womanhood was causing her to burn with a fire that threatened to consume her if it wasn't quenched immediately.

Unable to stand it any longer, she jerked her head away from him and moaned. "Don't make me wait, Chama. Take me now."

As though he had been waiting for the words, he lifted himself over her and plunged deeply into her body.

Mary Elizabeth sucked in a dizzying gasp of air as she felt his solidness against her softness and cried out with relief. But it was short lived. Because as he began to move inside her she could feel herself burning, burning, burning with a flame that rose higher and higher, threatening to consume her in its blaze as she gasped with pleasure, writhing against him, wild with an agony of desire that only he could relieve.

Chapter Fifteen

The mid-day sun shone down on the fiery-haired girl who stood on a gravel bar that extended into the middle of the stream. Her calf-length skirt was hiked up past her knees, the ends secured beneath the waist to keep it from getting wet.

Swishing the water around in the flat pan, Mary Elizabeth sloshed it out the sides, then stared into the bottom, searching for a few of the tiny, but heavy, yellow flakes of gold.

Finding no sign of color, she sighed and emptied the water from the pan, then dipped it into the gravel bed again.

They had been working this area for the past two weeks now. Although they found a few small nuggets, she had known the value was minimal; and when Chama suggested a few more days would surely see a big find, she had deferred to his greater knowledge, and they continued to pan for gold.

But, God! she was tired. She hadn't realized panning for gold was such hard work. Every muscle in her back ached, and when she straightened again, her movements were slow. They had very little to show for their hard work. It had been several days now since she had seen any sign of color at all.

As each day faded away, so did her dreams of getting rich, of returning to her brother with a sizeable poke of gold nuggets.

She looked downriver where Chama stood searching through the gravel for any sign of the shiny yellow nuggets. Although he had tried to get her to rest more, he'd stayed right with her and helped her search the streambed.

But not so Dawg.

The German shepherd had grown tired of waiting for them to finish their work and had chased after a rabbit. But she knew when darkness fell, the dog would return to the cabin, bedraggled and tired, but happy with its day's hunting and glad to see them again.

Realizing she was wasting time, Mary Elizabeth began to rock the flat pan back and forth, her gaze probing the bottom for some sign of gold color.

Something flashed in the bottom of the pan, and she paused. As she reached into the pan, her mouth dropped open.

Was she seeing things?

"Chama!" Mary Elizabeth whispered. Realizing that he couldn't possibly hear her, she raised her voice and yelled. "Chama! Come quick!" She peered at the gleaming nugget she held in her palm. She could hardly believe her eyes, but the sunlight glittering off the angles and planes confirmed her find. "Chama! Hurry! Come see what I found!"

When there was no response, she looked around to

where she'd last seen him a short distance away. He was still there, his body held curiously motionless as he watched her.

"Come on!" she shouted, raising her voice. Perhaps he hadn't heard her above the sound of the rushing water. "You've got to see this! I can hardly believe it myself!"

The warrior appeared not to realize the importance of her find, because he seemed incredibly slow as he waded toward her.

Finding she couldn't wait until he reached her, she hurried toward him, holding the gleaming nugget out to him in her outstretched palm. Excitement glittered in her cobalt eyes as she extended her hand toward him.

The back-breaking work had finally paid off!

God! With this nugget and the others they had found, surely there was no reason they could not leave immediately.

Suddenly, she sobered and slowed her steps, her hand closing over the nugget as realization flowed through her. Leaving this place meant their days together would come to an end, and curiously, the thought left her feeling unsettled.

Chama smiled at her, but it was a mere quirk of the lips, not quite reaching his dark eyes. "What have you found?" he asked.

She forced a smile to her lips. "A-a piece of g-gold," she stammered. "It's a big piece. Bigger than any we've found so far." She paused, opened her hand and frowned at the small nugget that seemed almost to pulsate on her palm. "I think it's gold. But it's not as bright as the other pieces we found."

167

He took the nugget from her and scraped a fingernail across it. "Yes," he agreed. "It is the yellow metal the white men seek. And it is big."

Yes. It *was* big. One of the largest pieces Chama had ever seen. It was twice the size of his thumbnail and weighed perhaps two ounces. And he wasn't the least bit happy about her finding it, but he allowed no sign of his feelings to show on his face as he continued to examine the yellow metal in his hand.

"I think it could be worth a lot of money," she said, her voice curiously husky. "We may not need any more."

He pretended not to understand. "Not need any more?" He frowned at the nugget, turning it over in his palm and poking at it with his finger. "How many horses is it worth?"

"Horses?" She looked up at him with troubled eyes. "I have no idea how many horses it's worth," she said.

"Buffalo robes, then." He looked at her, and for a moment a smile lit his dark eyes. He knew the pale-faces didn't deal in buffalo robes and horses. Although that was their way of trading goods with the Indians, they used what they called money in their own society. And the yellow nuggets.

Chama had made a point of learning the value of the white-eyes' money. To his people, a fine horse was worth ten buffalo robes, or ten weasel skins, while one buffalo robe could bring him three dozen iron arrow-points. But Chama knew as well that the trappers were after the beaver, greatly desired for the tophats the rich merchants wore. One good-sized pelt was worth at least fifty of the white man's dollars.

Paper money was worthless to the Apaches. And so

was the yellow gold. Horses represented wealth to all the tribes. They were a major medium of exchange for both the individual owner and the tribes, allowing them to travel great distances to trade the horses and other prized goods, such as buffalo robes and beaver pelts, at the trading posts established by the white merchants.

Chama had learned early on to be hardheaded in bartering for the goods he needed, for the merchants tried to dazzle him with mirrors and glass beads and shell ornaments that came from the big water.

"I don't know how much it's worth," Fire Woman said. "We'd have to take it to an assayer to find out." She took the nugget from him and mentally weighed it. "It's not very heavy," she finally admitted. "But it *is* big."

"Big enough to supply all your needs?"

She shook her head. "I don't think so." She looked down at the streambed again. "Maybe there's more where that one came from." Shoving the nugget into the pouch hanging at her waist, she tied it securely, then reached for the flat pan again. "Help me search here," she said, bending over to scoop up another panful of gravel.

Chama's movements weren't quite as eager, but he scooped up a handful of the gravel and sifted through it. Finding one of the bright yellow pebbles in his palm, he called her attention to it.

"I knew it," she said, her eyes glittering brightly as she caught the gold fever. "There's no telling how many we'll find here."

They worked through the afternoon until they were certain they had found all the gold nuggets to be had in that spot, then Chama suggested it was time to stop searching for the day.

"But there may be some more," she protested. "And if we don't find them while we're here, the water may wash them downstream."

"There is no more here," he said. "We are wasting time now. And I am hungry. It is long past time for a meal."

"You shouldn't have mentioned food," she groaned. "My stomach's carrying on something awful."

"Then, we will eat," he said. "There is always a new day to follow this one."

"We might have enough gold now," she said hesitantly, taking the leather pouch from her waist and hefting it in her hand.

"We must make certain you do before we leave," Chama said.

"I suppose if there's not enough, we could come back for more."

But even as she said the words, he knew how impossible they were. Once she reached her brother, she would have to remain. Her brother would never allow her to leave with Chama again.

He voiced his thoughts. "Would your brother allow you to leave again?"

She shook her head. "I don't think so. Not without him."

"And the man—the assayer—who determines how much the nugget is worth. Would he not want to know where you found it?"

"Yes." She nodded, her fiery hair dancing beneath the sun's rays. "He would. And then the white men— my people—would be rushing here to fight over the

170

gold."

"Then, perhaps it would be wisest to stay until you have more of the nuggets," he suggested.

Reaching out, he took a lock of her silky hair between his fingers and stroked it. His breath was warm and sweet against her uplifted face.

"Yes," she breathed softly. "You're right. It would make more sense to stay here until we have all the gold we need. There must be enough to last Jeb and me for the rest of our lives. That way it won't matter so much if the miners pour over this mountain."

His palm cupped her chin, his fingers softly playing around her lips. "I am glad you have reached this decision," he said. "And perhaps, since you have made such a good find, we could rest now and continue our search at the dawn of a new day."

He was afraid she would refuse, but strangely, she nodded her head in agreement. Unable to help himself, his head dipped lower, and his lips found hers. When her arms wound around his neck and pulled him closer, he scooped her up into his arms and carried her toward the cabin.

His heart thudded loudly in his chest. He had managed to buy a little more time, and he would use it to his best advantage, knowing he must make the most of the time they had left together.

The days that followed passed swiftly. Dawn would find Mary Elizabeth and Chama at the stream searching for more of the gold nuggets to fill their leather pouches. When one was full, they would start filling another, always working together, bending over the stream, scooping up gravel and washing it out of the flat pan. Oftentimes they would look up at the same moment, their eyes would meet and they would turn wordlessly toward the cabin together.

And as the days passed, Mary Elizabeth's feelings for Chama continued to grow. She refused to allow herself to dwell on the time when they would leave the cabin and continue their journey across the mountain.

But the day finally came when she could no longer ignore the rest of the world. It was the day when Broken Knife returned.

Mary Elizabeth was preparing the evening meal, and Dawg was sleeping peacefully at its place beside the stove. She filled a kettle with water, placed it on the stove, then bent to pick up a stick of wood from the woodbox.

Dawg lifted its head and growled low in its throat. She jerked her hand back and stared at the animal in confusion. What was the matter with it? Realizing the dog was staring at the open door, she crossed the room and looked for Chama.

The warrior was seated on a stump beside the woodpile, where he had been whittling on a chunk of aspen wood. His body was tense, his expression arrested.

Following his gaze, she saw two people leave the cover of the forest. Her heart gave a lurch as she recognized Broken Knife in the lead, holding a rope that he tugged occasionally to hurry along the captive he led behind him.

Ruth!

Mary Elizabeth was unaware that Dawg stood beside her until the animal gave a snarling growl, its neck hairs bristling with outrage, its muscles bunched as though it would attack the Indian who dared approach its territory.

"Stay," Mary Elizabeth muttered, although she would rather have ordered the German shepherd to attack.

She watched the pair approach, her eyes widening in horror as Ruth stumbled and the rope fastened around her neck tautened. When Broken Knife stopped before Chama, Ruth slumped wearily to the ground.

Chama laid his carving aside and rose to his feet, his gaze narrowing on the girl's bruised face. She had a cut on her chin, and one eye was swollen shut.

Mary Elizabeth ran to the girl and fell to her knees beside her. A quick examination of Ruth's limbs gave her a small measure of relief. At least there were no broken bones.

Fury surged through Mary Elizabeth. Leaping to her feet, she confronted the grinning warrior. "You should be whipped to within an inch of your life!" she grated. "It's a wonder she's not dead."

He ignored her and faced Chama. "My bird is now in hand," he said. "I have come to trade with you. My woman for yours."

Chapter Sixteen

Time ceased to exist for Mary Elizabeth. Each second that passed measured an eternity, each moment stretched itself into a hundredfold.

Finally, Chama spoke. "I have no wish to trade with you," he said contemptuously. "Your woman is barely alive. Perhaps she will even yet die from the beating you have given her."

Mary Elizabeth stared wide-eyed at Chama. His voice was so cold, so uncaring. But why should she be surprised? she wondered. Broken Knife and Chama were of the same tribe, raised with the same beliefs. For a while, she had actually forgotten that he considered her his property.

The thought caused a curious pain in the region of her heart. She realized at the same moment that he might even have agreed to the trade if Ruth had not been beaten so soundly.

The thought stabbed at her, and she tried to push it away; but it persisted, buzzing around in her head like an angry wasp.

Unable to bear such thoughts, she concentrated her

efforts on Ruth, working at the leather thongs that bound the girl's wrists. "Let me help you," she soothed.

Dawg licked sympathetically at Ruth's bound hands and whined softly. But the girl made no sound. She continued to stare straight ahead with her one good eye.

Suddenly Broken Knife whirled around to stare at Mary Elizabeth, quick anger in his flat black eyes.

"Leave the woman alone!" he ordered. "She tried to put a knife in my back."

Good for her!

Mary Elizabeth's lips tightened grimly, her eyes blazing blue fire as they met Broken Knife's momentarily before he turned back to renew his bargaining.

Ignoring his orders, Mary Elizabeth continued to work on the bonds that were cutting into Ruth's flesh, only vaguely aware of the two men arguing together as Broken Knife attempted to bargain with Chama.

Shutting out the sound of their voices, Mary Elizabeth concentrated on setting Ruth free. As the last strand parted, she heard Chama inviting Broken Knife to stay the night. Her head snapped up, and she stared at him with disbelief. He couldn't really be inviting that — that savage — to stay with them. "Chama!" she gritted. "I want to speak with you."

Chama's eyes narrowed on her, and she thought he was going to refuse her request. Her chin lifted, her hands clenched into fists, and she ignored his silent warning to stay out of it. A shutter seemed to drop over his expression as he joined her. "I don't want him here!" she whispered harshly. "Not even for an hour."

Chama's gaze was dark and inscrutable as he returned her look. "Be quiet," he warned. "It's not for you to say who will stay in my dwelling."

"The cabin is not yours!" she snapped. "If it belongs to anyone, then it is mine! And I refuse to let him step one foot inside that door!"

Broken Knife strolled over. "Your woman is insolent," he said. "If she were mine, I would beat her."

"Like you beat Ruth?" Fury almost choked Mary Elizabeth, and her blue eyes clawed him like the talons of an eagle. "I can only thank God I don't belong to you."

His broad-carved face twisted, his lips forming a smile, but his eyes were black and dazzling with anger. "This day you belong to Chama. But who can say what the dawn of a new day will bring."

A thin chill hung on the edge of his words, for she realized that he was right. In this insane world of the savage Apaches it was normal for one human being to own another. Why did she think she could make any difference to the way Chama thought? They were as far apart as the two poles of the world.

She must get away from here! She must escape from this place, must find a way to return to the civilized world, where people were kind to one another. She must return to her brother Jeb.

God! She must have been insane to delay her trip home. Had Chama ever intended for her to leave? Was he only playing with her emotions?

Even as the questions whirled around in her mind, questions she was unable to answer, she leaned over to help Ruth to her feet. Although Mary Elizabeth expected Broken Knife to interfere again, he made no objection as she helped Ruth inside the cabin and seated her in a chair. "I'm so sorry, Ruth," she whispered huskily. I had hoped you had found Saul."

As soon as Mary Elizabeth mentioned the mountain man, Ruth seemed to come out of her daze. Tears welled up in her one good eye and trickled down her cheek.

"Is there anything I can do?" Mary Elizabeth asked.

Ruth shook her head slowly. "I thought he was going to beat me to death," she whispered bitterly. "I should have known I couldn't escape from him. I'd rather be dead than have to continue like this."

"We'll get away from here," Mary Elizabeth said, keeping her voice low and her eyes on the doorway. "Tonight. When he's asleep. We'll leave together. And we'll find Saul. Someway. Somehow. Just hold on to that thought. Let it give you the strength you'll need when the time comes." She touched Ruth's shoulder gently. "And, Ruth," she added, "when the chance comes to escape, take it. And don't look back. You won't survive another beating like the last one."

"I know," Ruth muttered. She squared her shoulders. "He was right, you know. If I ever get the chance, then I'll kill him."

"Just be careful," Mary Elizabeth whispered, as the men stepped into the cabin. "And watch for the chance to run."

Mary Elizabeth was determined that someway she would help the girl. She didn't know how, but she would. She kept a close eye on the two men while she prepared the meal. When she reached for the roots she had gathered earlier in the day, her eyes fell on the butcher knife she used to pare them. Her muscles tensed. If only she dared attack Broken Knife with it, but she knew better. Although Chama didn't like the other man, they were from the same tribe, and he would not take kindly to her killing him.

But Ruth must have her chance at escape. She must survive until her husband could find her.

"Then I will take my woman and go!"

Broken Knife's voice, raised in anger, caught Mary Elizabeth's attention. Alarm rippled through her as he rose to his feet and started toward Ruth. The girl backed away from him, obviously terrified as she made for the open door.

Mary Elizabeth's hand found the knife and closed over the handle. If Broken Knife beat Ruth again, she would surely die. Ruth knew it as well and was not willing to chance it. She fled through the door.

Broken Knife gave a shout of anger and leapt toward the door. Mary Elizabeth sprang toward him, intent on stopping him from reaching the helpless girl.

They reached the door simultaneously, and Mary Elizabeth raised her arm above her head and swung the knife down . . . aiming it at the middle of Broken Knife's back.

If the blow had landed, the warrior would have been dead; but, as though sensing danger, he swung around at the last moment, and she struck him a glancing blow high on his shoulder.

Her eyes were wild as she yanked the knife out of his flesh and swung again, but he was too fast. One hand grabbed the wrist of her knife hand, his fingers tightening like steel bands. She was vaguely aware that Dawg had entered the fray with a furious growl. The warrior screamed out in pain as the German shepherd's teeth fastened around the ankle of the man who threatened its mistress.

The pain in her wrist increased, and she fought against it, vaguely aware of Chama beside the warrior, his hand on top of Broken Knife's. He seemed to be helping the other man. The pressure on her wrist was so great she feared the bones would snap.

Chama was muttering curses. Dawg was growling.

The noise and confusion and pain were almost more than she could bear. From the corner of her eyes, through a red haze of pain, she saw Ruth make a dash for the nearby woods.

Then suddenly she was struck a sharp blow on the back of her head that sent her senses reeling and blackness closing in around her.

When Mary Elizabeth regained her senses, she was lying on the bed and Chama was leaning over her. She gave a horrified gasp and jerked away from him. The sharp movement sent an aching jolt through her temples, and she winced with pain.

Why was it so quiet? she wondered. What had happened? She remembered fighting with Broken Knife, then remembered as well Chama and Dawg joining in. But that was all she could recall.

She lay there for a moment, still confused by the silence in the cabin. Her eyes roamed the small room. Dawg lay beside the fire, watching her steadily. But otherwise, the room was empty.

She lifted a hand and felt the large bump on the back of her head. "Why did you hit me?" she asked, her expression tight and bitter.

Chama drew back, his ebony gaze flickering with a curious expression.

Pain?

No. Of course not. She must have imagined it.

His eyes were dark, his expression cold and forbidding as he reached for the steaming cup on the table and held it out to her.

"This will clear your head."

"My head doesn't need clearing."

She knocked the cup aside, caring nothing that the liquid spilled over. Her lips were tight as she pushed herself to a sitting position.

"Where are Broken Knife and Ruth?"

"The girl fled into the forest, and Broken Knife is dead and buried."

Dead! Thank God, I killed him. Mary Elizabeth's relief was tempered with a bitter sadness. If Chama had had any feeling for her, he would have killed Broken Knife himself. Instead, she'd had to do it.

Dawg got up and padded across the room to her, laying its head in her lap and licking her clenched hands. She scratched behind its ear, feeling grateful for its sympathy. At least she could count on the German shepherd's loyalty.

The water in the stream shimmered and sparkled beneath the sunlight, but the man standing on the rock failed to notice. His thoughts were turned inward as he stripped the buckskin breeches from his bronzed body and savagely kicked them aside.

"Why would she believe such a thing of me?" he muttered. "She should have known I would never harm her."

Why didn't you tell her she struck her head on the cabin

door? a silent voice asked. *How could she know if you didn't speak out.*

"Explanations should not have been necessary. She should have trusted me."

An aching knot surrounded his heart, and it was almost more than he could bear. He had been so happy earlier in the day, before Broken Knife's arrival. He knew the instant he saw the warrior with Ruth that his time with Fire Woman was coming to an end. Among other things, it had served to remind her of the difference in their cultures. For a time he had hoped that she would come to love him and be happy with him, but Broken Knife had ended that hope.

Chama remembered the way the knife had felt as he'd plunged it into the other man, the way Broken Knife's flesh had yielded to the blade. The warrior's eyes had been disbelieving as they'd met Chama's . . . just before he'd crumpled to the floor.

But Chama felt no sympathy for the warrior, only a need to seek revenge for his brutal treatment of Ruth.

Realizing that his hands were clenched tightly at his sides, he dove into the stream and emerged halfway to the other bank. His arms cut cleanly through the water with powerful strokes, moving through the stream with the skill of an accomplished swimmer. His eyes were bitter, his mouth tight, as he continued to swim, the water rippling turbulently around his muscular body while he tried to ease his frustration by tiring himself out.

Mary Elizabeth had the meal prepared when Chama returned from his swim. She dished up the stew she had made and sat down at her place at the table as she'd been doing for the past few weeks. His nostrils twitched at the mouth-watering aroma coming from the plate she'd filled for him, and he took his seat across from her.

"This looks good," he said, offering her a smile.

She felt encouraged that he'd made no mention of the fight. But she couldn't help but worry about Ruth. She scooped up a bite of the stew and chewed it slowly. Finally, she could stand it no longer. She had to know about Ruth. "What happened to Ruth?" she asked.

"She ran away. By the time Broken Knife lay dead, she had disappeared."

She sighed. "I hope she got away."

He remained silent.

She looked up hesitantly. "You said before that you'd see me home to my brother Jeb."

His answer was a long time coming. He laid his spoon beside his plate and looked at her. Finally he spoke. "Yes. But we have not found enough of the yellow nuggets."

"There's enough," she said. "I want to go home."

"I am going to take you. But now is not a good time."

Her lips tightened bitterly. "I want to go now."

He sighed and reached for her hand, but she flinched away from his touch. Perhaps he was unwise to keep silent about the blow she'd received, but his pride would not allow him to speak. She must learn to trust him.

"I want to go home," she repeated. "You promised me."

"Then, we will go," he said heavily. "But it is too late

today. We will go at dawn."

She nodded, picked up her dish and started clearing the table. After she had finished, she began to prepare for the journey across the mountains. Her heart was heavy as she went around the cabin gathering together the things they would need. She took dried strips of venison from the drying racks and filled the parfleches until they were almost bursting.

Chama's gaze followed her as she worked, but he made no comment. Instead, he found a piece of aspen wood and began to whittle on it. He worked on the carving until darkness fell around the cabin. And then he came to where she stood.

"I have made this for you," he said, handing her the wood he had been carving. "Keep it with you. Perhaps it will serve to remind you of our time together."

She swallowed around a lump in her throat as she accepted the carving of an eagle in flight. It was a perfect likeness, and it fit in the palm of her hand; but she didn't need the carving to remind her of the time they had spent together. She felt she would never forget one day, one minute, of the time they had spent here in this wilderness cabin.

That night she lay in his arms for perhaps the last time. And when they made love it held a wildness, a bittersweetness that brought tears to her eyes and left a knot in the pit of her stomach.

Early the next morning they left the cabin behind. Mary Elizabeth kept her face forward, unable to look back. A lump formed in her throat, and moisture welled into her eyes. She blinked rapidly to dry them, unwilling for Chama to see her weakness.

They walked in silence, following no trail as they made their way along a ridge, through the underbrush and scrub growth, down a ravine and into a valley.

Darkness was falling when they heard the sound of rushing water. Soon they broke into a clearing and saw a narrow stream. On the far side of the stream was a rocky ledge, a perfect place to make camp.

Mary Elizabeth removed her moccasins and waded through the cold water until she reached the cliff overhang. The ground beneath the ledge was thickly strewn with leaves, which, when she walked through them, crackled and blew lightly. It was a good place to take shelter for the night, hidden away from the world, safe and dry, and she felt a curious longing to remain there.

Chama had killed a rabbit on the trail, and Mary Elizabeth cooked it over a small fire. They ate in silence as darkness closed in around them, shrouding the land in purple shadows. Using the subdued light provided by the small campfire, Mary Elizabeth gathered a bed of leaves and spread a blanket over them, adding another blanket to protect them from the chill of the night, then turned to look for Chama.

He was sitting outside the circle of firelight, just one more shadow in the darkness, yet even from where she stood, she sensed the tension coiling through his body.

"It is time for bed," she said, unlacing her blouse and slipping it over her head. She turned to gaze steadily at him, the flickering flames of the fire sending shadows dancing across the ivory skin of her breasts, creating valleys between the soft globes, inviting his attention.

He was hypnotized by the creamy mounds, his gaze riveted to her body. A flame of desire began to burn in his ebony eyes, but he sat motionless, unmoving, his face giving away none of his feelings.

Her fingers went to the lacings on her buckskin skirt, and slowly, her gaze locked with his, she unfastened the garment and let it drop to the ground. Walking over to him, she then stood before him in all her nakedness, her glorious body waiting, beckoning him to come to her.

Chama's body tensed, his fingers clenching into fists. But she remained undaunted, her lips curling into a smile, her eyes never leaving the pulse beating madly at the base of his throat.

There was no doubt in her mind that he wanted her, and the thought caused her heart to palpitate wildly. Although they would soon part, this night was hers. And she would use the hours of darkness to store up enough memories to last the lifetime she must live without him.

As he stood she loosened the lacings on his buckskin shirt and slipped the garment over his head. Then she opened her mouth and trailed moist kisses across his chest, pausing at one flat male nipple and flicking her tongue against it.

He drew in a sharp breath and clutched her against him. Thrilled with the response she'd incited, she circled the nipple with her tongue, then moved slowly across his chest to the other one. His breathing had become harsh and ragged, and she could feel his lower body growing, bigger and stronger, throbbing against hers.

She could hear the erratic thudding of his heartbeat

as she kissed his satin-smooth flesh. She was vaguely aware of his fingers fumbling unsteadily with the fastenings on his buckskin breeches. Suddenly they were free, and he was pushing them down and kicking them aside.

Lowering her to the blanket, he pressed rough kisses across her face until his lips finally fastened on hers and his tongue entered her sweet-tasting depths.

When he finally rose above her, she waited with bated breath. It almost seemed as though time had ceased to exist. It was as though they were the only people in the world, just the two of them beneath the star-studded sky. He remained poised above her for a long moment, and when he entered her, filling her with his strength until her desire was almost overwhelming, her body arched wildly against his, churning for a relief that only this man could give her.

They began the journey together, higher and higher, climbing toward some distant summit, and he seemed to know the moment when she reached the peak. He relentlessly stoked the fire that was consuming her until he was joining her, soaring together with a wild rapture that burst from within as they hung together . . . suspended in time and space until they reached their peak of release and collapsed together in a whirlwind of ecstasy.

Chapter Seventeen

Night sounds still echoed through the forest when Chama shook Mary Elizabeth awake in the half-light before dawn. "Get up, Fire Woman," he said urgently.

She stirred, and a soft sound escaped from her parted lips. When Chama shook her again, she opened sleep-blurred eyes and stared up at the bronze face so near her own. She was feeling completely relaxed, sleepy and warm, curled snugly as she was in her leafy bed.

"Get up!" he repeated. "We have no time to waste."

"Why?"

"There are others about who may present a danger. You must remain hidden until we know more about them."

Feeling as though she'd been drenched in ice-cold water, Mary Elizabeth was suddenly wide awake. "Who is it?" she whispered, pushing aside the blanket and reaching for her doeskin skirt. "Is it the Apaches?"

Even as she asked the question, she felt certain it was so. Chills ran across the back of her neck, raising the fine hairs at the nape, and fear rose like bile in her throat.

She should have known this would happen. She had feared it above all else. Ever since she'd escaped from the Apaches, she'd been afraid that somehow, someway, they'd find her again and exact their revenge for what she'd done to Ten Bears.

Mary Elizabeth pulled on her skirt, her gaze searching the shadows for the intruders, expecting at any given moment to see the war-painted Apaches burst from the forest, brandishing tomahawks and uttering bloodcurdling war cries.

But the forest remained silent.

Too silent.

There should be some sound, she mused. *The sound of a nightbird, or an owl . . . something.*

But there was nothing.

She listened to the silence, knowing that although she could see nothing out of the ordinary, Chama was right about the intruders.

Dawg knew too.

The German shepherd's four feet were planted firmly on the ground, its neck hairs bristling, its eyes fixed on the dense forest beyond the stream.

Becoming aware that Chama hadn't answered her question, she turned back to him.

"Who's coming?" she whispered. "Who is out there?"

"Not Apaches," he said, his voice showing his contempt for the intruders. "They could only be white-eyes. Only a paleface would sound like a blind bear stumbling through the forest."

"White men?"

She swallowed hard and pulled her blouse over her head. Her heart was racing madly as she forced herself to meet his gaze.

"Maybe you should leave me here," she suggested in a small voice. Her fingers trembled as she tried to fasten the leather lacing at her neck. "Perhaps it is all working out for the best." When he remained silent, she averted her gaze from his. "It wouldn't be sensible for you to take me all the way home. Jeb would most likely shoot you. And if there are really some of my people nearby, they would probably see me h-home."

Her efforts to control her voice had failed miserably, but he didn't even notice. He seemed completely unaware of her inner turmoil.

"Have you so easily forgotten what happened at the cabin?" he asked darkly. "The palefaces are not to be trusted."

"All white men are not the same."

But even as she protested, she fastened the pouches of gold at her waist and rolled the blankets up, not the least bit anxious to be left alone with strangers.

A low growl from Dawg, followed by an anxious whine, warned them the intruders were getting closer.

Mary Elizabeth's movements were hurried as she went about gathering their belongings together and fastening their packs securely. Then she helped Chama brush away their tracks with a leafy branch, carefully erasing all traces of the fire, covering the coals with cold dirt and raking it smooth, then scattering leaves over it.

But it had taken time, and when they were finished covering the evidence of their passing, there was no chance to flee. Nearby, a sharp crack, followed by a hoarse laugh, told her time had run out.

Snatching up their possessions, Chama pushed her toward the cover of some bushes that grew low against the forest floor. "Come Dawg!" he ordered.

Dawg seemed to understand what he wanted. As Mary Elizabeth crawled beneath the bushes, Chama followed, pulling brush and leaves behind him for extra cover.

Dawg scrunched in beside them, laying its head on its front paws, but its eyes remained fixed on the forest as though it could actually see through the shadowy darkness to the men who represented danger.

A low rumble began in Dawg's throat, and Chama leaned over, placing a warning hand over the dog's mouth, quietly ordering the German shepherd to cease its growling.

Although Dawg immediately fell silent, its neck hairs remained stiff, bristling a warning. Its gaze never wavered from the dense forest where the rumble of distant voices could now be heard.

Suddenly, a man appeared from the woods. "Told you they was a creek somewheres hereabouts," he said. "Good water in it too." As though to prove a point, he knelt beside the stream and scooped up a handful of water, slurping noisily at it.

"Don't know why we had to leave so early," a harsh voice sounded. "Makes no sense to be runnin' around up here in the dark."

The voice that answered was low and indistinguishable, but Mary Elizabeth could tell the man spoke with some kind of accent.

"Think you're wrong," said another voice, not the first one. That meant there were at least three men. "Sheriff ain't gonna come up here after us. Too easy to run across Injuns aroun' these parts."

"Injuns got more sense than to come up here before

summer sets in. Too much chance of bein' caught in a snowstorm. Heard they winter in the desert an' come back when the snow's all gone."

"If we run across a war party, I'll be sure an' tell 'em thet," said another voice. "If they give me a chance."

"It's a sure bet thet if any Injuns is hidin' out up here, they're gonna know we're aroun' with all thet noise you're makin'."

"Aw, hell, Jake!" said even another voice, making the count five now. "They ain't no Injuns out this early in the mornin'. Don'tcha know they're a lazy lot? I'd be willin' to bet my share of thet bank loot we're the only humans on this mountain."

"Hell, Carl," said the voice Mary Elizabeth had identified as Jake. "Thet ain't no kind of bet. Apaches ain't human. Ever'body knows thet. They ain't nothin' but animals walkin' upright like a bear."

"Don't make no difference what they are," said Carl. "I don't want to run into 'em. What about you, Sanchez?"

"I theenk you are making much noise, señor. If the Apaches are in these mountains, then I theenk they will surely keel us all."

Chama stiffened, every muscle in his body tensely coiled. If there was any race of people he hated more than the white-eyes, it was the Mexicans. Their cruelty to the Indian tribes went unmatched. It was the dark-skinned people who had initiated the art of scalping. The Mexicans paid silver coins for each Apache scalp brought to them. They were responsible for the deaths of many of his people. Warriors, women and children . . . all of them doomed to wander forever in the spirit world, for those who had been mutilated could never

191

reach the happy hunting ground. Only the presence of Fire Woman kept him in his hiding place. He could not risk the odds, could not take a chance on leaving her to face the men alone.

Chama counted his enemies as they passed by. *Six.* The last man had filed past when a low growl erupted from Dawg's throat. The man stopped, then turned, and the dog leapt forward, bursting from the underbrush, its jaws wide, teeth clamping over the man's leg.

The man cried out with pain and raised his rifle, but Chama was there, twisting it out of his hands. The weapon fell to the ground with a clatter, and so did the outlaw; but the noise had been enough to alert the others. Shouts sounded as they crashed through the underbrush, returning to help their fallen comrade.

Chama jerked Mary Elizabeth to her feet. "Go!" he said harshly. "Flee! While I lead them away!"

Although fear raced through her, she drew a deep breath, leapt to her feet and ran, knowing it was their only hope. Chama had been trained to fight in such circumstances and could run over obstacles at great speed for long distances. She could not.

"Stay with him!" she ordered Dawg.

Then she ran.

Fear tugged at her mind as she raced through the forest. It tingled up her spine and lent wings to her feet. Low-hanging branches brushed against her body as she leapt over obstacles. Sweat slicked her skin; thorny brambles tore at her garments. Her heart thudded painfully, her lungs seemed on fire, and her breath came in soft, raspy gasps.

In the distance, she could hear Dawg barking wildly and Chama's war cry echoing through the forest. It was a cry that had often chilled her blood in the past, but as long as she heard it, she would know that the warrior was still alive.

A sharp pain in her side brought her to an abrupt halt. She stopped, gripping a sapling for support and gasping harshly for breath.

Realizing the noise in the distance had stopped, she held her breath, cocked her head and strained her ears.

What was happening?

Had they killed Chama?

No! She refused to believe such a thing.

The wind gusted, and leaves whispered in the breeze. Nearby, there was a flutter of wings . . . a branch snapped, followed by a screech somewhere close by. Fear lurched through her, causing her heart to beat wildly within her breast until she realized the sound was only an early morning owl giving its poignant cry as it searched the woods for its food.

Worry creased her brow, but she forced herself to go on. Chama would expect it of her. But she found the silence unnerving and fought the urge to turn back.

I must go on.

Chama had told her to flee. She knew that he would join her as soon as possible. She found comfort in the fact that Dawg was with him. The German shepherd would help the warrior when the need arose.

As it surely would.

The sun lifted above the horizon, brightening the morning sky, sprinkling the pine trees with a shower of gold. But Mary Elizabeth had little time to admire the beauty that surrounded her. She continued her journey southward, knowing that way led to civilization.

The sound of rushing water in the distance reminded

her she was thirsty, and her waterskin was almost empty. Her steps quickened as she hurried forward. Breaking through the dense forest, she emerged into a glade dappled with sunlight.

She imagined it could be a peaceful place, almost magical at times, but at the moment there was no peace to be found there. The stream had turned into a raging river covered with muddy froth. The water was swollen beyond the banks, and logs swirled in fast-driven currents.

Her spirits plunged downward as she stared at the far bank, knowing that way lay home. She could never wade, or swim, across the fearsome water.

"Looks like they ain't gonna be no crossin' here." came a man's voice from behind her.

Icy fear twisted around her heart. Chama had failed to stop the outlaws, and they'd caught up to her.

She whirled around, her knife slipping from the sheath at her waist, her hand on the upthrust. He was on her in the blink of an eye, his fingers clamping over her wrist, holding the blade away from his chest.

His blue eyes glittered down at her. "Thet ain't none too friendly," he said.

Her eyes widened. "Saul!" she gasped. "What are you doing sneaking up on me that way?"

"Wasn't sneakin'," he denied, relaxing his grip on her wrist. "You gonna put thet pig-sticker away?"

"Certainly," she said, relief flowing through her. "You startled me. I didn't hear you, and when you spoke, I thought you were part of the gang I was running from."

He released her and rocked back on his heels, his big frame relaxing. "It'd be my guess you ain't feelin' friendly towards 'em."

"No. I'm not." She slid the knife back in the sheath at her waist. "Have you seen Chama?"

"Nope. But I wasn't lookin'." His gaze went back to the forest. "He back there?"

She nodded and explained what had happened.

"He's plannin' on takin' on six outlaws at once?" he asked.

"I think he's just leading them away from me." Her forehead wrinkled, and her troubled gaze scanned the forest behind them. "Dawg is with him. But I left before dawn. I've been worrying for hours, expecting Chama and Dawg to catch up to me."

"If he was just bent on leadin' 'em away, then he ain't gonna come to no harm. They ain't a white man alive can ketch an Apache in these mountains. Too many places to hide. 'Sides, you don't really need him no more. We ain't no more'n half a day away from Taos now. Reckon I can take you there myself."

"How will we get across the stream? The snow melt on the mountaintops has flooded it."

"Cain't cross here. But they's a good place downstream thet'll do. Water's not more'n knee-deep to a grasshopper. Purty wide, but thet ain't no problem." He began to fumble with one of the hide pouches hanging from a thong at his waist. "Ain't et since yesterday," he said. "Reckon my stomach figgers my throat's been cut. Guess this is a good place to remedy thet. You hungry?"

She nodded her head.

He'd already unfastened the hide pouch. Dipping in his fingers, he extracted two strips of dried venison and offered her one. Then, selecting the nearest large pine tree, he slumped down, leaned back against the trunk, and bit off a chunk of the dried meat.

Seating herself on the grass beside him, Mary Elizabeth chewed on her strip of venison.

"Didn't figger Chama'd really take you home," Saul said. "Know you told me he would, but it was my guess he was only tryin' to keep you happy."

She averted her eyes from his shrewd gaze. "He's not like the others," she muttered.

"Maybe so," he growled. "But I ain't got much likin' for no Injuns. 'Specially Apaches. Not since they took Ruth."

Ruth!

God! I forgot about Ruth!

She must tell Saul. He must find Ruth before anyone else did. "Saul." Mary Elizabeth's blue eyes were clouded as she faced the mountain man. "I saw her."

Saul bit off another chunk of venison and chewed slowly, his gaze on the swollen river. He seemed to be lost in thought, completely unaware of her words.

"Saul." She swallowed around a tightness in her throat. "Listen to me, Saul. I saw Ruth!"

Slowly, he turned his head, pinning her with eyes likened to blue chips of ice. His fist was clenched around the strip of venison, squeezing . . . squeezing.

"What did you say?" Although he spoke softly, there was a dangerous quality about his rigid frame, a menace, barely held in check.

Fear flickered in her eyes. She'd expected a totally different reaction from him. Certainly not this. "I s-saw her," she stuttered. "She came to the c-cabin."

He leaned forward, making his frame even more intimidating. "Ruth was at the cabin? Back yonder? Where you an' thet Injun was stayin'?"

"Yes." She nodded her head. "After you left."

He was up in a flash, his fingers gripping her shoulders, his blue eyes boring into her. "Then, where in hell is she?" he snarled. "Where is she now?"

Her eyes were wide with fright. He was like a madman. "You're hurting me, Saul. Stop it."

The madness slowly faded, and his fingers relaxed their grip. "Where is she?" he asked again, and his accusing voice stabbed at her.

She dropped her gaze, unable to bear the hope she saw burning in his eyes. "I don't know," she said miserably.

"You don't know?"

She shook her head, a gesture that set her fiery hair dancing around her face. "No. Broken Knife brought her to the cabin. He wanted to make a trade with Chama. Her for me. And Chama refused."

He stared at her with hot rage. "She was there an' you didn't try to help her?" His voice was cold and lashing.

"You got it all wrong, Saul," she said, tears welling into her eyes. "I tried to help her. I really did. I stabbed Broken Knife before I was knocked unconscious."

"Broken Knife knocked you out?"

She flushed miserably. "No," she admitted. "Chama did it. But not before I killed Broken Knife. But don't you see, Saul? Ruth got away. She's back there, somewhere. In the mountains. You've got to find her."

"I'll find her," Saul growled. "But Chama's a dead man. Next time I meet up with him, he's a dead man." His eyes were hard, narrow pinpoints of blue light. "I ain't got time to show you thet crossin'," he said. "I gotta find Ruth afore any more harm comes to her. You go on downstream until you come to a waterfall. The mountains come close together to form a canyon there. Looks like the way's blocked, but it ain't. They's a narrow ledge the goats use to get below. You can manage it well enough. You got guts. A mile or so beyond thet ledge you'll find a wide place, shallow enough to cross." Without another word he turned back into the forest and disappeared from sight.

Mary Elizabeth watched him go with a heavy heart, hoping he didn't run into Chama. She shouldn't have told the mountain man about Chama knocking her unconscious.

She traveled all afternoon, finding the trees and bushes growing so close together until, at times, her path was almost completely blocked.

All the while she traveled, her thoughts were on Chama. Why had he not joined her? She even contemplated turning back, but her chances of finding him were too slim.

She stayed close to the river whenever it was possible, at other times, detouring, then returning when she could. Always the sound of the rushing water guided her back to the stream. As she drew closer to the waterfall, the sound it made was almost deafening.

But Mary Elizabeth still wasn't prepared for the awesome power generated by the rushing water — not until she broke through a clearing thirty feet from the fall. She stared, wide-eyed, at the fearsome sight. Logs and upended trees swirled in the churning muddy froth, pausing momentarily before plunging over the edge to a raging pool at least twenty feet below.

Lifting her eyes, she scanned the sides of both mountains. There was only a distance of a hundred feet between them at this point, and she could see no way down, or around them. How could she possibly go any farther?

They's a narrow ledge the goats use.

Saul's words surfaced in her mind, and she studied the nearest mountainside. Surely that narrow ledge couldn't be the one Saul had spoken of.

It couldn't be more than eighteen inches wide. She'd never make it. She'd be sure to fall! And there was no way she could survive a fall into that angry water below.

No!

It's impossible!

God! I've come too far to go back!

Chama! Help me! she silently cried.

Her gaze slid to the forest behind her. There was no sign of Chama or the dog. She could either stand here and wallow in misery, or she could get on that ledge and cross it.

Clenching her jaws with determination, she stepped out onto the narrow ledge, picking her way carefully across loose rocks and shale, never forgetting for one moment about the long drop waiting only a few inches away.

Mary Elizabeth had only gone a few feet when she heard the sound of barking in the distance. Her heart gave a wild leap as she twisted around. But instead of Chama and the dog, Saul and Ruth stepped from the dense forest. The mountain man had found his wife!

Opening her mouth to call a greeting, she was forestalled by Dawg bursting from the shrubbery and stopping short at the sight of its mistress.

Although Mary Elizabeth's gaze fastened on the dog, her thoughts were on the absent warrior. Where was he? She started to backtrack, unaware of her footing, and tripped over a protruding rock.

Losing her balance, she flailed out with both arms, clutching at the face of the cliff, searching for some kind of support.

But there was none to be found.

Her right foot, too close to the edge, slipped . . . she felt the ground give way beneath her feet . . . and she was falling . . . falling . . . plunging toward the icy water below.

Chapter Eighteen

Chama was stretched flat on his stomach on top of a large rock, his gaze fastened on the three outlaws who moved cautiously toward him, unaware of the warrior's watching eyes.

Hidden in the bushes nearby, with orders to be silent and lie still, was Dawg. Chama had already killed two of the outlaws and sent another fleeing through the forest, leaving his companions to whatever fate awaited them, thoroughly convinced an Apache war party was intent on picking them off one by one and taking their scalps.

But the three remaining outlaws were not so easily frightened. They were older men, seasoned by years of fighting, and they had decided to track Chama down and kill him.

"You hear anythin', Carlos?" asked the man in the middle.

"Notheeng but you, amigo. And if the Apache is around, then I theenk he will hear you as well."

"He might," agreed Jake.

The man bringing up the rear spoke in a low voice,

barely distinguishable to Chama's ears. "You two're makin' enough racket to bring the whole damn tribe down on us."

Chama watched them come, his eyes contemptuous. They were fools if they thought they could outwit him. He drew his knife and waited for the first two to pass. When they had done so, Chama raised himself to a crouching position, lifted his knife hand, and leapt downward, landing behind the last outlaw, who was lagging behind his companions.

Something must have warned the man. He looked back, his eyes widened and he twisted, just as Chama struck. His blade missed a vital spot and sliced into the man's upper arm instead.

But the force of the impact, Chama's body slamming against the other man's, drove them against the ground with a bone-jarring jolt.

Chama's knife hand struck a rock with enough force that he lost his grip on the weapon. His opponent was quick to take advantage. Snatching up the knife, he rounded on the warrior.

Chama rolled quickly away, springing to his feet and coming in low and fast. His knotted fist met the other man's belly beneath the ribs. The man gave a coughing grunt and fell back.

Chama allowed the man no time for recovery. Instead, he followed him, delivering a blow to his opponent's solar plexus that stopped the man cold.

Then the knife was in Chama's hand, and he lifted it and swept down, feeling the blade penetrate the outlaw's chest.

Chama was vaguely aware of Dawg joining him as the warrior stood over the fallen man, shoulders slumped, his breath coming in harsh gasps.

But Chama knew better than to linger. The outlaws would soon discover their numbers were only two and would be warned. Dawg was by his side as he ran fleetly through the forest, traveling in a wide circle until he was ahead of the two outlaws. After ordering Dawg into the bushes to wait, he climbed a good-sized tree and waited atop the lowest branch.

The Mexican came first. Chama knew he would have to let the dark-skinned man pass and go for the paleface, the one they called Jake.

But, instead of passing by, the Mexican stopped beneath the sycamore tree and waited for his companion. "Do you wish to be the Apache's next victim?" he asked harshly, looking toward the other man.

"Hell!" grated Jake. "I ain't gonna be nobody's victim. I still ain't sure how he got the others."

"They were fools!" Carlos said. "But I am not. We should stay close together until we can leave these woods, amigo. The Apache dogs have the advantage here. We cannot delay much longer or the sheriff and his posse may find us."

"Naw," Jake said. "They'd be crazy to come up here. Like you said, they's too many places to hide. But you may be right about us leavin'. Maybe we should forget about thet Injun. Could be he's leadin' us straight into a trap." His head swiveled around, his eyes probing the dense shrubbery. "They could even be listenin' to us right now."

Chama reached carefully for an arrow, then stopped, realizing that the branches, growing in such abundance they shielded him from view, also kept him from drawing back his bow. He would have to use his knife. And unless the men separated, he stood little chance of killing both of them.

"He's already killed three men," Jake said. "And those three men was our partners. Seems like the only decent thing to do is to kill him before we leave."

"To kill him, we must find him," Carlos said. "And we take the chance he will find us first. Then we are the dead ones. And the money we carry will be his."

Chama's lips curled in contempt. He had no need for the palefaces' money.

"You got a point there," Jake agreed. "Thet ain't chicken feed we stole. An' since they's only two of us left, we get it all."

Carlos patted a wide belt strapped around his waist. "Perhaps the Apache did us a favor, amigo." He took the makings from his shirt pocket and rolled a cigarette. After running his tongue along the edge of the paper, he followed it with his thumb, stuck it in his mouth and struck a match to it. Taking a long drag, he blew the smoke out and gave a sigh. "What will you do with your share of the money, amigo?"

"Gimme the makin's, Carlos," Jake said. "I'm all out."

Carlos handed over the tobacco pouch and cigarette papers. Jake talked while he rolled his cigarette.

"When we leave these mountains, I'm goin' up north to Colorado City. Gonna hit the nearest saloon and buy me a bottle of good whiskey."

He stuck the cigarette in his mouth, lit it and smoked silently for a moment, his gaze narrowed on the bush where Dawg lay hidden. In the tree above Jake's head, Chama's muscles bunched, his body tensed, as he prepared himself for attack.

But the German shepherd's presence remained undiscovered.

Apparently Jake was only lost in thought, for he turned to the Mexican beside him. "You ever had a painted whore in a red dress, Carlos?"

"In my country there are many whores in red dresses, amigo."

"Yeah, but you ever had one?"

"I have had many of them. The señoritas like me, amigo."

Jake gave a snort of disbelief. "Don't know why they would," he said. "You're a mean son-of-a-bitch."

Carlos laughed. "You know notheeng of women, amigo. A man must be forceful."

"Maybe I know more'n you think. I heard stories about you, Carlos. They ain't none of 'em purty. An' most of 'em was told by women you'd bought."

"If they speak of me, amigo, it is proof they like what I give them."

"You got a funny way of thinkin', Carlos. But thet ain't neither here nor there. Just so long as you stay away from my woman."

"You got a woman, amigo?"

"Not yet. But I'm gonna get me one. She's gonna have a red dress on. A shiny red dress."

"Then, she will be a whore, amigo."

"She'll be a woman, Carlos. Don't matter thet she's a whore. She's gonna bring me luck wearin' that red dress. I'm gonna find me thet woman, then find me a poker game. I might even wind up ownin' Colorado City before I'm done."

"Perhaps you would do better to invest your money," Carlos suggested. "Or buy a sheep farm."

"Sheep?" Jake snorted. "Don't be stupid. I don't like

sheep. Wouldn't have no sheep farm if it was given to me."

"You will lose your money in a card game and be broke again before the month is gone," Carlos predicted, taking another drag off the cigarette and tossing it on the ground. "Then you will be looking for another bank to rob."

"What if I do?" Jake jeered. "They's plenty of banks around waitin' to be broke into. An' not enough sheriffs to keep me from doin' it."

"You will die by the gun, amigo," Carlos said. "But that does not concern me. This place has a bad feeling to it. Like the eyes of the Apache, it feels dangerous. Let us leave here."

"I don't believe in feelin's, Carlos. But I don't mind movin'. We ain't gettin' thet Apache by stayin' in one place."

Jake moved off in a northeasterly direction, and Carlos followed.

Chama's lips thinned, and his dark eyes glittered. He was unwilling to allow the men to escape. He lowered himself from the tree, and motioning for Dawg to stay hidden, the warrior started after the two men.

The Mexican was caught unawares. Chama could have knifed him in the back, but he wanted the man to see him before he died, to realize an Apache had taken his life. The warrior swung Carlos around and brought the knife up in one instant, plunging it downward as the man gave a fearful cry.

"Jake!"

His plea for help came too late to save him. The blade entered his chest with a heavy thud, and blood gushed from the wound. Chama would have liked to twist the knife in his enemy, but from the corner of his eye, he saw Jake headed for him.

Chama yanked the knife from the Mexican's chest and turned to meet Jake's attack. But Jake's strength was greater than the Mexican's had been. Chama had a fight on his hands. Despite Jake's size, he was swift on his feet. His foot came out and hit Chama's wrist, and the knife went spinning out of his reach. Before he could react, Jake had doubled up a fist and sent it slamming into the warrior's solar plexus.

The breath went out of Chama's body, and while he gasped to draw air, Jake made a dive for the knife. His fingers had barely grasped it when the warrior stomped on Jake's wrist. The man's fingers loosened their grip, and Chama kicked the knife away.

Jake regained his feet and circled just out of Chama's reach. "You're gonna die," he growled. "They ain't no way you can kill me."

The words were so unexpected that the warrior laughed. The sound sent the other man out of control, and he made a dive for the warrior. Chama leapt aside and sent a hard kick into his opponent's stomach that dropped him in his tracks.

Becoming aware of a movement nearby, Chama spun to see the Mexican dragging himself toward the rifle lying on the ground a few feet away. So . . . he had not killed the Mexican dog yet. Chama turned back as Jake regained his feet and came toward him again.

Chama's eyes glittered as he shifted from side to side, seeming intent on retreat, but actually each noiseless shift of his body carried him nearer to Jake, like a big stalking cougar.

The white man was becoming confused by the constant clumsy turning he was forced into in order to face the warrior's circling. Chama cast a swift glance toward the Mexican, who was drawing nearer the rifle on the ground, and decided it was time to act. The warrior came in low and fast, again with his foot. His heel met the white man's belly beneath his left ribs with the force of a lightning bolt. Then he leapt to regain his knife while the other man was gasping for breath.

A moment later the two men lay dead, and the warrior raced through the forest, intent on finding Fire Woman as quickly as possible.

An hour later Chama heard Dawg barking in the distance, and his heart leapt with hope. Had the German shepherd found Fire Woman? Feeling certain it was so, he hurried forward, leaping over the obstacles in his path as he went to meet his woman.

Bursting through the trees, Chama stopped short.

Fire Woman was poised at the edge of a waterfall, looking back toward the forest. He had only a moment to see her face before she lost her balance and flailed out with both arms.

His limbs seemed to be frozen to the spot as he watched her topple over the edge of the cliff.

Chapter Nineteen

For a moment Chama remained motionless, almost frozen as he stared at the place where Fire Woman had stood.

Then he was moving, his heart beating wildly in his chest as he raced forward, unaware that Dawg was keeping pace beside him.

They reached the ledge simultaneously, and the color drained from Chama's face as he stared down into the churning water far below. There was no sign of Fire Woman.

Without a thought, he drew air into his lungs, leapt outward, then curved his body and plunged down into the foaming pool.

He struck the icy water with enough force that it carried him to the bottom. He could feel the numbing influence of the water immediately, and his iron control took over.

He would not allow the cold water to slow his search for Fire Woman. He must find her—and as quickly as possible. He gave a hard kick that carried him upward. After drawing another breath, he plunged beneath the icy surface again. But the water was muddy and swift. The current swept him downstream before he had covered even a small portion of the area beneath the waterfall.

With a sinking heart, he faced the realization that finding her was next to impossible. His mind dealt with this fact even while he was fighting the pull of the water, struggling toward the surface for a breath of air. When he broke the surface of the water, he saw that Dawg was there before him. And amazing though it was, the dog was clutching the neck of Fire Woman's deerskin blouse between its teeth but was having difficulty keeping her head above the water.

The current was carrying the two swiftly downstream, and Chama's strong arms stroked through the water toward them. He saw Dawg lose his grip, and Fire Woman's head submerged — but only for a moment. Although the dog was obviously tiring, it plunged its head downward and came up with the girl again.

Desperation gave Chama the strength he needed to reach them. When he had her in his grasp, he found it took all his strength just to keep her afloat. How could she weigh so much?

Suddenly he remembered the gold pouches fastened at her waist. There were three of them, and it could only be their weight that was making her so heavy.

He must free her of the gold. Even as he made the decision, he realized he couldn't accomplish the task. He had only two hands. One kept Fire Woman beside him; the other was needed to keep them afloat.

Chama's strength was nearly spent when he saw the log coming toward them, carried along with the other debris in the strong current. It would strike them unless he could take evasive action.

Suddenly he realized the log could be their salvation. He waited until the end swung toward him, then lunged for it with his free hand. His head went under, and he swallowed a mouthful of muddy water; but his fingers clutched the rough bark. Then he was pushing Fire Woman onto the log as the dog scrambled up beside her.

Only then did he allow himself to rest momentarily, knowing he must control his breathing and regain some of his strength before he could push them toward the shore.

Mary Elizabeth coughed, and water spurted from her mouth. Her stomach roiled and churned. She turned on her side and gave way to her nausea. For a brief time she lay in a stupor, then slowly she became aware of feeling cold . . . wet.

What happened?

She felt weary beyond belief . . . too weak to move. Becoming aware of the sounds beside her, she raised her head and stared with dazed eyes at the warrior who lay beside her.

"Chama," she whispered.

His breath came in strangled gasps; his buckskin-covered chest heaved with the exertion of his breathing.

A cold, wet nose pushed against her arm, and she turned her head to see Dawg beside her. The German shepherd looked wet and bedraggled, completely exhausted.

Sudden realization dawned on her, and her eyes widened. She had fallen from the cliff, almost drowned. Chama must have saved her.

211

She turned back to the warrior and found his eyes on her. "There . . . was an . . . easier way to get to the other side," he rasped. "All you had to do . . . was ask."

She shuddered. How could he joke about such a thing? If he'd drowned, she'd never have forgiven herself.

She curled tightly into a ball, her body shaking with chills.

Don't be a fool! a silent voice chided. *The worst is over now.*

She firmed her jaw and squared her chin; but despite her efforts at control, her teeth began to chatter, and her body shook even harder.

"Come, little one," Chama said, gathering her into his arms. "You are safe now, and we are together."

But no matter how hard Mary Elizabeth tried, she couldn't stop shaking. It was as though the icy water had penetrated her very bones.

Muttering curses beneath his breath, Chama released her and gathered wood for a fire. A few minutes later the wood crackled and popped as the flames leapt and danced, warming the surrounding area.

Chama pulled handfuls of the new spring grass and rubbed them across Mary Elizabeth's wet buckskins. "With the extra moisture removed from the doeskin, the heat generated by your body combined with the warmth of the fire will soon dry your clothing," he said. "It would be easier if you were wearing the garments of the pale-faces. They could be removed and hung out to dry, but the soft deerhide you are wearing would only become stiff and uncomfortable."

When he had finished rubbing away the excess water, he did the same for his own clothing, then pulled her into his arms and held her tightly against him. Soon, combined warmth of his body and the fire began to penetrate the flesh beneath her damp garments. Her chills slowly passed and her doeskin clothing began to steam.

The penetrating warmth was making her drowsy, until she suddenly remembered the mountain man.

"Did you see Saul?" she whispered.

"Saul? The mountain man who came to the cabin?" When she nodded, he looked confused. "Was he with you?"

"No. But I saw him just before I fell. And, Chama . . . he had Ruth with him."

"He found her?"

"Yes. After so long a time, he finally found her."

"That is good."

His words startled her. Did he really mean them?

As though guessing her thoughts, Chama gave a long sigh. "How could you believe I would ever strike you, little one? Have you not learned by now that I would never cause you harm?" He pressed his lips against her eyelids.

"Chama . . . was it Broken Knife who hit me?"

"No. You struck your head against the door."

She knew he spoke the truth. Whatever Chama did, he would never lie about it. But why hadn't he told her before? If he had done so, then they would probably still be at the cabin.

Chama wondered what Fire Woman was thinking as her arms found their way around his neck. Her fingers twined through his hair, and she laid her head against his chest.

"I should have known," she whispered in a voice so low that he had to strain his ears to hear. "I've been such a fool. And so worried about you."

"There was no need to worry," he said, working his fingers through her tangled hair. Even wet, he loved the feel of it against his skin. Had any other ever had such wondrous hair?

"Do you think the outlaws will try to follow us?"

"No."

"You put yourself at great risk to lead them away from me." She lifted her head, and tears sparkled in her eyes. "You could have been killed."

"Would it have bothered you?"

She drew back, and her blue eyes flashed indignantly. "Of course it would have bothered me! How could you even ask? It's because of you that I'm alive. You've rescued me countless times in the past few months." She paused, her face reflective. "I'm afraid I'm going to miss you when we part."

The words stabbed deep through him. How would he live without her? And yet, how could he live with her? The white-eyes would never accept him, even if she would allow him to stay near her. He sighed deeply. There was no way they could be together, unless she were willing to remain with him. But she had not been willing. And now they could not go back.

How could fate be so cruel as to give him a love that was impossible for him to keep? He could not even fight for her; he must step aside for the sake of her happiness. But he knew it would be the hardest thing he'd ever done.

Mary Elizabeth slept in Chama's arms, waking several times during the night in the grip of a nightmare;

but the warrior held her tightly until the terror had passed, and even Dawg crept nearer to offer support.

When the morning came, Chama killed a rabbit, and they roasted it over the campfire, barely waiting until the meat was done before tearing it apart and devouring it.

Then it was time to resume their journey.

When she noticed the area was beginning to look familiar, Mary Elizabeth started looking for landmarks.

Wasn't that gnarled tree by the stream familiar? Her heart beat faster as she realized they must be near her home. Her forehead wrinkled in a frown. She didn't remember the willow tree nearby.

"What bothers you?" Chama asked from beside her.

"I thought I recognized that tree over there," she said, pointing at the gnarled oak. "But the willow isn't familiar."

"You must remember it has been four years since you were here," Chama said. "The willow is young, with only three seasons' growth. It would not have been there when you were taken captive."

She looked quickly at him. Something about his words gave her pause. Her mind worried the matter until she was able to grasp it.

When you were taken captive.

It was the first time he'd said the words, the first time he had admitted she had been a captive instead of a daughter of the tribe. What had happened to change his mind?

But she really had no time to worry the matter over now, because she suddenly realized he was right. Her gaze had found the wild rose bush growing near the creek. And beyond it stood the fig tree her mother had planted when they'd first moved to these mountains.

If her memory served her right, there should be a spring nearby. She hurried forward, her moccasins crunching over fallen leaves until she reached the rocks that surrounded the spring, a pool measuring about two feet across that was formed by water bubbling from beneath the ground.

Her blue eyes glittered with excitement and goose bumps broke out on her arms. "This is the spring," she said. "The cabin is only a short distance away." She turned around, got her bearings and tried to find the path that led to the cabin.

But it wasn't there.

A spidery chill crept beneath her sun-warmed flesh.

"What is wrong?"

"There should be a path leading to the cabin from the spring. It's not here. But surely Jeb still uses the spring for his water."

"Perhaps he found another source," Chama suggested quietly.

"No," she insisted, fear clutching her tightly in its grip. "There would have been no need. Look for yourself. The spring is good water. And the cabin is not far. It would be the natural place to come . . . if he were still here."

"Do not upset yourself," he said. "If the cabin is there, then we will find it."

If the cabin is there.

Mary Elizabeth found something ominous in his words. What would she do if the cabin wasn't there? She had placed such hope in Jeb being alive. All these years it was the only thing that had kept her going.

The cabin will be there!

And so will Brother Jeb!

They must be!

Chama's eyes never left her face as she began a systematic search for the trail. But it was nowhere to be found. The weeds had completely covered the path.

Something is wrong.

Fear formed a knot in the pit of her stomach.

"Perhaps this is the wrong place," he suggested softly.

"No!" she said angrily. "It was here." Moisture filled her eyes, but she blinked it away. The trail was here. It had to be. Her gaze skittered here and there, searching. "That rise," she said, her voice grating harshly, her hand shaking as she pointed the way toward a dense growth of trees. "It has to be that way."

"Come," he said, reaching for her trembling hand. "We will look together."

Mary Elizabeth jerked her hand away and glared up at him. She didn't want to look with him! She would find the cabin alone! It was because of his people that she had been taken away.

She didn't want him to touch her.

Her brother Jeb would be waiting at the cabin!

He would!

She hurried up the rise and searched the area for something familiar: the blackberry thicket to the left.

Yes.

This is the way.

Mary Elizabeth was lost in the past as she waded through waist-high weeds, hurrying past the blackberry thicket, intent on getting home as quickly as she could. When she broke through the forest into the clearing, her blue eyes widened, and she stood frozen, staring at the remains of the cabin.

Chapter Twenty

Mary Elizabeth's hands clenched into fists. She was unaware of her whitened knuckles, of her fingernails digging into her palms. Her gaze was fixed on all that was left of the cabin: the blackened remains of the fireplace.

Standing there, shaken to the core, she heard the high-pitched, drawn-out lonely wail of a coyote somewhere in the distance. She shuddered, for the sound seemed to come from the past, a ghostly echo of the war cries uttered by the painted savages who had descended on them.

The wind gusted, blowing her fiery hair around her pale face, carrying with it the scent of pines . . . and the acrid smell of charred wood left by the fire that had gutted the cabin so many years ago.

Pine needles cushioned her feet as she went closer, searching amid the fire-blackened ruins where her family had once lived, fearing at any given moment that she would find their remains.

She stopped short at the sight of the old kettle her mother had kept hanging in the fireplace. The blackened pot was almost hidden among the overgrown weeds. Overturned, it rested on its side, half-filled with soil. And within the pot, carried by the wind, nurtured by the rain and sun, was a yellow daisy.

Mary Elizabeth's eyes filled with tears as she stared at the daisy. The daisy . . . her mother's favorite flower. Daisy . . . her maternal grandmother's name.

Grief and despair tore at her heart. She dropped to her knees beside the kettle, reached inside the pot and plucked the daisy. Clasping the dainty yellow flower to her bosom, she rocked back and forth while tears rained down her face.

Why? she silently cried. *Why did this happen to my family? They're all gone. All of them!*

She'd known Ma and Pa were dead, known Melissa and Clem were gone as well. She'd faced that and dealt with her loss years ago.

But not once in all the time she'd been with the Apaches — not once during all the time she was their captive — had she allowed herself to believe Brother Jeb was dead.

Never!

"Come away, Fire Woman," Chama said softly, putting a hand on her arm.

Bitterly, she shook it off, lifting her head to stare with accusing eyes at the warrior beside her.

"They killed him too!" she cried. "Your people killed Jeb too!"

Chama's eyes were dark with a pain she was too overwrought to see. "No, Fire Woman," he rasped harshly. "You were right. Your brother was not killed that day. If he is dead, then others are responsible. Not my people."

"How could you know?" she cried, scrubbing at her

tears with the back of her hand. "You weren't here."

"No," he admitted. "But I have spoken with the warriors who raided your home. They told me of two white men who had died at their hands. Not a third."

Lifting her chin in the palm of his hand, he held her gaze, forcing her to believe his words. "You must hold on to that belief, little one. Your brother still lives. And I will not rest until you are with him."

"No," she snapped, jerking away from him. "You and your kind have done enough to me and my family. If my brother Jeb is alive, I'll find him! And I'll do it alone!"

Her legs refused to cooperate when she tried to stand. She stumbled over a rock and would have fallen, but Chama wrapped an arm around her and pulled her into his embrace.

"No!" Mary Elizabeth cried, struggling against him, but her efforts were weak, ineffectual and finally ceased.

Chama waited until her sobs turned into hiccups before he spoke. "Let us leave this place of death," he said. "We will journey to the town, and you will surely find your brother there."

The mid-afternoon sun found them in the foothills of the Sangre de Cristos. Off in the distance they could see the town of Taos.

Chama felt numb inside. The muscles in his jaw tightened as he steeled himself against the pain of losing her. All the way from the burned-out cabin site, a fierce battle had been raging within him. The reality of losing her was worse than he'd ever imagined it would be.

She's mine! his heart cried silently. It was written in the stars, etched in his heart, burned into his brain. He could not bear to let her go, and yet, how could he keep her?

Everything within him urged him to scoop her up in his arms and carry her away from this place, back to the cabin in the mountains where they had found happiness.

But he could not.

For the sake of Fire Woman's own happiness, he must let her go.

Deep inside, he had always known the day would come, and nothing would be gained by giving in to the pain he was feeling. But how could he even contemplate life without her? And yet he knew he must. Somehow, he must find a way. Perhaps knowing that she was finally truly happy would be enough to warm his lonely nights, but he didn't think so.

Her face was pinched when she turned to him, lifting her gaze to meet his eyes. "Don't come any farther," she said quietly. "It would be dangerous for you to journey there."

He knew she was right. Taos was a favorite trading place for the Comanches, Navajos, and the Utes, all of them his enemies.

"Will you be safe among them?"

She nodded, and her fiery curls danced around her shoulders. "There are men like the trappers there. But there are decent people as well. They'll see I'm not harmed. And I'm sure someone in town can tell me what happened to my brother."

"Will you promise me one thing?"

221

"What?"

"Will you return if your brother is not there?"

"Why?"

"I need to know that all is well with you."

"All right. If Jeb's not in Taos, then I'll come back. But only if you promise to let me leave afterward."

He wanted to protest her terms, but knew if he did, she would be lost to him. However, if her brother was not in Taos, Chama had not the slightest intention of leaving her there alone. He kept his face free of emotion as he agreed. When she turned to leave, he reached out a hand and grasped her wrist.

"You would go without a farewell?" he asked softly, pulling her into the circle of his arms. He knew he was only making the parting harder, but couldn't seem to help himself.

When his mouth found hers, it was a kiss of infinite sweetness and tender longing. He had to force himself to release her and watch her walk away from him when every particle of his being screamed out in protest. A strange numbness crept over him as he watched her walk away, a numbness that didn't leave, even as the sun crept down and darkness fell over the land . . . and still he was alone.

Mary Elizabeth left Chama behind, feeling a curious heaviness in her chest, an ache that spread to the pit of her stomach leaving an emptiness that could never be satisfied by mere food. Although she told herself she hated Chama, she knew it wasn't true. Hate would have been easier for her to bear.

When she arrived in Taos, followed by her faithful

companion, Dawg, she found it had changed little in the four years she'd been gone. Built around a square, the buildings were made of adobe brick. Bathed in a golden hue, they seemed to bask in the sunshine.

Mary Elizabeth made her way down the crowded street to the square, feeling self-conscious about her doeskin garments, expecting any moment to hear a hoot of laughter, to see heads turning, fingers pointing at her. But her passing went unnoticed. Soon it became obvious why. There were many others dressed in hide garments. Indians and mountain men mingled with prosperous businessmen dressed in suits and gaudily dressed New Mexicans. Since the annual fair began in August 1780, Taos had become a favorite trading place for Indians as well as the Spanish. Indians arrived by the hundreds, carrying chamois, buffalo skins, horses and other goods to trade for blankets, beads and their other needs.

Mary Elizabeth looked for a friendly face, someone to question about her brother, but no one looked familiar. She passed Juan Diego's Cantina, unwilling to enter the rowdy establishment. Across the street was Carpenter's General Store, where Lije Carpenter, owner and operator, was busily stirring up dust as he swept the sidewalk out front.

As she hurried toward him, he became aware of her gaze and stopped suddenly, leaning on his raggedy broom while he looked her up and down. His eyes narrowed on her fiery curls, dropped to her doeskin garments, then swept up to her face again.

Suddenly, his mouth dropped open, and the broom fell to the ground; the Adam's apple on his scrawny throat worked up and down.

223

"Mary Elizabeth?" he croaked. "Is that you?"

She offered him a tentative smile. "Yes, it's me, Mr. Carpenter. I've come home. And I'm looking for Brother Jeb."

"Well, Lord Almighty, youngun," he said. "Ever'body hearabouts figgered you was long since dead. It's been nigh on to five years now, ain't it? What happened to you?"

"It was the Apaches," she said. "They came from the mountains. They killed my family. All but Melissa . . . and Brother Jeb?" The last words were more a question than a statement.

"We knew that," he said. "Clint Hollister saw the smoke from the fire and raised the alarm. We got there 'bout the same time your brother Jeb did."

Her heart gave an excited leap. Chama had been right! Jeb was alive! But where was he?

"When we saw your folks was dead and you and Melissa was missin', the town formed a posse and took off after them 'Paches what took you." His eyes darkened with sadness. "Sorry we didn't find you. But we lost thet trail 'fore we'd gone more'n a few miles. Couldn't find nary a track to follow, Mary Elizabeth. It was like you dropped right out of sight. Where you been all these years anyhow? And where is Melissa?"

"We've been all over," she said. "The Apaches move around a lot." She swallowed hard. "Melissa is dead." Tears misted her eyes, but she blinked them away. She wouldn't stand in the middle of town and cry. The worst was over now. She was back home with her own people. And Jeb was alive!

But for some reason she felt uncomfortable. A crowd had begun to form. Some of the faces were familiar;

224

others she'd never seen before. "I didn't know about the cabin being burned," she said. "I went there first. Could you tell me where I can find my brother Jeb?"

He eyed her sadly. "He ain't been here for more'n three years now, youngun. He gave you and your sister up for dead a long time ago. He was so broke up over what happened thet he up and left town."

Mary Elizabeth's heart plummeted to the ground. "Left? Where did he go?"

"He told me he was goin' to Texas."

"Texas?" Her blue eyes widened. She'd heard Texas was a big place. "Do you know where in Texas?"

"He told me," he said, scratching his grizzled head. "Stood right there where you're a standin' an' told me where he was goin'. Trouble is, I didn't think nobody'd be askin' fer him, an' I cain't rightly recall what he said. Coulda been Houston." He frowned and scratched his head again. "No. I take thet back. Wasn't Houston neither. Maybe it was Forth Worth." He didn't seem so certain about that either, because he looked up, his gaze scanning the crowd. "Anybody here know where Jebediah Abernathy went?"

"Texas." The answer came promptly.

Mary Elizabeth looked at the man who had spoken. He was a Mexican of short stature, dressed in the gaudily embroidered garments of a caballero.

"Do you know where in Texas?" she asked. "Was it Houston or Fort Worth?"

"I think it was neither, señorita. Your brother, he tell me he is going to the hill country."

"Where is the hill country?"

"I do not know, señorita."

"Once I heard it was slap-dab in the middle of Texas,"

another man said.

"Ain't Austin somewheres in the middle of Texas?" asked another.

"Somewheres in there."

She turned their words over in her mind. They all seemed so vague, but the need to find her brother Jeb had intensified since she knew with a certainty that he was alive. There was nothing to stop her from following him. She still had the gold. Although she didn't know how much it was worth, she could find out at the assayer's office. She could cash it in there. Perhaps the assayer could even provide some information about Jeb.

She sighed heavily. The task seemed almost insurmountable. Texas was a long way from home.

Home.

Mary Elizabeth thought about that for a while. The cabin, her old homeplace, had been burned. She couldn't stay there. And all her family was dead, except for Jeb, and he was gone to Texas.

Squaring her shoulders and firming her chin, she looked at the man facing her. "Where is the assayer's office?" she asked.

The storekeeper's eyebrows lifted slightly, and his eyes narrowed. "What would a girl like you be needin' with the assayer?" he asked curiously. "You find somethin' back in the mountains?"

She remained silent, having no intention of telling him about the gold she carried—not with the whole town listening.

"I'll take you there, little lady," said a heavy-set man, pushing his way to the front of the crowd. "It'd be a pure pleasure to help you."

"I expect it would," said another man. His collar

226

identified him as a clergyman. "But I consider it my duty to escort the young lady to her destination."

"There's no need!" came a strident voice from the crowd. "What Mary Elizabeth needs is a woman. I'll take her wherever she needs to go." A woman in a heavy purple dress bustled forward, pushing past the men to stand before Mary Elizabeth. A small smile softened the woman's features. "You poor child. You've been through quite an ordeal."

Mary Elizabeth tried hard to place the auburn-haired woman. Her face seemed familiar, associated with spicy cookies warm from the oven and—Sarah Jane! Little, rebellious Sarah Jane Grimes.

Yes.

The woman facing her was Sarah Jane's mother, Martha.

"Mrs. Grimes?" she asked hesitantly.

"Yes. You poor dear." The woman gathered the young girl into her arms and pressed her against a heaving bosom. "Your mother was my dearest friend. I could do no less than help her daughter in her time of need. You come right home with me, dear."

Mary Elizabeth found herself following meekly behind the woman with Dawg trailing closely. When they neared the cantina, a woman's raucous laughter floated through the batwing doors, and Martha Grimes' face took on a disapproving look. She stepped into the street and crossed to the other side. Mary Elizabeth felt confused for a moment as they went only one block before crossing the street once again.

But suddenly her brow cleared as she remembered the code the white women, the good women, lived by. It wasn't the cantina itself they were avoiding; it was the painted women, the tarnished ladies who worked there. Mary Elizabeth remembered visiting Sarah Jane in town at a birthday party and learning that the painted women were different than the rest of them. Sarah Jane had whispered they did bad things with the men and were to be avoided, lest they contaminate the rest of the women.

What bad things did they do? she wondered. But only for a moment, for her mind was taken up with the excitement of being with her own kind again. She had actually left the Apache life behind and returned to live among her own people. As she had often said she would.

No matter that her brother was missing. Somehow, she would find him.

Wherever he was.

Chapter Twenty-one

Martha Grimes opened the gate to the adobe brick fence that surrounded the hacienda where she lived, and motioned Mary Elizabeth to follow her. They went up a gravel path lined with pots filled with gardenias and wild roses. When they reached the wide veranda that ran the length of the dwelling, Martha pushed open the door.

"That dog will have to say outside," she said.

"Of course," Mary Elizabeth murmured. "Stay, Dawg!" she ordered.

The German shepherd immediately sat back on its haunches and watched her enter the dwelling.

Mary Elizabeth had only been in the parlor once before, the day of Sarah Jane's birthday party, but the room hadn't been changed since then. It was handsomely furnished, with a curved, high-backed sofa and marble-topped tables. The whitewashed walls were hung with portraits of holy characters and crosses in the Spanish style, and interspersed with mirrors framed with gold. The windows were decorated with crimson worsted curtains, and an Oriental rug was spread over the wooden floor.

Mary Elizabeth waited for Martha to invite her to sit down; instead, the woman crossed the room to the foot of the stairs.

"Sarah Jane!" she called.

There was no answer.

"Sarah Jane!" Her voice was sharper this time. "Get down here!"

Mary Elizabeth, realizing she couldn't be seated until she'd been invited to do so, crossed to the window and pulled back the curtains. Dawg lay in the shade of a rosebush, its eyes fastened on the house, as though the animal felt the need to keep guard over its mistress.

"What is it, Ma?" asked a slightly bored voice from the top of the stairs.

"Sarah Jane!" Martha sounded like she had eaten a sour pickle. "How many times have I told you not to call me Ma. Get down here! We've got company."

"I *do* beg your pardon, Mama."

Mary Elizabeth stifled a grin as she let the curtains fall in place and turned to greet the girl who entered the parlor.

Sarah Jane had changed little during the past four years. She still had the same thick black hair, but now her braids formed a crown at the top of her small head instead of hanging down her back. Her mouth opened in a shriek, quickly stifled by the small, black lace handkerchief that she carried.

For a moment Sarah Jane looked as though she expected Mary Elizabeth to attack her. Then her gaze went to her mother, and her deep blue eyes, if possible, opened even wider.

Martha Grimes showed her annoyance at her daughter's flagrant emotional display. "Don't carry on so, Sarah Jane! It's only Mary Elizabeth, come home after all these years!"

"Mary Elizabeth?" Sarah Jane's voice was questioning. Her gaze dwelt on the copper hair and a weak smile surfaced. "It *is* you. We — we thought you were — dead." She gulped. Her gaze dropped to the deerskin dress for a long moment, then quickly darted upward again.

Mary Elizabeth smiled at the girl who had been her childhood friend and held out a hand. "It's good to see you, Sarah Jane. But I wouldn't have known you. You've changed a lot since your twelfth birthday."

"So have you," the other girl said, her smile becoming more genuine. "Lordy, Mary Elizabeth! I'm so glad you survived!" Sarah Jane pulled her friend into a warm embrace. "It's still hard to believe," she enthused. "After all this time, you've come back!" She pulled back, her expression suddenly hesitant. "Is Melissa with you?"

"No," Mary Elizabeth said, blinking back the tears that were so quick to come. She shook her head, feeling suddenly unable to speak. How could she tell them what had happened to Melissa? But she found there was no need. Sarah Jane seemed to understand her feelings and wrapped her arms around her again. "God! It's so good to have you home! So good! We've got so many things to talk about. So much catching up to do."

Martha pulled the two girls apart. "There's time enough for all that later," she said. "Her dear mother, Grace, would expect me to look after her child. And what Mary Elizabeth needs right now is a bath. Sarah Jane, put some water on to heat and help her get the bathtub in off the back veranda. Then get the lye soap and scrub brush. And she's going to need some clothes." Her eyes appraised Mary Elizabeth. "She's a mite smaller than you. Perhaps those gowns you've outgrown will do."

"Only until we can get some more made." Sarah Jane's face glowed with enthusiasm. "We'll go shopping later and buy some material and find some patterns. Oh, it will be lots of fun."

Everything was going too fast for Mary Elizabeth. She wanted to tell Martha Grimes that she didn't need a bath, that she had bathed earlier in the day, but the woman seemed so set on her purpose that Mary Elizabeth remained silent.

Mary Elizabeth felt tears were very near the surface again. Why after all these years was she so prone to cry? Perhaps it was because she knew these people had loved her parents and mourned them too.

Yes, that must be it, she silently decided.

Martha Grimes' sympathy for Mary Elizabeth was apparent, but it had been a long time since anyone had been sympathetic toward her. That must be the reason she continually felt like crying.

When the tub had been carried upstairs to Sarah Jane's bedroom and filled with steaming water, Mary Elizabeth waited for Martha to leave them alone. But to her extreme embarrassment, the woman showed no sign of leaving the room. Martha Grimes watched as the girl unfastened the rawhide bag that held the gold and laid it aside before removing her clothing.

Mary Elizabeth stepped into the tub, then sat down in the water, and Sarah Jane handed her a bar of scented soap.

"Not that!" Martha said sharply, her brows drawn into a frown. "I told you to bring the lye soap, Sarah Jane."

"But, Ma," the girl protested. "The lye soap is strong enough to peel the hide off Mary Elizabeth. She hasn't been wallowing in a mudhole."

Martha rolled up her sleeves. "The lye soap," she insisted. "And don't talk back to me, Sarah Jane."

When Sarah Jane returned with the lye soap, Martha picked up the scrub brush and, after rubbing the bar over the bristles, proceeded to scrub Mary Elizabeth until her skin was red and scratched. If Sarah Jane had not been protesting most of the time, Mary Elizabeth would have crawled out of the tub. But the girl's obvious distress kept her silent and grim until the woman decided she was clean enough.

Martha's eyes glittered when she rose to her feet and rolled down her sleeves. "Take that—that—abomination away Sarah Jane!" she said harshly.

"What—what abomination, Ma?" the girl asked, obviously intimidated.

"That—that Injun outfit. Those—clothes—made out of animal skins."

With her face looking as though she'd eaten a bushel of lemons, the woman stalked out of the room and banged the door behind her.

Sarah Jane seemed ashamed to look at her friend. "I'm sorry, Mary Elizabeth," she whispered, her gaze directed at the floor. "Ma's not usually so mean. I don't know what got into her. Did she hurt you?"

She had. But although Mary Elizabeth's skin was scratched in several places by the harsh bristles on the brush, she wasn't going to tell the other girl. It was ob-

233

vious Sarah Jane was feeling badly enough already. "No. She didn't hurt me," she lied.

Picking up the dress Sarah Jane had laid out for her, Mary Elizabeth lifted it over her head and was stopped by the other girl. "Aren't you going to put your undergarments on first?"

Mary Elizabeth blushed. She'd been unused to such feminine garments for so long that she'd forgotten they must be worn. After spreading the dress carefully on the bed, she picked up a pair of pantaloons and slipped them on over her hips. Then she frowned at the corset and chemise.

"Do I have to wear all this?"

Sarah Jane giggled. "Mama would be horrified if you didn't."

Picking up the undergarments, Mary Elizabeth donned them and several petticoats her friend insisted must be worn as well. Then she fumbled at the unfamiliar fastenings of the dress.

Sarah Jane found a pair of high button shoes for Mary Elizabeth, and although they were a perfect fit, the leather felt stiff and uncomfortable after the years of wearing nothing but soft moccasins on her feet.

Mary Elizabeth felt hot and uncomfortable in the heavy clothing, and she had barely finished dressing when the visitor arrived.

The two girls heard Dawg bark and only moments later a sharp rap on the front door. It was only a few minutes before Martha called them to afternoon tea. Mary Elizabeth felt conscious of her reddened skin as she entered the parlor behind Sarah Jane.

Martha was seated on the high-backed sofa beside a woman wearing a heavy gray skirt and a white pleated blouse.

The two women looked up as they entered.

"Come sit down beside me, Mary Elizabeth," Martha said, patting the sofa next to her. "This is Gladys Miles, a dear friend of mine. She's brought us a fresh cake just hot from the oven."

After Mary Elizabeth acknowledged the other woman and took her seat, the questions began.

"I didn't know your dear parents," Gladys said. "We only moved here last year. But I understand they were God-fearing folks."

"Yes, ma'am," Mary Elizabeth said, accepting the cup of tea Sarah Jane held out to her.

"Gladys's husband, John, is the governor's aide," Martha Grimes said.

"How nice," Mary Elizabeth held the fragile cup in one hand and its china saucer in the other while she sipped at her tea. And, although she watched the other woman politely, her thoughts had strayed as she tried to deal with the unreality of the situation. Could she really be sitting here, taking tea with these women as though the past had never been, when only a short time ago she had been a captive of the Apache Indians, the fiercest and most savage warriors of the plains? She had suffered deprivations these women could never imagine, even in their worst nightmares.

"Martha tells me your poor sister was killed," Gladys said, her small, curious eyes on the younger girl. "The whole thing must have been terrible for you." She clucked her tongue. "Just terrible. A young girl like yourself, all alone and surrounded by those naked savages."

Mary Elizabeth's hand trembled as she lifted the cup

to her lips and took another sip. Gladys's words had brought back the memory she had tried so hard to suppress. Realizing the woman would report her actions to the townfolk when she left the house, Mary Elizabeth forced her hands to steady. She would not let the woman upset her. Nor would Gladys catch her slurping her tea or some other such mannerless action. Although it had been four years since Mary Elizabeth had held a teacup in her hand, the years of training she'd already received from her mother had not been forgotten.

"I've heard the Apaches strip the clothes off their prisoners," Gladys said. "Is that true?"

Sarah Jane gave a shocked gasp, and Mary Elizabeth's teacup clattered against the saucer. She knew her cheeks must be flaming. "I'd rather not talk about it," she said stiffly.

Gladys paid no attention, intent on having her pound of flesh. "However did you manage to survive?"

Mary Elizabeth looked at the woman, at her tight, pursed lips, the disapproval in her narrowed eyes. "I was adopted by Three Toes."

"Three Toes?" The woman's nose wrinkled with disgust. "Adopted, you said?" She took a long time considering the words, and when she spoke again, her voice held a curious speculation. "What does it mean. This . . . Three Toes person . . . adopting you?"

"I don't understand," Mary Elizabeth said.

Gladys pursed her lips, her small eyes narrowed on Mary Elizabeth's face. "You said he . . . adopted you," she said sharply. "People usually adopt children. Did he treat you like a child? Or a woman?"

"I was only twelve years old. Still a child," Mary Elizabeth stated.

"Yes," the woman said firmly. "I know that. But did he *treat* you like a child? Or did you fill another role, as his wife?"

"Mother?" Sarah Jane's voice intruded. "Is this necessary?"

"Hush, Sarah Jane," Martha Grimes said. "Gladys is only asking what everyone in town will want to know."

Gladys's words had conjured up the image of Melissa in Mary Elizabeth's mind, of the way her sister had looked just before she died. But the fury, barely tempered with bitterness at Gladys's assumption, snapped Mary Elizabeth's chin up, and her eyes locked with her inquisitor's. It was bitterly ironic that Mary Elizabeth had been the victim of a violent act, and yet her morals were being questioned. Would Gladys be more content if she hung her head in shame? Perhaps. But Mary Elizabeth refused to do so.

"I did not fill the roll of a wife for Three Toes," she said stiffly. "Most of the time he treated me as he would his own child."

"Most of the time?" Gladys prompted.

"Yes." Mary Elizabeth's voice could have melted icicles.

"What about the other times?"

"He beat me until I was senseless."

A silence hung heavy over the room. But the woman wasn't done yet. After a few long moments, she spoke.

"What caused the beatings?"

"My attempts to escape."

"Were you violated in any way?"

Mary Elizabeth sucked in a sharp breath. She had been certain the question would come. "No. Not the

237

way you mean."

"What about Melissa?"

Mary Elizabeth's throat closed. She swallowed hard, but made herself hold the other woman's gaze. "Yes. That's what killed her."

Sarah Jane drew in a sharp breath. "Would anyone like some tea?" she asked in a slightly hysterical voice.

"Be quiet, Sarah Jane," her mother said harshly.

Gladys's gaze was shrewd as she studied Mary Elizabeth. "Don't think I'm not sympathetic to your plight," she said. "I've heard what the Indians do to women. And none of it's good."

"All the Indians aren't like that," Mary Elizabeth said.

"Far as I'm concerned, you can lump them all in one basket. In my opinion, none of them are fit to be called human beings. And I'm surprised you were able to get away from them." Her gaze probed Mary Elizabeth. "You are still a virgin, aren't you?"

Mary Elizabeth could feel the heat in her cheeks and knew they had flushed, but she refused to feel shame. She had known all along that that was where the woman's thoughts lay. And it was past time to put a stop to her questions.

Willing her hand to remain steady, Mary Elizabeth carefully placed her cup and saucer on the marble-topped table; all the while her gaze never wavered from the woman bent on tormenting her.

"I really don't see what business it is of yours." She spoke quietly.

"Does that mean you're not?"

"But you said you weren't violated," Martha Grimes interrupted. "And if you weren't, then you must have

238

allowed—allowed—" Her eyes widened perceptibly. "Land sakes alive!" she exclaimed. "How could you let one of those dirty savages touch you?"

"This has gone far enough, Ma!" Sarah Jane's voice was sharp. "I'm ashamed of you both."

"Sarah Jane!" her mother said. "Watch your tongue!"

"No!" the girl retorted. "I won't shut up! You claim to be her mother's friend. Do you think she'd want Mary Elizabeth put through this? It wasn't her fault the Indians took her and Melissa. And you don't know what she had to do in order to survive."

"A decent woman would kill herself before allowing one of those savages to touch her," Gladys stated coldly. She stood up, looking at Martha Grimes. "I'm sorry, my dear, but I can't possibly stay in this house with such a woman here. It would be unthinkable."

"Gladys," protested Martha. "Please don't go."

As Mary Elizabeth listened to the two women, the terrible reality of her situation began to sink in. She had slept with an Apache Indian, therefore, she was a tainted woman. Everyone in Taos would look at her either with contempt or pity. And she wanted neither one. She couldn't stay here. She wanted desperately to find a safe haven, someplace where she would never have to deal with pain again. But there was no such place, no one left to care whether she lived or died.

Except Chama.

Her head thumped painfully as she stood up.

"There is no need for you to leave," Mary Elizabeth said. "Since I'm the intruder here, then I'm the one who should go. I had no intention of staying anyway. It was at Mrs. Grime's insistence that I came." She looked sorrowfully at her friend. "If you'll tell me what you did

239

with my clothing, then I'll leave."

"Ma!" Sarah Jane snapped. "You apologize instantly! I won't have Mary Elizabeth made to feel as though she's done something wrong."

"I'll just show myself out," Gladys said, headed for the door as though afraid she would contract some dreadful disease unless she made a hurried departure.

"Good riddance," Sarah Jane snapped, putting a comforting arm around Mary Elizabeth.

"Sarah Jane Grimes," her mother said. "I don't know what's gotten into you."

"What's all the racket in here?" called a gruff male voice. "And why is Gladys leaving in such a huff?"

Mary Elizabeth recognized the voice of Harry Grimes, Sarah Jane's father, and it was the final straw. She couldn't go through the whole thing again. She made a dash for the front door and hurried out of the house. Dawg gave a wild bark and came around the corner to join her. She knelt on the ground and gave him a quick hug. She would leave this place. But first she must get the bag of gold she'd left in Sarah Jane's room.

"I'm sorry," Sarah Jane said from beside her. "Please come back inside. Pa will make Ma apologize."

Mary Elizabeth shook her head. "No," she said. "I won't stay here. It's obvious your mother doesn't want me here." She looked at the other girl. "Sarah Jane, I must have the bag I left in your room. And my clothing. But I don't want to go back inside. Will you get them for me?"

"Yes," the girl said. "But I wish you would change your mind."

"No." Mary Elizabeth shook her head. "I can't do

240

that. I'm going to find Jeb. It was never my intention to do anything else."

Sarah Jane went into the house and returned a short time later with a carpetbag.

"What is this?" Mary Elizabeth asked.

"I put your things and some of mine inside," the girl said. "Also a few dollars that I had put by." She held the bag out. "We can get you a room at the hotel until we can think of something else."

Mary Elizabeth nodded. "That would be best. But I don't need your money, Sarah Jane. I have some gold. But I'll need direction to the assayer's office."

"Soon as we get you a room, I'll show you where it is."

Dawg kept pace beside the two girls as they left the yard and hurried toward the town.

Chapter Twenty-two

Mary Elizabeth's eyes widened when she entered the hotel lobby. She hadn't expected such lavish furnishings, the gold brocade couches, marble-topped tables, gilt-edged mirrors and red velvet curtains.

She felt completely intimidated by the opulence, and Mary Elizabeth realized if Sarah Jane hadn't been with her, she'd have been tempted to turn tail and run. But she didn't, for the other girl's presence gave Mary Elizabeth the courage she needed to stay.

Her feet seemed to sink amid gold designs in the red wool carpet that covered the floor as she crossed to the registration desk.

Although she could only see the upper half of the man behind the counter, she supposed he was dressed in the fashion of a Spanish gentleman. His black jacket was plain, except for the gold embroidery and braid that edged it, and at the moment, he was reading a newspaper.

"Hector." Sarah Jane demanded his attention. "My friend needs a room."

He looked up from the newspaper, and when he saw

Sarah Jane, his face broke into a smile. "Señorita Grimes," he exclaimed. "I am surprised to see you.".

Sarah Jane offered him a smile. "I didn't expect to be here," she said. "But my friend needs a room."

Although the clerk's dark eyes were curious, he reached for a long black book and pushed it toward Mary Elizabeth. "How long will you be staying, señorita?"

"I don't know," Mary Elizabeth replied.

He handed her a pencil. "Please sign your name and address in the register," he said, before turning around to reach for a room key hanging on the wall behind the counter. After placing it on the counter, he turned the register around to read her name. "You have room number eighteen. You will find it up the stairs and down the hall to your right. Will you need help with your baggage, Señorita, uh—" his gaze dropped to her signature, squinted for a moment, then flew up to narrow on her face— "Abernathy. You are Jebediah Abernathy's sister?"

Mary Elizabeth's blue eyes widened. "Yes," she breathed, hope flowering within her breast. "Do you know where Jeb went?"

"No," he said shortly. "I do not know your brother."

"But—I thought—" She broke off, staring at him in confusion. After swallowing hard, she went on. "You seemed to know about me."

"I think everyone in town knows of you, señorita." His eyes were dark and assessing. "The good people speak of the girl who lived with the Apaches without harm, and they wonder how such a thing could be possible. But me, I do not wonder." His tone was slimy, insulting.

243

Sarah Jane gave a gasp of outrage, and Mary Elizabeth's lips tightened, her eyes glittering brightly. No one had to tell her what conclusion the *good* people, and the clerk, had arrived at. But Mary Elizabeth had no intention of discussing it. Instead, she picked up her carpetbag.

The desk clerk had not finished with her. He pointed at Dawg. "You cannot bring the dog into the hotel." His voice was sharp, bordering on the insolent. "He must stay outside."

"Dawg goes where I go!" Mary Elizabeth snapped, keeping her back turned firmly against the man as she headed toward the stairs.

"Señorita!" he called angrily. "I must insist. The beast will not remain inside the hotel."

Mary Elizabeth clutched the room key tightly in her hand. If she left the hotel, she would have no place to go. But she would not give up Dawg. The animal was her only means of protection.

"Hector!" Sarah Jane chided. "Mary Elizabeth shouldn't be left alone. She's been through an ordeal. The dog won't hurt your precious hotel."

"The señorita has my sympathy, of course," the desk clerk said. "But we must abide by the rules. The owner of this hotel has decreed there will be no animals inside. Is not the dog an animal?"

"I think it's debatable who is the animal here," Sarah Jane replied. "You haven't seen the old man who owns this place in two years, and you probably won't see him for at least another two. In fact, he's so old, he may not live that long. So stop making such a fuss. Unless . . ." she paused for effect, "you want me to speak to my father about this incident. He wouldn't be happy to hear

244

about the way you treat his friends."

The clerk sucked in a sharp breath. "The governor's aide is a friend of the señorita's father?"

"Yes," she said firmly. "The *governor's aide* is my godfather!"

"Godfather! Oh, a thousand apologies, señorita. I did not understand. Of course you must keep your lovely dog with you."

The clerk hurried around the counter and continued to mutter apologies to Mary Elizabeth, reaching out a hand to pat the German shepherd on the head and snatching it back when Dawg growled and bared its teeth. The clerk flinched away, then tried to take the carpetbag from Mary Elizabeth, intent on carrying it for her, but again he was foiled. She clutched it tightly against her chest and hurried up the stairs with the dog and Sarah Jane following.

Mary Elizabeth heaved a sigh of relief when the door to room number eighteen was closed behind them. She laid the carpetbag on the bed and sat beside it.

"You shouldn't have lied to him," she said. "He'll be angry when he finds out."

"Not half as angry as I am," Sarah Jane said, sinking down beside her. "What's wrong with everyone? You'd think you were carrying typhoid or something?"

"I think they'd probably feel better if I did have typhoid," Mary Elizabeth said. "At least it could be treated. I didn't realize everyone would feel this way. I actually thought they'd be glad I had survived." She turned saddened eyes on her friend. "Perhaps I was wrong to come back."

"Oh, balderdash!" Sarah Jane said, putting a comforting arm around her friend. "Don't ever think that way. Just because a few small people act as though you've contacted a contagious disease—" She broke off and was silent for a long moment. When she spoke again, her voice was sad. "I don't know what to say to you. All these years I've gone to the chapel to light candles for you, prayed for you to come back safe. Even dreamed about the things we'd do, the fun we'd have. But I never once thought you'd get such a reaction from the townspeople."

"Neither did I," Mary Elizabeth said, keeping her gaze away from the other girl, afraid Sarah Jane's sympathy would be her undoing. She certainly hadn't expected what she'd found. Not only was her brother missing, but she had been rejected by her own people. What had she done to deserve it?

Suddenly Dawg laid its head in her lap and whined, claiming her attention. She scratched behind its ear, but the animal moved back, crossed to the door and pawed at it, turning its head to look back at her.

"Even Dawg wants to leave me," Mary Elizabeth said, her voice showing her utter misery.

Going to the door, she opened it for the German shepherd. It went into the hallway and stopped. When she stayed where she was, it slipped inside the room again and padded back to the bed. The dog seemed to be telling her it would rather go, but if she insisted on staying, then it would stay with her.

"Dawg wants to go outside, and I need to find the assayer's office," Mary Elizabeth said. "Could you show me where it is?"

"Of course," Sarah Jane sad. "Anything is better than sitting here and moping." She seemed relieved for the excuse to leave the cold, impersonal hotel room.

"Where did you find nuggets this size?" the assayer asked, rolling the gold back and forth in his palm.

Mary Elizabeth knew better than to tell the man. "How much are they worth?" she asked.

He frowned down at them. "Umm . . . they ain't quality stuff," he muttered. "More rock than gold."

"They look good to me," Sarah Jane said, reaching for one of the nuggets that lay on the counter. She put it in her mouth, bit down on it, then frowned at the imprints of her teeth. "What do you think they're worth?"

"It's kinda hard to say," the assayer said, scratching his unshaven chin. "Would be easier to determine was I to know where they came from."

Mary Elizabeth kept silent as she watched the man. He didn't seem trustworthy to her. But she had no choice in the matter. She needed the money the gold would bring.

"I don't understand why you must know where she found them," Sarah Jane insisted. "It shouldn't make any difference to their value."

"Well, it does!" the man retorted sharply. "Gold is my business. An' I know what I'm talkin' about. They's lots of cheap gold layin' out in the desert, an' they's a little better gold in the streambeds; but the best gold is found in the mountains. And they's a difference in the quality of thet gold. Now, if she was to tell me where it come from, might be she's got some of thet quality stuff. But I can't decide until she tells me."

"Do you want the gold or not?" Mary Elizabeth demanded.

She had no intention of telling the man where the

gold came from. Chama might return to the cabin, and it wouldn't be safe for him if anyone knew gold had been found there.

The assayer's expression darkened. He thumped the nuggets down on the counter and looked at them with scorn. "I ain't so sure I do. This ain't quality stuff!"

Mary Elizabeth was about to ask what the assayer would give her for the gold, but Sarah Jane forestalled her, scooping the nuggets off the counter and dropping them into the leather pouch. Then she took her friend's arm and pulled her toward the door.

"Now, hold on there," the assayer said, hurrying around the counter to block their way. "I thought you wanted to sell thet gold."

"She's decided to consult someone else about the gold," Sarah Jane said.

"But—" Mary Elizabeth started to protest, but was silenced by Sarah Jane's fingers squeezing her arm.

"You sell to me or you don't sell at all! They ain't no other assay office in town, missy," the clerk said sharply. "But I guess I could make you a good deal on them rocks. Seein' as how you're in such bad need. I could prob'ly give you—" he pursed his lips, pretending to think it over—"oh, maybe as much as fifty dollars for the lot of 'em. But it's only because it's plain you're in a lot of trouble."

"She's not in that much trouble," Sarah Jane said, hurrying her friend from the shop and slamming the door behind her.

"Where are we going?" Mary Elizabeth asked.

Sarah Jane's lips curled in a secret smile. "We're going to see someone who'll be glad to help you anyway he can."

They went to the middle of town and entered a square building that housed several offices. "Is Wesley upstairs?" she asked the manager.

He nodded, and Sarah Jane motioned for Mary Elizabeth to follow, went up the stairs and knocked softly on the first door on the right.

"Enter!" a voice muffled by the door called out.

Sarah Jane pushed open the door and pulled Mary Elizabeth inside the room with her.

Thick, dark hair famed the even features of the man behind the desk. He looked up at them, and the natural lines at the corners of his mouth curved upward.

"Sarah Jane," he said, pushing back his chair and hurrying forward. "I wasn't expecting to see you."

"Mary Elizabeth, meet my fiancé, Wesley Parker," Sarah Jane said.

Murmuring a polite greeting, Mary Elizabeth listened as the other girl explained her predicament, ending with, "I think the assayer is trying to cheat her."

"He probably is," Wesley said. "Just a minute while I get my hat. I'll come with you and see she gets a fair deal."

It was less than an hour before Mary Elizabeth left the assayer's office with over four hundred dollars. And the crooked assayer was trembling in his boots at the anger directed toward him by the lawyer who threatened to report him to the governor if he should ever attempt to cheat anyone again.

"Little good that did," said Sarah Jane as they left the assayer's office. "He'll cheat the next innocent who walks inside."

"Very likely," Wesley said. "He needs to be replaced. I'll have it looked into." He turned to Mary Elizabeth.

"What are your plans now?"

"I'll buy a stagecoach ticket to Texas. I'm going there to find my brother."

"It's not wise to travel alone," Wesley said. "It could be very dangerous."

"I have no choice," she said quietly. "I have to find my brother. He's all the family I have left."

Wesley checked the gold pocket watch he carried in his coat pocket. "The last stage has already gone. The next one doesn't leave until dawn. You'll have to have a place to spend the night."

The sun was sinking low on the horizon, and it was hard to believe that so few hours had passed.

"I've already checked in at the hotel," Mary Elizabeth said. She put out her hand, and he took it in his. "Thank you for your help."

"Don't mention it," he said, then he turned to Sarah Jane. "Could I walk you home?"

A smile lit her face as she accepted eagerly.

Mary Elizabeth's gaze dwelt on the couple. They were obviously content in each other's love, and Wesley seemed like a nice man. She hoped so, because if anyone deserved to find happiness, it was most certainly Sarah Jane.

Thoughts of Chama intruded, and she pushed them away, refusing to think about her feelings for the warrior. With Dawg beside her, she returned to the hotel and went up to her lonely room.

She was nearly asleep when the knock sounded at her door. Wondering who it was, she threw back the covers and hurried to the door, opened it a crack and peered out into the hallway. A man, dirty and disheveled, stood there with a bottle in his hand.

"There you are!" His words were slurred, and she realized he was drunk. His small close-set eyes were knowing as he leered at her. "Come on, honey. Open the door. I need some company."

"Go away!" she hissed, attempting to push the door shut.

But he had stuck the toe of his boot into the crack, effectively stopping her. He leaned forward, pushing the door wider. "Don't be thet way," he muttered. "You been layin' with them bucks so long, you don't know what a white man's like. I'm aimin' to show you." He kicked the door, and it crashed into the wall.

Dawg was up in a flash, growling furiously, jaws wide open as it went for the man's leg.

"What'n hell!" the man shouted, turning tail and partly running, partly staggering down the hallway, intent on getting away as fast as possible.

When Dawg would have given chase, Mary Elizabeth called it back. Then, with tears raining down her face, she shut the door, locked it, and threw herself across the bed.

She felt so alone and frightened.

Chama! she silently cried. *Help me!*

But Chama couldn't help her. She had left him in the forest. Guilt stabbed through her. How desperately she needed him. And it was her own fault she was alone. She had walked away from him—walked away without once looking back—determined to put him from her life.

And for what? she asked herself. Her brother was gone! Her people despised her, considered her soiled, used.

Chama.

Pushing the damp hair back from her face, she sat up, determined to be strong . . . courageous. But she didn't feel that way. She felt weak, frightened and alone.

Chama.

He said he would wait in the forest until you returned, a silent voice whispered.

Wiping at the tears with the back of her hand, she lay back down on the bed. She couldn't go back. And anyway, he would have given her up a long time ago and returned to the mountains.

Chama.

God! What could she do?

"I'll go to Texas and find Brother Jeb," she muttered.

Chama.

She tried hard to conjure up her brother's image, but instead, she saw the black hair of the warrior she had left in the forest. She saw now the dark pain in his ebony eyes as he'd held her when she'd cried for her family . . . a pain that she'd refused to allow herself to recognize.

Why should he feel pain on her account? Was it possible that he really cared for her?

Somehow, the thought gave her comfort.

When she finally fell asleep, she dreamed of the man with hair dark as a raven's wing.

Chapter Twenty-three

"Chama!"

The cry woke Mary Elizabeth, jerking her from a dream in which she was trying to follow the warrior through a dense green forest. But she couldn't catch him, because hands with eagle talons instead of fingers were reaching out for her, ripping, tearing at her clothing and flesh.

She shuddered and rapidly blinked sleep-fogged eyes, trying to clear her mind of the nightmare that still surrounded her.

An anxious whine caused her head to jerk around.

Dawg!

The animal's front paws rested on the bed, its neck was stretched out to its fullest and its anxious eyes fixed firmly on her face.

Mary Elizabeth forced herself to take deep, calming breaths. "Everything's all right, Dawg," she soothed.

But it wasn't.

She could still feel the hands tearing at her, ripping away her clothing and rending her flesh. A sound in the corner of the shadowy room caused icy chills to creep down her spine.

Pushing herself to her elbows, her gaze narrowed on the corner, indistinct in the gray light before dawn. Something small and gray darted from the shadows; claws scraped against the wooden floor as it crossed the room and scuttled beneath the empty wardrobe.

A mouse!

She stifled a hysterical laugh, knowing the sound of the mouse had been magnified because of her dream. Her gaze returned to the German shepherd. "Why didn't you chase the mouse?" she asked it. "Not important enough? We'll let it pass this time. But it's a good thing I'm awake. We've got to buy a ticket on the stage."

The sound of her own voice gave her comfort, so she kept up a one-sided conversation with the dog as she slid her legs to the floor and dug through the carpetbag for fresh clothing.

"Do you like this blue gingham dress?" she asked, holding the garment up against her. "It's a mite wrinkled, and I don't think it's the thing for traveling, do you?"

She searched in the bag again and pulled out a brown flannel dress with gold braid, shook it out, and held it up against her. "I think this is a walking dress, Dawg. And it's not nearly as wrinkled. Do you think the stagecoach driver would let me ride his coach in a walking dress?"

The animal gave a long sigh, as though to say it didn't find its mistress's jokes the least bit funny. Dropping to all fours, it went to the window, ducked its head under the curtains, put its paws on the windowsill and stared down into the street.

"The stage's not coming yet, is it?" She crossed the

room and pulled the curtain aside. "There's not a soul stirring, Dawg. We've got plenty of time. Come away from there."

The German shepherd left the window and padded after her. When she poured water into the washbasin, the animal plopped to the floor on its belly, laid its head on its front paws and watched her.

After washing up, she began to dress. "I don't know who said women had to wear all this stuff," she grumbled, stepping into the pantaloons and chemise. "Did you ever see anything like this?" she asked the dog, holding up an elaborately trimmed, pink whalebone corset with lacings at the back.

"How did Sarah Jane expect me to fasten this thing alone?" *Alone.* Mary Elizabeth had never imagined her return to civilization would be like this. She'd always thought Jeb would be there for her. "What am I going to do, Dawg?" she whispered shakily, her eyes filling with tears.

The dog woofed, its eyes never wavering from its mistress's face.

"Chama said he'd wait for me in the mountains," she told the animal. "Do you think he's still there?"

Dawg raised its head and howled, a long, drawn-out, mournful sound. "What's wrong with you?" she asked, her eyes suspiciously bright.

Shoving the corset back into the carpetbag, she slipped the money inside her chemise, donned the dress and picked up the stiff, uncomfortable shoes that Sarah Jane had provided.

"It wouldn't do to wear my moccasins," she muttered, pushing her feet into the shoes. "They'd just remind folks where I've been these past years. But I'd stake my life Jeb's got a farm. When I'm there, I'll wear whatever I please."

After brushing her hair and tying it back with a ribbon, Mary Elizabeth packed the carpetbag. She would leave it there until she bought her ticket and had some breakfast.

It was only moments later when she left the hotel and made her way down the street.

The German shepherd seemed eager to be outside and frisked along behind her, but when she opened the door to the stagecoach office, the dog stopped and sat back on its haunches, its head turned toward the distant mountains.

"Come on, Dawg!" she said sharply.

The animal paid her no attention.

"Dawg!"

"It appears he ain't wantin' to come in," said a masculine voice behind her.

Mary Elizabeth spun around to face the clerk behind the counter. Expecting to meet with hostility, she felt surprised to see the man smile at her.

"I don't know why he's being so stubborn," she said, but even as she denied knowledge of Dawg's reasons, she realized he was missing Chama.

"Would you like me to try to coax him inside?" the clerk asked.

"No. I guess he'll be all right out here. I need to buy a ticket to—" Suddenly she broke off. "What about my dog? Does he need a ticket too?"

The clerk laughed. "We don't allow dogs on the coach."

When she looked stricken, he added, "I'm sorry, miss. But it's company policy. The passengers wouldn't like havin' to ride with animals."

"But how will I get him to Texas?"

He looked sympathetic. "I wish I could sell you a ticket for him, miss. But it would be worth my job."

Mary Elizabeth's lips tightened grimly. She couldn't abandon the dog. She should have left him with Chama.

Chama.

Her gaze turned toward the mountains.

"Do you know somebody you could leave him with?" the clerk asked.

"No. There's nobody," Mary Elizabeth said, turning back to face the man.

"I'm sorry, miss," he said again. "That does present a problem. Do you want a ticket for yourself?"

"I don't know."

"I hate to rush you, but the stage will be here shortly."

"Will it stay long?"

"About an hour. Just long enough to change horses and drivers. But if you need more time, there's another one out late this afternoon."

Mary Elizabeth gave a long sigh. An hour wasn't very long to find a solution to her problem. Sarah Jane would probably keep Dawg for her, but Mary Elizabeth had imposed on her enough already. And the animal wouldn't be happy left with a stranger.

"Thank you for your kindness," Mary Elizabeth told the clerk.

"Not at all, miss," he muttered, looking discomposed.

Realizing he was aware of her identity, she thanked him again, told him she'd be back later, then stepped outside and closed the door behind her.

Her gaze dwelt on the German shepherd for a long

moment. What was she to do about the animal? She couldn't bring herself to leave the dog, and yet, she couldn't take it with her.

"I should have left you with Chama," she murmured.

"Woof!" barked Dawg. It raced forward a few steps, then turned back, its gaze fixed on her face. She realized the dog wanted her to follow.

Curious as to what the dog wanted from her, she followed it to the end of town before realizing he was headed for the mountains.

And Chama.

But Chama wouldn't be there. He would have decided she'd found her brother and left.

Will you promise to return and tell me?

A frown marred her forehead. Had she promised to return if she found her brother or if she didn't find him? For some reason she couldn't remember.

"Is Chama still there?" she asked hesitantly.

"Woof!" Dawg barked. "Woof! Woof!"

Suddenly it seemed imperative that she find out if Chama was still waiting. It seemed absolutely necessary for her to know. And if he was still there, she could leave the dog with him.

Leaving you to go on alone, a silent voice whispered.

"Eeeyaaah!" The sound sent chills running down Mary Elizabeth's spine and she jerked her head up.

"Hah! Hah!" The creaking of the stagecoach wheels and hooves beating against the hard-baked earth identified the sound. "Hah! Hah!" the driver yelled again, cracking his whip over the horses as the stagecoach lurched into town, amid a cloud of dust and spurting gravel.

Mary Elizabeth stepped back against a building, giving the grizzled driver all the room he needed. He pulled back on the reins, slowing the six-horse team as he passed her and made for the stagecoach office.

When the Concord Coach lurched to a stop, the door opened and a man stepped down, turned and held his hand out to a woman passenger.

"Careful with those bags!" he ordered brusquely as the driver prepared to toss them down.

The woman beside him fussed with her bonnet and straightened her skirt, grumbling about the carelessness of the driver all the while.

Mary Elizabeth saw the grin on his face, just before he tossed the smallest bag at her feet.

"Land sakes!" she shouted, jumping back. "Watch what you're doing!"

"Yes, ma'am," he muttered, tipping his hat to her. "Sorry about that."

A moment later he turned the coach around and headed back toward Mary Elizabeth. It was only when he pulled the coach up a few feet away that she realized she was standing in front of the livery stable.

"Howdy, miss," the driver said, stepping down from the coach and tipping his hat to her. "Red!" he called. "Get out here!"

A redheaded man stepped from the livery and approached them. "You don't have to yell, Burl. I heard you drive into town."

"You wasn't fixin' to stir yourself neither," Burl said. "You better get them horses changed fast. Walter's takin' 'em from here, an' he's bent on always leavin' on time."

"I'll have 'em ready," Red said. "But I got more to do than unhitch horses." He looked at Mary Elizabeth.

"Was you needin' somethin', miss?"

"I did—" She broke off. She'd been about to say she didn't need anything but had suddenly changed her mind. "Do you rent horses?" she asked.

"Yep," he said. "I rent 'em for however long you need. Or I'll make you a fair deal was you wantin' to buy."

"I plan on leaving on the afternoon stage," she said. "But I'd like to rent a horse for the day."

He nodded. "Consider it done."

"I'll be back in a little while," she said. "I need to get some breakfast and make arrangements about my things."

"Anytime will be fine," he said. "I'm open until sundown."

How long would it take to find Chama? she wondered. Hopefully, it wouldn't take long. She didn't want to spend another night at the hotel. Especially alone.

And she would be alone, she realized—Alone until she found Brother Jeb.

The thought left her feeling curiously bereft.

Chapter Twenty-four

Entering the hotel, she approached the clerk, Hector. "I won't be able to leave on the morning stage, so I'd like to make arrangements to leave my belongings here for the day."

"That would be impossible, señorita. To leave your luggage you must pay for another day." His gaze narrowed spitefully. "I am certain you could find many uses for the room while you wait, but we have our reputation to think of. And men are not allowed into the single ladies' rooms."

Mary Elizabeth's eyes glittered, and her hands tightened into fists. She knew what the hateful clerk was inferring and would have given anything to be a man for just one moment, long enough to demand satisfaction for the insult. Instead, she lifted her chin and marched up the stairs.

Only moments later she entered the lobby again with the carpetbag in her hand. With her shoulders squared and her eyes fixed firmly ahead, she left the hotel with her belongings.

She passed a restaurant and went inside to have

breakfast, leaving the German shepherd outside to wait. When she'd finished her meal, she ordered bacon and biscuits for Dawg, then waited in the shade of a building while the animal ate. When she reached the stables, the livery man was waiting for her.

"What about the gray stallion?" she asked, after he'd shown her several horses.

"Not for rent. That one's for sale."

She eyed the stallion. It had the look of Chama's big gray, the one he'd been riding when they left Bent's Fort. Because of her, the warrior now traveled on foot. An idea began to form in her mind. The animal had strength, could most likely carry Chama any where he wanted to go.

Even to Texas.

The thought continued to buzz around in her head as she looked over the rental horses.

Chama would make a perfect guide to Texas. And she wouldn't have to leave Dawg, or make the journey alone.

"How much do you want for the gray stallion?" she asked.

"He's mighty expensive, ma'am," the livery man said. "He's bred for strength and endurance. I'd have to get a mighty high dollar for him."

"How much?"

"Four hundred dollars."

"Mighty steep, don't you think?" came a gruff voice from the door.

Mary Elizabeth jerked around to see Burl standing behind her, a toothpick stuck in his mouth. "Run into Saul Jacobs at the way station," he said conversationally, stepping around Mary Elizabeth to join Red.

262

"Had his wife with him."

Mary Elizabeth gave an inward start. *Saul had found Ruth. Thank God!*

"She all right?" Red asked sharply.

"No lastin' harm was done," Burl said. "She'll mend in time." He ran a hand down the gray stallion's neck. "Mighty fine animal," he commented.

Mary Elizabeth's fingernails dug into her palms. She had business to transact, but the two men seemed to have forgotten her presence. It was only when Burl spoke that she realized she was mistaken.

"You know who this little lady is?" Burl asked, jerking his head toward Mary Elizabeth.

Her lips thinned, and a flush swept over her cheeks. It hadn't taken the driver long to discover her identity.

Red's eyes slid past the stagecoach driver and stopped on her. "No," he said gruffly. "Never seen her before."

"Her name's Mary Elizabeth Abernathy. She's Jebediah Abernathy's sister."

"The one the Apach —" The words were suddenly bitten off.

"The same one," Burl said, keeping his voice low and even. "Saul figgered she'd be in town. Said she helped Ruth escape from the Apaches. He kinda guessed how the good folks in town'd be treatin' her an' ast me to look out for her. See she got a fair shake. Now the way I see it, thet horse ain't worth what you're askin'. Not for the lady thet helped Ruth Jacobs when she was aneedin' it. Not for Jebediah's sister. Don't you agree?"

Red seemed to consider Burl's words. "Guess I could let that stallion go for a hunderd dollars, miss. If you've a mind to buy him."

Mary Elizabeth's eyes were suspiciously bright as she

gratefully accepted the man's offer. She hadn't expected to find kindness here. "I still want to rent a horse," she said. "Just for the morning."

"Pick any one of 'em you want, Miss Abernathy," Red said. "I'm glad to help in any way I can. You got a good horse in that stallion there. He could take you clear across Texas and back again without workin' up a sweat."

She wondered at his choice of words, then realized he must know Brother Jeb had gone to Texas. "What about the black gelding?" she asked.

Clear across Texas and back again! Across Texas! Across Texas! Red's words echoed in her mind over and over again.

Chama knew Texas and would be a perfect guide.

"Would you sell the black gelding?" she asked.

"Yes'um," Red said. "Paid fifty dollars for him. You can have him for that."

"Thank you, Mr., uh, Red," she said, lifting her chin proudly. "But you've already lost your profit on the stallion. I couldn't ask you to do the same on the gelding."

"That's all right, ma'am," Red said. "Me and Burl will split the difference."

"What'n hell does that mean?" inquired Burl.

"Means you'll give me half my profit loss on the gelding."

"Hey . . . I ain't gonna—" He broke off, his gray eyes on Mary Elizabeth's flushed face. "Considerin' the way the rest of the town's been actin', I'd be more'n happy to do it. An' let me say, ma'am, that I hope you find your brother."

She swallowed hard, unable to express her feelings. "Thank you," she said huskily. "I didn't expect—thank

264

you." The men shifted uncomfortably, seeming to be embarrassed by her gratitude.

"Could I leave the horses here while I buy some supplies?" she asked.

"Yes, ma'am," Red said. "Be happy to oblige. I got a couple of saddles that're kinda wore out. You can have em if you're of a mind."

"I'm of a mind," she said. "And again, I thank you."

"Ma'am . . ." Burl scratched his grizzly head. "You ain't thinkin' on ridin' them horses to Texas, are you?"

"Yes," she said.

" 'Scuse me, ma'am," Red said quickly. "But that wouldn't be too safe. Better plan on takin' the stage. A woman alone would be fair game for anybody that passed by."

"I won't be alone," she said. "I'll have a guide, and he'll protect me."

If you can find him! a silent voice warned.

"Ma'am, you ain't talkin' about goin' back to the Apaches, are you?"

Her gaze fell on Dawg, waiting patiently near the wide door. Would Chama still be waiting? If he had left, she might not be able to find him.

Realizing the men were waiting for her answer, she said, "Not the Apaches. Only one man, one warrior. He'll guide me to Texas. If I can find him."

"Are you sure?" Burl asked. "Them Apaches are mean devils."

"I know that," she said. "But you can't lump them all in one basket. It seems that all races have a streak of cruelty in them. Some people subdue it, others don't."

"Reckon you'd know best about that Injun, ma'am," Red said. "I just hope you're right about him."

"He brought me home."

"Them Apaches know the desert," Burl said. "An' I guess they ain't no better guide to be found." He squeezed her shoulder gently. "Ma'am? You're aimin' to go into Comanche Territory. An' that could be mighty dangerous for a woman. You take my advice, Miss Abernathy, and get you some breeches and a hat. You'd be safer wearing boys' clothes."

After thanking the two men again, she left them and made her way to the general store. With her hand on the door, she turned to the animal beside her. "Dawg, stay here." The dog dropped down on its belly and watched her enter the store, empty except for a plump middle-aged woman standing behind the counter. She gave Mary Elizabeth a tight smile.

"New around here?" she asked.

Mary Elizabeth nodded, wondering where Lije Carpenter was. The woman, possibly his wife, was obviously curious about her, but Mary Elizabeth had no intention of satisfying that curiosity. She wouldn't be surprised to learn the woman had already heard about the girl who had lived with the Indians for four years. Mary Elizabeth had already felt the effects of Gladys's loose tongue.

Feeling the need to hurry, Mary Elizabeth turned her attention to the merchandise on display.

In addition to a large selection of canned goods, barrels of dried beans and sacks of flour and potatoes dominated most of the floor space. On one side of the store, shelves held bolts of material, while the other side offered a variety of weapons: flintlock muskets and pistols, muzzleloaders, and bowie knives.

After selecting the foodstuffs she would need for the

rip, Mary Elizabeth's gaze narrowed on the weapons. She would need some means of protection, but the flintlocks looked big and heavy, as did the muzzle-loaders.

"You lookin' for a rifle?" the woman asked.

"Yes."

"If you're aimin' to use it yourself, them's all too big." The woman reached beneath the counter and drew out a pistol. "This'd be more your size, but it ain't for sale."

"Why not?" Mary Elizabeth asked, picking up the pistol and hefting it in her hand. She'd never seen one quite like it.

"Just bought it a few minutes ago," the woman said. "Salesman rode in on the stage. Had it with him. My man ain't even seen it yet. It's a new kind of pistol. Called a Colt Navy Revolver. Salesman said it was .36 caliber. He seemed right taken with it." She frowned down at the weapon. "Don't know much about guns myself, but the salesman insisted there'd be a big demand for them. I kinda like the pearl handle myself. It makes the pistol look purty."

"Do you know how it works?"

"No. But it's all writ down on a piece of paper." The woman fumbled beneath the counter, then handed a sheet of paper across to Mary Elizabeth. "There it is. Don't know what it says. Never did learn to read. But my man does. He's right good at it too."

The woman continued to extoll her husband's reading abilities while Mary Elizabeth read the instructions, silently giving thanks to her mother for insisting that all her children learn to read.

According to the instructions, the cylinder was loaded from the front with paper cartridges. The compression of the charge in the chambers was effected by a loading lever under the barrel; then copper caps were placed on primer points on the front of the cylinder. Cocking the hammer with the thumb turned the cylinder sixty degrees, bringing chamber after chamber into the axis of the barrel. When the trigger was pulled, the hammer was released and set off the cap by percussion. Colt claimed it to be a real breakthrough in weapons.

"How much do you want for it?" Mary Elizabeth asked.

"Like I done said, my man ain't even seen it yet. Wisht I knew if he'd want to keep it."

The woman looked uncomfortable, and Mary Elizabeth guessed she was wondering if she'd made a mistake in buying the pistol. "The handle is pretty," Mary Elizabeth said. "Do you think he'll like the looks of it?"

"Lije don't care much about looks," the woman said, biting her bottom lip and looking at the pearl handle.

Mary Elizabeth placed the pistol on the counter between them. "Pearl handles don't really matter," she murmured, letting her eyes wander over the assortment of weapons on the wall, and frowned. "I think you're right about the other pistols being too heavy for me," she said. "If you don't want to sell the smaller one, then I'll pass on a weapon."

"Well . . . I guess if you really wanted it, I could sell it for a hundred dollars."

The pistol's not worth that, Mary Elizabeth silently told herself. *She know's it, but she's trying to put one over on me.* Shaking her head, she spoke. "Don't have much more than a hundred. And the supplies have to be paid for."

The woman looked at the goods on the counter. "This all you're goin' to need?" she asked.

"No. I'll need some ammunition, breeches, a shirt, hat, socks and a pair of boots."

"Then, I guess you could have them all and the pistol for a hundred dollars."

"Then, we have a deal," Mary Elizabeth said. "Do you have a place where I can change clothes?"

A few minutes later she left the store clothed in men's garments, and she had purchased enough supplies to last her for a month. Dawg followed along behind as she picked up the horses, then returned for her purchases.

After fastening the supplies on the gray stallion, she turned her face toward the distant mountains and rode out of town, with Dawg trotting eagerly along behind.

Chapter Twenty-five

The morning sun burst over the horizon, touching the top of the pine trees with a bright burst of color. Its rays penetrated the purple shadows hovering beneath the branches of a giant willow tree that grew beside a creek, rousing the warrior from his restless sleep on his bed of fern.

Chama rose dispiritedly to his feet and went to the stream, feeling weary beyond belief. Bending over, he splashed water on his face, then carried a handful to his mouth. Although the water was cool and quenched his thirst, his troubled mind could not be so easily soothed.

When Fire Woman had not returned before dark, Chama felt certain she'd found her brother. Even so, he could not bring himself to leave, not with her promise to return still ringing in his ears.

Why has she not returned?

He felt certain if Fire Woman had found trouble in Taos, Dawg would have come for him. Since the German shepherd had not done so, Chama could only believe her absence was deliberate.

You are a fool for staying! an inner voice chided. *Anger*

smolders within Fire Woman's breast and could erupt any time.
She could, even now, be planning her revenge. Her brother and
other palefaces may come for you. You must go! Leave this place
while you are still able.

"No!" he argued. "I told her I would wait. I will
honor my promise to her."

As she honors her promise to return?

Chama willed his mind to be silent, but his thoughts
remained in turmoil. Suppose she needed him.

Dawg would come.

Something was wrong.

You want something to be wrong.

He was tempted to go into the white man's town and
search for her, reassure himself that all was well with
her.

Such a thing would be foolish. It would accomplish nothing
but your death. And she would not welcome your presence. It
would only serve to remind her of her years as a prisoner.

His ebony eyes darkened with sadness. Why couldn't
he have made her love him? Although he tried, she had
resisted and continued to mourn her paleface family.

Sighing heavily, he rose to his feet, turning his face
toward the desert . . . and the town of Taos. Although
wild flowers grew in abundance around him, he had no
eye for their beauty. Nor did he care about the buck,
standing quiet and still, watching him from the verdant
green bushes only a short distance away. Instead, his
thoughts were turned inward as he silently cursed himself.

Why didn't I tell her how much I cared? Why didn't I swal-
low my foolish pride and beg her to stay with me?

His anger erupted, and he lashed out with his foot,
kicking the heads off several daisies that were in his

271

path.

Suddenly he remembered the daisy she'd plucked from inside the iron kettle, remembered how she'd clutched it to her breast and rocked in agony. Bending over, he picked up one of the daisies he'd so carelessly used and held it in the palm of his hand.

The stem was broken, the petals crushed; soon it would wither and die. And the fault was his.

Chama lifted the daisy to his lips and brushed the petals softly against them. His stomach knotted with a pain that spread, growing, until it became a fiery gnawing in his gut. *You are a fool!* an inner voice chided. *Put the past behind you. Fire Woman is gone. You must accept it and go on from there.*

How can I? his heart cried.

The ache in his gut continued to grow, becoming almost unendurable. But endure it he must. Fire Woman was with her brother now, and among her own people . . . as she'd always wanted.

He would never see her again.

Uttering a sigh, he opened a rawhide pouch that hung from a thong at his waist, carefully placed the crushed daisy inside and closed it again.

One last time Chama narrowed his gaze on the distant town of Taos, but there was no sign of the woman he sought.

His voice husky with pain, he whispered, "My heart will never forget you, Fire Woman . . . my love."

Feeling more alone than he'd ever felt before, even as a boy when he'd watched his tribe walk away from the sickness he carried inside his body, he turned his face to the mountains and strode toward the verdant green forest in the foothills of the Sangre de Cristos.

* * *

Even though Mary Elizabeth had told herself Chama might already have gone, she hadn't really expected it. The knot that had been forming in her belly worked its way up into her throat as a flash of wild grief ripped through her. He must be here! He must! Surely he couldn't just walk out of her life so easily. Surely she meant more to him than that!

Her eyes were glassy as she tried to hold back the tears that threatened. "Chama!" she called. "Chama, where are you?"

Only silence greeted her question. A heaviness centered in her chest, then became an ache that she refused to put a name to. She felt hurt and disillusioned beyond belief. Chama had promised to wait for her! Dammit! He'd promised to wait!

For how long? an inner voice chided.

Mary Elizabeth wiped away the tears that managed to slip past her defenses, and a curious bitterness spread through her. How could he put her out of his mind so easily? He could have waited.

For how long? the inner voice asked again.

But she refused to listen to the voice of her conscience. Instead, her blue eyes darkened and became stormy as anger mingled with her pain. Her gaze fell on Dawg, lapping up water from the stream.

"Dawg! Go find Chama!" she commanded.

The animal's head jerked up, and it stared at her for a moment.

"Find Chama!" she said again. "Take me to Chama!"

The German shepherd barked as though to say it understood. Lowering its nose, it began to sniff the surrounding ground. Only moments later the dog picked up the trail, barking as it raced toward the mountains. She urged the gelding forward, intent on keeping the dog in sight. But she needn't have bothered. They had only gone a short distance when Chama stepped out of the dense forest.

Dawg barked crazily, cavorting happily around the warrior.

Mary Elizabeth's gaze locked with Chama's, and she fought the overwhelming need to fling herself from the horse, to run to him and wrap her arms around his neck. She was so glad to see him! She waited with breathless expectation for him to speak, feeling as though she would melt beneath his turbulent gaze.

Why didn't he speak? Why?

The prolonged anticipation was almost more than she could bear.

Suddenly, he moved toward her, and her heart gave a leap, then fluttered wildly, beating inside her breast like a bird trapped in a cage. A quivering sensation raced down to her feet, and her nostrils were filled with his manly smell.

It seemed anti-climatic when he reached her, kneeling beside Dawg and stroking the German shepherd's head. When he straightened and faced her again, his face was expressionless.

"You bring only two horses," he said gruffly. "Not the hundred I paid for you."

Sucking in a sharp breath, Mary Elizabeth stared at him. Whatever she'd expected from him, it certainly wasn't a reminder of the bride-price he'd paid for her.

Anger glittered in her eyes as she slid from her mount. "You'll get your horses," she snapped. But you'll have to wait until I find my brother."

He showed no reaction to her words as he turned to examine the horses. "The animals are strong," he commented. "They will carry us over great distances."

Out of the corner of his eye, Chama saw Mary Elizabeth's lips tighten. "Don't you want to know about my brother?" she asked.

"Only if you wish to tell me." He gave no indication that the need to know her brother's fate was almost overwhelming. Nor did he show any sign of the agony he'd felt during the hours she'd been absent, knowing his future happiness depended on that same brother's fate.

She looked at the ground, nudging at a rock with the toe of her boot. "He left town three seasons past."

Chama remained silent, studying her bent head.

"I thought — thought perhaps you'd go with me to find him."

His pulse picked up speed, and his heart lightened. To conceal his feelings, he bent over and plucked a twig from Dawg's neck fur. "I have nothing better to do," he said. "Will the journey take long?"

He raised his head in time to see her nod. "I'm afraid so," she sighed. "My brother has gone to Texas."

Texas! He bent over and patted Dawg's head to hide the elation he knew must be glittering in his eyes. *Texas!* It would take days to journey to the Texas border.

"Do you know where the hill country of Texas is?" she asked.

"Your brother is there?"

"Yes."

"I know the hill country," he said. "It was there we found She-Who-Heals, the woman you call Johanna.

275

But the journey will be a long one. It would take . . . perhaps two full moons to reach the hill country of Texas." His eyes met hers. "Perhaps your brother will not have stayed there."

She looked away from him. "That is a possibility," she admitted. "No one has heard from him since he left."

"Would you not rather return to the cabin in the mountains?" he asked gently. "Everything we need to make a good life is there . . . just waiting for us."

"I can't," she murmured. "I must go on to Texas. I must find my brother Jeb."

"Then, we will go," he said. "But first, we must eat. I am suddenly very hungry."

When she pointed out the pack containing the food, he opened it, and they sat down on the grass and ate together. After they had finished their meal and fed the dog, he handed her the waterskin, waited until she'd quenched her thirst, lifted it to his own mouth, then fastened it to the back of the saddle.

"Come, Fire Woman," he said. "It is time we left this place. It is much too near the paleface town for my liking."

He watched her mount the black gelding, then leapt on the back of the gray stallion and settled himself in the saddle. "You have done well in selecting a mount for me, Fire Woman. The stallion will have endurance and will enable me to outrun my enemies."

"I thought you'd like him."

Chama felt at peace with the world as he urged the stallion forward. He had his woman again, if only for a while. He had a strong horse and plenty of food for his belly. And he had Dawg to guard them.

The Great Spirit had looked down on him with favor.

They rode in a half circle, always keeping close to the mountains, hidden from prying eyes by the forest. Darkness found them on the east side of the mountain. Tomorrow they would ride through open country, easily seen by those who cared to look. While they traveled that way, he would have to be cautious, always alert. But tonight he could relax . . . and he could enjoy his woman.

With these thoughts in mind, he made camp and hobbled the horses while his woman prepared the evening meal. They were seated beside the fire when she told him she had a gift for him.

"A gift?"

"Yes," she said, her eyes glittering with excitement. "I think you'll like it."

When she brought the pistol to him and explained the way it worked, he examined it closely. With such a weapon, he could kill many of the white-eyes. The thought brought his gaze up quickly to meet hers, and he felt ashamed. She had given him a gift, and his first thought had been to use it against her people.

"Thank you, Fire Woman," he said humbly. "It is a very good weapon. I will use it wisely."

She nodded her head, and her fiery hair danced around her shoulders. "And only against those who would harm us," she said.

"Agreed."

"Load it," she said. "I want to see you shoot it."

"What would you have me shoot?" he asked. "Perhaps you would have me kill the dog?"

"Don't you dare!" she gasped. When she saw the twinkle in his eyes, she laughed. "You could try it out on your gray stallion."

"So I can lope behind you like a dog all the way to Texas? No, thank you. I think we shall test it on a pine cone."

"That might be best," she said. "How about that one?" She pointed toward a spot a short distance away.

The pistol was loaded and duly fired, and both of them were amazed to see the pine cone fall, then another and another. When the weapon was empty, they stood stunned. Neither had really believed it would work.

Leaning over, he placed a light kiss on her lips. "It is truly a wondrous gift," he said. "Now I must give you something in return."

"No," she said. "You don't have to do that."

"But I must," he said, opening the pouch at his waist. He took something from it, something that glittered with blue and pink speckles and dropped it in her hand.

"Chama," she murmured, fingering the turquoise bracelet. "It's beautiful. Where did you get it?"

"I bought it from a merchant," he said.

"But when . . ." She looked at him with puzzled eyes. "Did you get it from William Bent?"

"No. It came from a merchant in the land of the dark-skinned people."

"But . . . Chama. We haven't been near Mexico for three years."

"I know."

"Then, you bought it for someone else?"

"No. I bought it for you."

"But why?"

"Because the color of the stones reminded me of your eyes." His voice was thick and unsteady.

Mary Elizabeth saw the heartrending tenderness of

278

his gaze and swallowed hard, feeling touched beyond belief. She tried to speak, but seemed to have lost her voice. A slender delicate thread began to form between them, and she felt a curious stirring inside her.

"Chama," she whispered achingly, leaning closer to him.

Reaching out, he gathered her into his arms and dipped his head toward hers, his lips hovering only inches above her own. The very air around them seemed vibrant with electricity. Mary Elizabeth was caught up in his nearness, aching for the fulfillment of his lovemaking.

Her hands seemed to move of their own accord, sliding around his neck to bring his head down to hers. With a husky groan of passion, his mouth closed over hers in a kiss of intense longing. He pressed eager kisses on her neck, her shoulders, her breasts, then moved back to greedily devour her mouth again before he hurriedly removed her clothing.

A devastating hunger overpowered her, and she slid her hands down the tensed muscles of his back, feeling him shudder against her. Excitement raced through her as Chama's tongue entered the secret places of her mouth, and a moan of pleasured torment escaped her lips. A flame lit deep inside her body, leaping and dancing, swirling higher and brighter until his lovemaking became wild and savage.

Quickly he shed his own clothes, and when he entered her, animal sounds of pleasure broke from her throat, and her body bucked beneath him. He was driving her wild with desire, prolonging his loving until the waiting became almost unendurable. Finally, he began to thrust deep inside her body. She moaned with pleasure, withholding nothing from him. Her body raised up to meet his while she reveled in the savagery until they were climbing together, striving to reach a distant peak that was growing ever nearer. Finally, with a long gasp of pleasure, they hovered together . . . balanced on the edge of eternity. Then they were falling . . . plunging over the edge until they lay spent and exhausted in each other's arms.

It was early when Mary Elizabeth woke. She lay quietly, listening to Chama's soft breathing beside her, remembering the wildness of their coming together the night before.

She realized she shouldn't have allowed it to happen. But she had felt so alone among her own people, alone and despised. Perhaps that was the reason she had responded so wildly to his embrace. Chama must care about her. The bracelet was proof of that. And, unlike her own people, he was kind to her.

His voice, when it came startled her. "You are restless?"

She looked up to see him watching her. "Yes."

"Tell me why?"

"The people in the town weren't happy to see me," she said. "I hadn't expected that."

"Were they not glad you still lived?"

"They didn't care. I think they'd have felt better if I had died like Melissa."

He tilted her chin up with his fingers. "Forget about them, Fire Woman. Come with me to the mountains." His voice was soft, persuasive. "We could be happy there. We could make a good life together."

She jerked her chin away. "I've already told you I can't," she said. "I know my brother is alive. And he'll want me back. It's said that blood is thicker than water. No matter what's gone before. We're kin . . . of the same blood. He'll be different than the others. And he'll want me with him."

"Does it not matter that I want you?"

Mary Elizabeth realized that he must never know just how much it mattered. She must be careful to keep her emotions under control. If Chama ever knew how much she cared for him, he could never let her go. And she must. A love like theirs would never be allowed to blossom. The world would never let it. Both the white man and the Indians had their prejudices.

Her eyes misted, and she turned her head away from him, unwilling for him to see her tears. "If you cared about me, you would let me go," she said.

"How can I, Mary Elizabeth?"

She brought her head around at his use of her name. Her eyes met his, and the pain she saw there almost proved to be her undoing. How could she continue to deny him? How could she?

"Suppose we cannot find your brother. Will you return with me then?"

Avoiding his eyes, she pushed back the covers briskly. "We will find my brother," she said. "Now, come on. Get up. We have a long way to go."

"Must we hurry?"

"Yes," she said, reaching for her clothing. "Why are you being so lazy this morning?"

He reached for her hand, but she eluded him. "Get up," she insisted. She moved to the fire, raking through the ashes searching for live coals, aware of him dressing behind her.

The turquoise bracelet on her wrist caught her eyes. Chama had said he'd bought it three years ago. Had he known even then that he would want her for his own? The thought left her feeling curiously unsettled, even as she stacked wood on the coals and coaxed a flame from it. She wouldn't allow herself to consider the implications as she went about preparing breakfast, but the bracelet was a heavy band around her wrist, binding her to the man who had bought it.

Mary Elizabeth tried to push the bracelet to the back of her mind as they mounted and began the long journey to Texas, but the turquoise bracelet seemed magnetized, continually drawing her attention to the glittering stones, just as the warrior who rode ahead of her continually occupied her thoughts.

Chapter Twenty-six

The late morning sun hung hot and heavy in the eastern sky, and the wind blew dust into Mary Elizabeth's face. Even at this early hour, damp tendrils of hair curled around her face, and her tongue felt thick from thirst. They had been traveling through the staked plains for the last few days, a harsh land where the vegetation was sparse, the arid earth unable to supply enough moisture to grow more than stunted cedars, or the stubby, spindly cottonwood with its twisting, turning branches reaching for the barren sky.

Their passing alarmed a collared lizard basking on top of a layered rock of gypsum and sand. Raising up on its hind legs, the creature streaked across the ground, dragging its long tail behind it.

She remembered the last time she had journeyed through this desolate area, traveling by foot with Johanna and the other women on the long trek to Bent's Fort, where the Apaches would trade goods with William Bent. It was on that journey that she and Johanna managed to escape from the Apaches.

Mary Elizabeth's thoughts turned to Johanna and Hawkeye, her warrior husband. Hawkeye had come to

Bent's Fort searching for his wife. Had he found her? Were they even now together? Mary Elizabeth hoped it was so. Johanna had been kind and deserved to find happiness.

Realizing they were nearing the Palo Duro Canyon, Mary Elizabeth wondered what Chama would do if they happened across a hunting party from his tribe? Would he fight them to protect her? It was a question she couldn't answer.

A movement in the distance sent fear shivering down her spine, and she pulled the gelding up short.

Chama turned in the saddle and looked back at her. When he saw the expression on her face, he reined his mount up beside her. "There is no need to fear," he said. "Up ahead is a lone buffalo, somehow separated from the herd."

His voice soothed away her apprehension, and she silently called herself a coward. Even so, she remained tense and watchful until the sun had gone down and they were miles past the entrance to the canyon.

Chama seemed to understand her fears, and instead of making camp when the sun went down, they continued riding. Mary Elizabeth guessed it was near midnight when Chama finally stopped. She felt weary beyond belief, hardly able to stay in the saddle when they found a shallow gulley and made camp. She was stumbling toward the blankets he'd tossed down when she noticed that Dawg was limping.

"Chama!" she called. "Something's wrong with Dawg."

The warrior hurried toward them, knelt beside the dog and examined its feet.

"His feet are blistered," he said.

Mary Elizabeth bent over and rubbed behind the German shepherd's ear, crooning softly to him. "Poor Dawg. You didn't know we'd mistreat you so. You should have stayed in the mountains."

Dawg licked her hand and laid its head down on its sore paws. When they broke camp the next morning, Dawg rode in front of her.

When they first saw the dust cloud, they thought it was a herd of buffalo. By the time they knew differently, they had no hope of hiding, or outrunning the travelers, and they continued to ride forward, hoping for the best.

It was only when the bugle sounded that she realized the horsemen were cavalry.

The group stopped a short distance away from them, talking among themselves. There was a flurry of movement, then a horse and rider came forward. Mary Elizabeth was aware of the coiled tension in Chama's body, of his hand hovering beside the pistol stuck in his belt.

"No, Chama!" she said. "You can't fight all of them."

The clip-clop of the horse seemed to echo her heartbeat as the lone rider came closer.

"Hello," Mary Elizabeth called. "We didn't expect to see anyone out here."

At the sound of her voice, the trooper's gaze traveled the length of her, taking in the baggy breeches she wore, the damp shirt that did little to hide her curves.

Anger darkened Chama's eyes, but he remained silent.

"What're you doin' with the Apache?" the trooper asked.

"He's my guide."

Keeping his eyes on Chama, the trooper waved the other horsemen forward, and suddenly, amid thudding hoofbeats, choking dust and creaking saddles, they were surrounded by the United States Cavalry.

285

Mary Elizabeth's gaze roamed the troopers that surrounded them, searching for the commanding officer, stopping on the young lieutenant who was obviously fresh out of West Point. The officer was eyeing Chama with trepidation when Mary Elizabeth kneed the stallion toward him.

"State your business," the young lieutenant said.

She smiled at him and pushed her hat off her head. His eyes widened as her fiery curls cascaded around her shoulders. "I'm Mary Elizabeth Abernathy," she said. "Chama, my Apache friend, is guiding me to my brother's farm in the hill country."

"Well, I'll be damned," the lieutenant said, a flush creeping up his cheeks. Snatching his hat off his head, he held it in front of him, staring at her in surprise. "I had no idea you were a woman."

"Please put your hat back on." She laughed. "The sun is much too hot for those unused to it. As for my clothing, Lieutenant . . ." She paused, waiting expectantly.

"Tucker," he supplied. "Lieutenant Samuel Tucker. At your service, Miss Abernathy."

"I'm glad to meet you, Lieutenant Tucker. And I'm traveling in these clothes because it's safer than traveling as a woman."

"I'm afraid even such garments do little to disguise your beauty," he said gallantly. "Traveling by horse is much too rough for a woman. Why didn't you take the stagecoach?"

Her gaze found Chama's, willing him to remain silent. He had to trust her to handle the soldiers. In fact, it would probably be best if they didn't know he understood their words. "I trust Chama," she said quietly. "More than I trust strangers on a coach."

"Your brother must trust him as well," Lieutenant

Tucker said. "You said your brother lives in the hill country. I've just come from Llano. Perhaps I know him."

"His name is Jebediah Abernathy," she said eagerly. "And I hope you do know him. Somehow, I—I lost the letter with his address, and I'm not sure where he's living. Just that it's in the hill country."

"I'm sorry, ma'am," he said. "I never heard of him. But perhaps some of my men know him." Turning to his aide, he said, "Ask around and see if anyone knows Jeb Abernathy."

Moments later, a man wearing the stripes of a sergeant rode forward. His face was weather-burned and, at the moment, set in disapproving lines. She didn't know if it was her attire he disapproved of, or the warrior who was with her, but she suspected a little of both.

"You know Miss Abernathy's brother, Sergeant Johnson?" the lieutenant asked.

"Not personally, Lieutenant." The sergeant worked his chaw of tobacco around to his other jaw, all the while studying Mary Elizabeth a moment, before turning his shrewd gaze on the warrior beside her.

"Well, Sergeant Johnson?" the lieutenant prompted.

Sergeant Johnson spat a long brown stream of tobacco at the ground, then wiped his chin with the back of his sleeve. All the while his eyes never left Chama. "Don't it set you wonderin', Lieutenant, what an Apache's doin' in Comanche territory?"

"Miss Abernathy has already explained the Indian is guiding her to her brother's farm!" the lieutenant snapped. "Now answer the question, Sergeant. Do you know something about her brother or not?"

"Only hearsay, Lieutenant, only hearsay."

"And do you plan on letting us in on this . . . hearsay

. . . information, Sergeant Johnson?" The lieutenant's voice had become angry, hard.

"I got no objection," the sergeant said. "Folks in Llano say a man called Abernathy bought out Carter Smith. His farm was south of Llano, somewheres along the Colorado River."

"That must be Brother Jeb," Mary Elizabeth said eagerly. "Surely there couldn't be more than one Abernathy in the hill country."

"You didn't happen to hear the fellow's first name did you, Sergeant?" the lieutenant asked.

"Nope. Never did."

"I'm sorry we couldn't be more help, Miss Abernathy," the lieutenant said. "I suggest you go to ranger headquarters when you get to Llano. Perhaps they'll be able to help you find your brother. I wish I could see you to your destination, but I have orders to report to Fort Bliss. Some kind of trouble with the Indians."

"The Apache Indians!" the sergeant said.

"That will do, Sergeant," Lieutenant Tucker said. "You're dismissed."

"You ain't really gonna let that Apache go, are you, Lieutenant?"

"I said you're dismissed, Sergeant!" the lieutenant snapped. "Get back in formation!"

Jerking the reins of his mount, the sergeant rode back into the middle of the troopers. Mary Elizabeth controlled a grin. She couldn't see any kind of formation, or order, among the troopers.

"Thank you for your help," she told the lieutenant. "There's no need to trouble yourself about me. Chama has seen me safe this far. He'll stay with me until I find Jeb."

288

After bidding them good-bye, Lieutenant Tucker ordered his troopers forward, intent on making up for lost time.

Only after they were out of sight did Mary Elizabeth draw a sigh of relief. She felt they had been lucky. If the commanding officer had been an experienced man, they would not have gotten away so easily, with so few questions—especially since there was reported trouble with the Apaches, a tribe that Chama so obviously belonged to.

Looking at his bronzed skin and shoulder-length hair, she realized he wasn't safe. They were in a land settled by his enemies. He would be lucky to leave it alive.

Had she sealed his death warrant by asking him to guide her on her search? Perhaps she should send him back. But even as the thought came, she knew how impossible it was.

Chama would never leave her. He had known better than she the dangers he faced by coming with her. And he had come anyway.

Dawg left them when they reached the hill country.

They had crossed the Colorado River, running wide and clear, washing along its path over the high marble falls of the Llano Uplift. When they saw the clearing, bordered on three sides by the wooded bottomland filled with mesquite, cedar and oaks, lush with range grass and brightened by a carpet of bluebonnets, Chama decided it was the perfect place to spend the night.

He built a campfire in a small depression, and after they had eaten, they fell asleep in each other's arms. Sometime during the night, they heard the lonesome call of a coyote, and when they woke the next morning, Dawg was gone.

"He will return," Chama said, lifting the tin coffeepot off the coals and pouring a hot stream of coffee into his cup. "It is the mating season, and he is lonesome. But when it is time, he will come back." A gust of wind whipped through Chama's dark hair as he put the coffeepot back down on the coals and sipped at his coffee.

"We can't wait for him," she said. "We have to go on."

"It makes no difference," he answered, slanting a narrowed glance toward a grove of nearby trees. "Dawg is smart enough to find you."

She noticed he'd said the dog would find her. Obviously he didn't expect to be there. The thought brought pain to her heart.

But she had no time to worry about it, for the skin at the back of her neck prickled uneasily. She had the uncanny feeling they were being watched, and that Chama knew. He continued to sip at the hot coffee, but she noticed his gaze slide cautiously toward the fallen log where their saddles and supplies were stacked.

And the pistol, she suddenly realized. Chama had laid the pistol in the saddlebag to keep it away from the morning dew.

His eyes seemed to send a signal as he splashed the dregs of his coffee onto the dirt beside the fire, set his cup down and stood, slowly, almost leisurely unfolding his big frame.

Chama drifted to the fallen log, settled himself beside the stack of supplies where he could reach the pistol and guardedly watch the grove of trees, his legs sprawled in front of him.

Unable to sit still wondering what he had seen, Mary

Elizabeth rose to her feet and moved toward the campfire. "Is there any coffee left?" she asked casually, reaching for the coffeepot.

"Some," he replied.

Picking up the cup he'd abandoned, she swirled the coffeepot absently, listening to the slosh of coffee against the sides, but intent on studying the grove of trees he seemed so interested in.

"I am going for a swim while you pack and make ready to leave," Chama said, rising to his feet.

Even while Mary Elizabeth poured the unwanted coffee, she noticed Chama now held the pack that contained the pistol. She brought the cup to her mouth, pretending to sip at the hot brew, while her heart beat fast with trepidation.

Chama reached the riverside, seemed to be measuring the depth of the river, then headed farther upstream, near the grove of trees.

Mary Elizabeth jerked around as a twig snapped behind her. The hair at the base of her neck stood on end with fear. Another crack sent her gaze scurrying toward the ground, in time to see a frog leap across a fallen limb that blocked its way to the river.

Coward! She uttered a short laugh, quickly smothered when she heard a heavy crashing somewhere inside the grove of trees. A shout was followed by the sound of a shot, and she dropped the coffee cup. The tin cup struck a rock, but she barely heard the clatter it made. Her ears were tuned to the sound of cries, shots and branches snapping.

Finding she could wait no longer, she started forward. Whatever had happened, Chama was in the middle of it, and she would not leave him alone.

Chapter Twenty-seven

Mary Elizabeth sprinted across the clearing as Chama burst from the grove of cedars.

"Comanches!" he shouted, sending another shot into the woods. "Get the horses and ride!"

Sheer black fright swept through her, and she stood frozen to the spot. *God, no!* her mind screamed. *This can't be happening. Not again!*

"Go, Mary Elizabeth! Get Away!"

Chama's voice galvanized her into action. Whirling around, she ran to the horses, made skittish by the noise. Her fingers trembled as they worked at the ropes Chama had used to hobble the horses.

Hurry! Hurry! Hurry! her mind screamed.

After a quick glance over her shoulder, the color swept from her face. Two painted warriors had left the cover of the woods and were racing toward Chama. He fired the pistol, and one of the warriors fell. Another shot halted the other warrior, but only momentarily. Lifting his warclub over his head, he raced toward Chama.

The gray stallion side-stepped nervously, and she

grabbed for its reins. She couldn't lose the horses. If she did, then all would be lost. Clutching the reins of both horses in her left hand, she leapt on the gelding and dug her heels into its side, urging the animal forward, toward Chama and the attacking Comanche warrior.

Chama sent off another shot and downed the Comanche, but two more took his place, then three more and another and another.

Mary Elizabeth's eyes widened in horror. Was the whole Comanche nation attacking them?

"Go, Fire Woman!" Chama shouted, springing on the back of the stallion. "Ride hard and don't look back!"

She didn't once think of disobeying him.

Bending low over the gelding, she rode as she'd never ridden before, her heart pounding in time with the gelding's hooves. The wind caught her hair and sent it swirling around her shoulders in a wild, fiery dance.

Close behind, she could hear the clatter of unshod Indian ponies as they raced across hard-baked earth. A quick glance over her shoulder told her that Chama was following close behind.

But only for a moment. Suddenly, even as she watched, his body flinched as an arrow struck him high in the shoulder.

"Chama!" she screamed.

"Go!" he shouted, his body swaying as he tried to hold himself upright.

God! Please don't let this be happening, she cried silently. *We were nearly there. Nearly home.*

Realizing the only way to help Chama was to escape, she dug her heels into the gelding's flanks, urging her mount to even greater speed, shivering with apprehension as one of the war-painted Indians shot ahead of the others. His long black hair flowed in the wind, his lance, trailing rawhide squirrel tails, was thrust forward from his right hand.

Everything seemed to be in slow motion as he drew back his lance and sent it forward, straight toward Chama.

"No!" she screamed.

But it did little good. The lance, tipped with a stone warhead, struck Chama in the back. Mary Elizabeth watched in horror as he toppled from the saddle.

Stop! her heart cried. *Go back! Help him!*

But her mind told her to run. She could not help the fallen warrior. It might be too late to even help herself. But the least she could do was try.

She headed for the distant woods, realizing her only hope was to hide from the warriors who were after her.

But they seemed so close.

Deafening heartbeat.

Thundering hooves.

Blood-curdling war cries.

These were the sum total of her world.

She screamed at the gelding, urging it to greater speed. She had to escape the warriors. She had to.

She was almost to the woods, only another fifty yards, just over that rise. She clenched her teeth to stop their chattering. *Please, God! Let me make it!* she silently cried. *This time, let me make it!*

Her heart lurched as four braves topped the rise, cutting her off from her only hope for survival. Still she refused to give up. Wrenching on the reins, she guided her mount to the west.

But the act put her closer to the Comanches behind

her, and the gelding was already giving everything it had.

And she was alone.

Chama was gone.

His riderless horse attested to that fact.

Suddenly the warriors were no longer behind her but riding alongside and keeping pace with her mount.

Mary Elizabeth turned a terrified face toward the nearest warrior. He was so close that she could see the red and blue paint slashed across his forehead and down his cheeks in the shape of lightning bolts.

His ebony braids were flying in the wind, his face savage and wild. He reached out a bronze-colored arm, his hand wrapping around her reins, and she struck out at him, trying to break his hold.

"Get away," she screamed. "Leave me alone!"

But it was no use. His pony, a well-trained war stallion, was guided by only the slightest pressure from its rider's knees, and it left the warrior's hands free to deal with his enemies. Now he held on grimly, pulling hard on the reins until the gelding faltered and slowed its stride.

The warriors surrounded Mary Elizabeth, and amid the dust and noise, she was dragged from the horse and flung to the ground, landing with a hard thump that succeeded in taking her breath away and snapping her head back. Her head began to spin, and she heard a loud ringing in her ears; spots floated in front of her eyes, and her muscles loosened as consciousness slipped away and she sank into a gray mist.

When Mary Elizabeth regained consciousness, she

was tied belly down across a horse that was splashing through a stream. She found it hard to breathe in that position, and her body ached all over from being jolted and tossed about.

Chama! she silently cried.

But even as she cried his name, she knew there would be no help from him. He had been wounded at least twice, and could even be dead. The thought caused an agonizing pain in her heart.

Chama!

Chama!

Chama!

His name drummed in her heart, just as the pounding of hooves striking against hard-packed ground drummed in her head, over and over again, until she finally welcomed the darkness that swept over her.

Consciousness slowly returned to Mary Elizabeth. Groaning, she opened her eyes and stared up at the star-studded sky. The pale moon wavered fuzzily, and she squinted, attempting to bring it into focus.

Why did her head pound with such vigor? she wondered. And why did her body seem to be a mass of bruises?

She tried to straighten her arms and legs . . . and discovered she couldn't. Strips of rawhide bound her wrists and ankles, making movement next to impossible.

Terror streaked through her as her memory returned, striking her with the force of a hard blow. They had been attacked by a war party of Comanches . . . and Chama was dead.

Grief and despair tore at her, and she felt weighted down by a terrible guilt. It was all her fault! All her fault! She should never have asked him to come to this terrible country. Only selfishness had kept her from taking the stage.

Turning her head, she saw the warriors talking quietly among themselves beside the campfire. One, two . . . she silently counted them . . . Ten!

At that moment, one of the warriors, taller than the rest, looked up and met her gaze. He spoke to his companions in a guttural language she couldn't understand, then rose to his feet and came toward her.

"So . . ." he said, surprising her with his use of English. "My paleface captive has awakened." Kneeling beside her, he cupped her chin in his palm, lifting her face for his inspection. "I am Sky Walker, white woman. I am Comanche. Why do you travel over Comanche land with an Apache warrior?"

Mary Elizabeth jerked her head away from him, trying to hide her inner misery from his probing stare. She felt numb with pain and grief, and her body ached all over; but she would not allow him the satisfaction of seeing her distress. Neither would she answer his questions.

His expression hardened; he was obviously angered by her defiance. Grabbing a handful of copper hair, he gave it a hard yank that sent pain streaking through her scalp and brought tears to her eyes. "Do not try my patience, woman!" he growled. "You are now my captive. And your fate rests in my hands. Although it pleases me that you are a woman of fire, for you will bring me many horses should I decide to sell you, you will show proper respect to your owner."

His head lifted, and he stared across the clearing. "This was a good day," he muttered. "We have taken a prize and captured an enemy. The villagers will be pleased."

Following his gaze, Mary Elizabeth's heart gave a lurch. Across the clearing, spread-eagled between two saplings, was Chama.

Her heart leapt with hope. Chama must be alive! Otherwise, the Comanches would not have bothered to bring him along. But, with her own eyes, she had seen him wounded. He was undoubtedly in a bad way, and it was up to her to help him.

But how could she, bound hand and foot as she was? Her only hope was to trick the Comanches into releasing her.

She curled her lips in contempt and struggled to sit up. "I hope you tortured the Apache dog!" she snarled. "He has been cruel since the day he captured me." She narrowed her eyes, pretending to see more than she did, then she made her voice scornful. "You said you had a prisoner! Do you consider a dead man a prisoner?"

"He is not dead," he said, frowning down at her. "He still breathes."

Mary Elizabeth gave a harsh laugh. "Maybe he does right now," she said, "but he won't last through the night. From the looks of him, he'll bleed to death before the sun rises."

His gaze narrowed on the warrior whose body hung limp, and he seemed to be considering her words. Rising to his feet, he left her and spoke to his companions. Several of them went over to Chama and stood in front of him. Sky Walker lifted Chama's head and looked at him for a long moment, then he dropped it suddenly. Chama's head lolled against the base of his neck.

Sky Walker returned to his companions around the fire. He broke off a section of meat roasting on a spit and brought it to her.

"I can't eat with my hands tied," she said.

Surprisingly, he seemed to agree, for he laid the meat aside on a rock and unfastened the thongs that bound her hands. Her heart thumped loudly in her breast as she took the meat he offered. Although she felt it would choke her, she forced herself to eat it. She couldn't help Chama if she fainted from hunger.

Her mind worked frantically as she ate, devising and discarding plans, trying to find a way to help Chama. She could worry about escape later. At the moment Chama's life hung in the balance.

When she'd finished eating, Sky Walker handed her a water gourd, and she lifted it to her lips, let the water trickle down her throat, then handed it back to him. She offered no resistance when he reached for the leather thong to bind her wrists. Instead, she let her eyes wander across the clearing to the man hanging between the saplings.

"The Apache dog looks dead," she said conversationally. "It feels good to finally get revenge for his cruel treatment." Her gaze was steady as she met his. "Will you carry his body to your village?"

Sky Walker frowned down at her, then looked across the clearing at the warrior. "It is not my wish to take his body to the village," he said. "Hawkeye will want him alive. He cannot feel the pain of Hawkeye's revenge if he is dead."

Hawkeye! God, was it possible there could be two

Comanche warriors called Hawkeye? "Does Hawkeye have a white woman for a bride?" she asked.

"How do you come to know about She-Who-Heals?"

It was the same tribe! If she could get Chama to the village alive, then Johanna could save them.

"When the Apaches learned about the healing powers of She-Who-Heals and stole her from the Comanches, I helped her escape from them. She would be unhappy if harm came to me. As would her husband, Hawkeye."

The warrior's movements had stilled; he seemed to be weighing her words.

God! She must convince them. She must help Chama. Hardening her expression, she said, "I care nothin' for the cruel Apache. When he is tortured, then I will spit on him. But for my friend, She-Who-Heals, I would be willing to keep him alive." She must have been convincing, because she sensed him relaxing.

"You are a healer?" he asked.

"I know how to stop his bleeding," she said.

Seeming to make up his mind, he bent down and worked at the bindings on her ankles.

Mary Elizabeth realized she had won a reprieve. At least for now.

But when she went to Chama, she wondered if she had done any good at all. His face was completely colorless, and blood covered his buckskin shirt.

He looked lifeless.

Chapter Twenty-eight

During the journey to the Comanche village, Chama wavered in and out of consciousness. Although he'd lost a lot of blood, Mary Elizabeth had managed to staunch the bleeding with spider webs.

When they reached the village, the sight was enough to strike terror into her heart. Nearly a hundred tepees were spread out in a clearing, and alerted by the warrior who had been sent ahead, when the war party rode in with their captives the Comanches left their dwellings to witness the warriors' triumphant return.

Hands clutched at her, nails scratching her legs, ripping her clothing as she was pulled off her mount. Panic-stricken, she looked for Chama, but was unable to see over, or around, the wall of human flesh that surrounded her.

Her mouth felt dry, her skin cold and clammy, and terror formed a fist in the pit of her stomach.

Mary Elizabeth's hands were forced together, and leather thongs were tied around her wrists, mercilessly tight. The sound of drums thundered through her head as she was dragged to the center of the compound and fastened to an upright pole.

Her pulse raced with fear, her heart thundering in her breast in time to the pulsating drumbeats, and she strained against the bonds that fastened her wrists to the wooden pole, even though she knew her efforts were useless.

She was poked and prodded and pinched, but she stood with head erect, trying to look brave in the face of the savages.

Suddenly, Sky Walker pushed through the crowd. He spoke sharply, and her tormentors fell back. After assuring himself they had not damaged her person, he strode away and left her standing there.

Mary Elizabeth's knees collapsed beneath her, leaving her hanging by her wrists. She looked around, searching for some sign of a familiar face, but there was none. Where were Hawkeye and Johanna? And what had become of Chama? Had they already killed him?

The thought of his death was almost more than she could bear, even though she realized that he would at least escape the torture they had in store for him if he still lived.

She tried to still her fears, realizing Sky Walker did not mean to kill her. He had said she would be sold or traded. And Mary Elizabeth had discovered long ago that where there was life, there was hope.

But did she want to face a future without Chama?

No! her heart cried. Without Chama, the future could only hold emptiness and despair. For the first time, Mary Elizabeth faced the fact that perhaps she had made a mistake. Perhaps her happiness didn't lie with her brother after all.

With that thought, came another. She would give up

all hope of ever seeing her brother again if she and Chama could return to the cabin in the mountains.

But it was too late.

Tears welled into her eyes, but she blinked them away, knowing the Indians admired bravery and despised any show of weakness. She must never allow them to see her fear.

It seemed hours had passed when a girl with dark-blond braids brought her some water. Mary Elizabeth drank greedily, uncaring that water spilled down her chin. The girl had turned to leave when Mary Elizabeth stopped her with a whispered plea: "Help us."

Although the girl's blue eyes expressed sympathy, she shook her head. "I can do nothing for you."

Despite her efforts at control, a tear found its way down Mary Elizabeth's cheek. "Him," she cried. "Chama. Surely you have some sympathy for us. What happened to the warrior who was with me. Is he . . . dead?"

"Not yet. He was taken to medicine woman to be healed. He is still there."

"Your medicine woman . . . is she called Johanna?"

"That is the name the white-eyes gave her," the girl replied.

"You speak as though you are Comanche, but your blue eyes and blond hair deny it."

The girl lifted her chin, her expression set. "I am Comanche. My name is Naduah. Never again will I answer to the name of Cynthia Ann Parker."

Mary Elizabeth had no time to wonder why Cynthia Ann denied her parentage. Instead, her thoughts were on Chama. Why did the Comanches want him healed? She voiced the question.

"He is our enemy. He must be well enough to feel the pain when he's burned at the stake."

Mary Elizabeth swallowed the bile that rose in her throat. She could only hope that Johanna remained adamant in her refusal to heal Chama. Somehow, she doubted that he could last much longer, and she didn't want his last hours on earth to be filled with pain.

"Would you go to Johanna?" Mary Elizabeth asked. "Tell her Mary Elizabeth is here. Tell her I need help."

She watched the girl leave, then she waited . . . for what seemed an eternity, with the sun beating down on her head, the heat throbbing in time with the drums sounding throughout the village.

God! Help us! she silently prayed. *If he's to die, then let it be quick.*

A shout roused Mary Elizabeth from a near stupor. It was followed by a babble of voices sending fresh alarm surging through her. She twisted around, her gaze falling on several warriors who were dragging a limp body toward her.

"Chama!" she cried.

But there was no answer. He looked more dead than alive as they tied him to the pole standing upright beside Mary Elizabeth.

The sight of his bruised and bleeding body proved to be her undoing. Tears rained down her face. Why hadn't he died? God! Why hadn't he?

As though feeling her anguish, Chama opened his eyes and looked at her. "Be strong," he whispered huskily. "Do not let them see your fear."

Swallowing around the lump in her throat, Mary Elizabeth's gaze locked with his. Even now his thoughts were of her. But how could she be strong in the face of his pain? "Please forgive me," she whispered. "It's all my fault this happened."

"Do not blame yourself." His chest rose and fell with his efforts to draw breath into his body. "Never blame yourself for what has happened."

"Who else is to blame?" she asked. "If we had stayed in the mountains, you would not be . . . dying." The last word was barely a whisper, but she knew it must be said. She loved this man, loved him above all else, and because of her stubbornness, her refusal to accept his love, he would die.

Suddenly a warrior approached, and her bonds were loosened. She jerked her head around, her heart leaping with hope. Perhaps they'd reconsidered and were letting them go.

The young girl with the blond braids reappeared beside her. "She-Who-Heals demands that you be released, and Hawkeye has heard her words. You will not have to watch the torture."

But what about Chama?

"Please," she said, aware there was little time. "Go to her. Tell her I must see her! Quickly."

Hands were on Mary Elizabeth, dragging her toward a tepee as the girl turned away, moving slowly in the opposite direction. Didn't she realize how desperate the situation was?

Hurry!
Hurry!
Hurry!

The words resounded in her head as Mary Elizabeth was dragged closer to the tepee. She glanced back at Chama to see that he had gone limp and the blows aimed at him by the women and children would not be felt. He would not be conscious of the pain they were inflicting on his already bruised body.

They had nearly reached the tepee when she became aware of the commotion. The racket had been covered by all the other noise, the loud yells, the sound of the beating drums. The crowd had parted to allow a small dark-haired woman through.

"Johanna!" Mary Elizabeth cried. "Thank God! It is you!"

The girl hurried toward her. "Mary Elizabeth," she said, gathering the younger girl in her arms. "I would have come sooner, but Hawkeye has just returned and the others would not allow me to leave my dwelling."

"They've got Chama!" Mary Elizabeth cried. "You've got to help him."

"I can't," Johanna said. "As soon as Hawkeye returned, I tried to make him put a stop to this madness. But he won't listen to me."

"You must do something."

"I did the best I could for him by doing nothing. Chama is gravely wounded. He won't live through the night. Be grateful he will be spared the torture of death by fire."

Mary Elizabeth looked back at Chama. How could she be glad about his death?

"This is a part of my husband's culture that grieves me," Johanna said. "But I can do nothing. It is the way of his people. We punish our lawbreakers by putting them in prisons or choking the life out of them with a rope around their necks. Is it less cruel than the Comanche way of punishing their enemies?"

"How can you ask that?" Mary Elizabeth cried. "How can you stand to live here with them?"

"I love my husband," Johanna said. "Now come to my tepee and rest."

Mary Elizabeth allowed herself to be led to the tepee with the hawk painted on the side. She was racked with agony, knowing Chama's only hope was to die before the Comanches tortured him. If only she could cry, give vent to her pain. She felt Johanna's sympathetic gaze, saw her beckon to the warrior who guarded the entrance.

"Bring Hawkeye to me," Johanna said.

Moments later a dark-haired man dressed in fringed buckskins entered the dwelling. His features were sharply cut, and he had the blackest eyes Mary Elizabeth had ever seen; but what caught and held her attention was the fact that he looked more like a gunfighter than an Indian. Heavily armed, he wore a double holster fastened to a wide belt around his waist, and a big-bladed bowie knife rested in a sheath behind the left-hand Colt. Ignoring Mary Elizabeth, he looked at his wife.

"You sent for me?"

"Yes," Johanna said. "Hawkeye, you owe Mary Elizabeth a debt for helping me escape from the Apaches."

"I know," he said. "But I cannot give her the warrior's life. He knew the risk he was taking when he came to our land, knew he would forfeit his life if we found him." He shook his head. "I'm sorry, little one. I cannot show weakness before my people. And to give in to a woman's pleas would be taken as such. Ask anything else of me, but not that."

"I don't want anything else from you," she told him. "Nothing but the warrior's life."

"Be reasonable, Johanna. He kidnapped you. Took

you away from here. It was only luck that I ever found you again. How could you want him to live?"

"Mary Elizabeth loves him," Johanna said. "Surely you understand that."

"Of course I understand, Johanna. But my hands are tied. The people would not follow a weak leader. I have a duty to them, and I will honor it."

"Then, get out of here!" she snapped. "Let Mary Elizabeth have some time alone with her grief."

"Don't be angry with me, Johanna. I only do what I must."

"Hawkeye," Mary Elizabeth said. "If you won't set him free, at least let me stay with him for the few hours left."

"No," he said gruffly. "I can only spare you the pain of seeing him die." Without another word, he turned and left them alone.

"Wait," Johanna whispered. "When night falls, the villagers will sleep. Then we'll try to set him free."

The hours seemed to be endless while they waited.

Darkness cloaked the village, and the crowd dispersed one by one. When no one was left except the guards, Johanna attempted to leave the dwelling and was stopped at the entrance.

Mary Elizabeth tried to push past the guard, but was met with resistance. Fire illuminated the compound, and her eyes went to the man tied to the pole. As she watched, he lifted his head and stared directly at her. His lips tried to form a smile, and she swallowed around a lump in her throat.

Suddenly there was a movement in her peripheral vision. She narrowed her gaze on the dog, barely visible in the pale light of the moon, that crept toward Chama

308

No one paid it any attention . . . except Mary Elizabeth. Her heart skipped a beat as she saw the scruffy-looking German shepherd, coat matted with dirt and twigs, move quietly behind Chama. Lifting its head, the animal seemed to be licking the warrior's bound hands . . . over and over again.

Dawg had found them. And unless Mary Elizabeth was mistaken, he was chewing away at the bonds that held Chama prisoner.

"Johanna," she whispered. "Is it true that you have the power to heal?"

"It is not my power," Johanna said. "The gift comes from a higher being than myself."

"Yes. But can you do it?"

"Sometimes."

"Will you try to heal Chama if he is free?"

Johanna whirled around, saw the dog behind Chama and whispered, "We must get to the woods behind him. If he can reach us there, perhaps you will get away. Come on," the girl said, taking her friend's arm. When the guard moved to stop her, she held up a hand. "We are going to the river to bathe," she said in the Comanche tongue. "My husband would be angry if you try to stop us."

The guard fell back, allowing the girls to leave. Only moments later they had retrieved Chama and Mary Elizabeth's mounts from the rope corral and were waiting when Chama stumbled weakly toward them, Dawg at his side. Fear for him tightened Mary Elizabeth's throat. His chest heaved with the effort he expended trying to fill his lungs with air. When he tripped and fell, she hurried forward and dropped to her knees beside him, vaguely aware of Johanna joining her.

Becoming aware of a change in the rhythm of hi breathing, Mary Elizabeth turned to the girl beside her. "Help him, Johanna," she pleaded.

Johanna spread her hands across his breastbone and closed her eyes. Her head fell forward, and Mary Elizabeth knew something was happening. Although Johanna's head was bowed, her body quivered as though she'd released some kind of energy and set it traveling through her body until it surged forth, pulsing through her extremities. It seemed to flow over the wounded flesh as her hands moved lightly over Chama's chest and shoulders. At first there was no visible change, then suddenly the warrior's breathing became easier, less ragged, and his violated body relaxed.

When Johanna fell back on her haunches with her arms hanging limply at her sides, looking drained and exhausted, Mary Elizabeth stared at her in awe. How could such a thing be possible? She had heard the tales of Johanna's gift, but until now she had been sceptical. Never again, she told herself. Realizing there was no way she could express her gratitude, Mary Elizabeth kissed Johanna's forehead. As she watched Chama rise to his feet, Mary Elizabeth blinked and stared. Then feeling completely amazed at Chama's miraculous recovery, she mounted her horse. With Chama and Dawg at her side, Mary Elizabeth rode away from the Comanche village.

Chapter Twenty-nine

They rode hard through the night, and by the time dawn brought a rosy blush to the eastern horizon, they had put at least forty miles between them and the Comanche village. Mary Elizabeth felt in awe of Chama's endurance. He seemed tireless while she slumped wearily over the gelding.

"Hadn't we better keep going?" she asked when Chama pulled the stallion up in the shadows of a wooded hill.

"No," he said, pulling his mount up nearby. "You are weary. We will stop to rest."

"But they may be after us," she protested.

"It makes no difference," he said. "They will never find us where we are going."

Dismounting, he took her reins and led the horses up the side of the wooded hill, picking his way over granite rocks, through cedar brakes growing so thick the way looked impassable. When they reached the top of the hill, Chama stopped and tied the reins of both animals to a tree.

"Wait here," he said.

Feeling too tired to do anything else, Mary Elizabet[h] watched him stride toward a granite rock overlookin[g] the valley they had just left. Shading his eyes with hi[s] hand, he searched for any sign of movement in the dis[-]tance. A moment later, he left the rock and rejoined he[r].

"All is well," he said. "There is no sign of our enem[y]. We will go to a cave I found on my journey here man[y] moons ago. We will be able to rest in safety there."

Rest? How could she possibly rest until they were ou[t] of this godforsaken country. The whole Comanche na[-]tion wanted to kill him! *No!* She could never know peac[e] of mind until they were away from this place, back in th[e] hidden valley on the mountaintop. *But you'll never go back* a silent voice said. *You'll be living with Brother Jeb.*

No! she silently argued. *I don't know where Jeb is. It's to[o] dangerous to search for him. We must return to the mountains.*

She felt a weight leave her shoulders as she made th[e] decision. She'd tell Chama in the morning.

A musky smell emanated from the cave. "It's the bats[,]" Chama explained. "They live inside and come out a[t] night. Although the cavern is large, it is riddled wit[h] holes at the top. We will not need a torch while the su[n] lights the sky."

Whining softly, Dawg followed them into the shadow[y] interior, keeping close to Mary Elizabeth. They ha[d] only gone a short distance when the passageway opene[d] onto a large cavern measuring about twenty feet in cir[-]cumference. Farther on, Mary Elizabeth saw anothe[r] tunnel leading off the main cavern.

"We will leave the horses here," Chama said.

After fastening the reins to an outcrop of rock, the[y] entered the passageway which ran for a short distanc[e] before opening up into a smaller cave. Toward the bac[k] was yet another tunnel. Chama told her it led to the other side of the mountain and would act as a natural flue to carry the smoke from their campfire away from them.

Mary Elizabeth, weary beyond belief, slumped to the ground and only moments later was fast asleep.

It was morning when she woke. Her lashes fluttered, then slowly lifted. She was immediately aware of the silence.

"Chama!" she cried, leaping to her feet, her gaze searching the small cave for the warrior.

Dawg, although having been asleep, was instantly on all fours beside her. Whining softly, it lifted its nose and queried the air for intruders.

"Chama!" she cried again. "Where are you?"

Silence was her only answer.

She hurried through the passageway, with Dawg keeping pace beside her. When she reached the outer cavern, she stopped short. *Chama's stallion is gone!* Her gaze fell on her mount, placidly munching on the grass the warrior had obviously gathered for him.

"Chama! Where are you?" Rushing through the tunnel to the brightness outside, she scrambled on top of the granite boulder, shading her eyes to search for him.

Nothing moved within her range of vision. Where was Chama? Why had he left her? Cupping her hands over her mouth, she called, "Chaaaamaaa!"

A covey of quail lifted out of the bushes nearby, startling a rabbit which fled from the noise, racing across a small meadow and diving beneath the cover of a concealing bush.

But there was no human movement. No sound indicated she'd been heard. Why had Chama left without a

313

word.

She had a quick and disturbing thought. Suppose he hadn't left voluntarily. Suppose the Comanches had come into the cavern while they slept and taken him away. In her mind's eye, she saw Chama bound to the stake. The fearful image built in her mind until she saw flames leaping and coiling around him, his body twisting and turning in agony.

She had worked herself into a state by the time he returned, and he had no more than slid from the stallion when she rounded on him. "What do you mean by leaving without a word?" she demanded.

He put his arms around her, but she pulled away. "Leave me alone!" she cried. "You had no right to leave me that way! No right at all! Where have you been?"

His gaze hardened. "You are overwrought, therefore I refuse to take offense at your words."

"I'm not overwrought!" she yelled. "I'm angry! Where have you been? We're in Comanche country. If you don't care about your own damned hide, then you should at least think about mine. Don't you know what will happen if they catch us again? There's no way in hell Johanna could help either one of us! Is this your way of getting rid of me?"

"Why should I want to get rid of you? You owe me a hundred horses."

"Horses! Horses!" she raged. "That's all you can think about. Your damned horses! If you weren't so set on traipsing around the countryside, you'd find my brother and he'd give you the horses. Then you could go back to the mountains and forget about me."

"I found your brother," he said quietly.

His words stunned her. For a moment she couldn't

314

speak. Then, "You found Jeb?" Her voice was a ragged whisper.

"Yes. Not far from here. It would be dangerous to travel now. We will leave just before dawn."

Mary Elizabeth's legs felt weak, unable to support her. Reaching out, she steadied herself against the cavern wall. *No!* her heart cried. *Don't leave me!* But she made no outward protest, gave no sign of her distress.

"I returned to the place where we were attacked and picked up what was left of our supplies," he said. "Most of them were gone, but they missed the pack in the bushes."

"Are we so close to the Llano River, then?" she asked, fear streaking through her. "You shouldn't have taken a chance on returning there."

"We needed the supplies."

He remained silent while she prepared the rabbit he had brought with him, skewered it over the fire, then turned to him. "Did you see my brother?"

"Yes." He rose to his feet. "There is a stream nearby if you would like to bathe."

She nodded silently, took fresh clothing from the pack and followed him to the stream. But instead of joining her in the water, he left her there alone.

Did he no longer desire her? she wondered as she watched him walk away into the woods.

The question was uppermost in her mind when darkness shrouded the land and he spread two blankets several feet apart, bid her good night, then rolled up in one with his back to her, seeming intent on sleep.

Was he bent on cheating her of their one last night together? It would seem so. Dammit! How could he do this to her. He had made her love him, and now he couldn't wait to be rid of her? Hurt stabbed at her, expressing itself in anger. Well, she'd damn well see about that!

Stripping her garments away, she knelt naked beside him. He stiffened when she gripped his shoulder.

"Are you angry with me?"

"No," he grated, barely turning his head to acknowledge her. When his gaze touched on her naked shoulders, he sucked in a sharp breath as though he'd been struck in the middle with a club. His gaze dipped to the creamy swell of her breasts, lingering for a moment before sweeping down to her rounded hips. When his gaze met hers again, she saw a smoldering flame.

Encouraged, she slipped her fingers inside his shirt and lightly stroked his naked flesh. "Stop." His voice was harsh, sounding almost pained.

Ignoring him, she fumbled unsteadily at the lacings on his buckskin shirt. Fingers of steel wrapped around her wrist, effectively staying her hand.

But Mary Elizabeth refused to be deterred. Leaning over, she placed a wet kiss on his chin, then began trailing moist kisses across his neck. When she met with no resistance, she pushed his shirt up and closed her mouth over one flat male nipple.

"Fire Woman," he groaned. "You must not."

Feeling encouraged, she moved to the other nipple and laved it with her tongue. His breath became harsh, raspy, and she pushed the shirt higher, nipping and biting at the skin with her teeth.

He groaned again, his body becoming hard with tension, but still he didn't try to push her away.

Emboldened, she pushed the shirt over his head and fitted her naked body against his. His arms found their way around her, and he buried his mouth in the crook of her neck. But she would have none of it; she wasn't fin-

316

ished with him. She worked her hand into his trousers until she felt his hardness. Then, taking him in her hand, she stroked his silky skin.

He muttered harshly, his teeth nipping at her neck. She continued to stroke him until he pushed at her, trying to get more distance between them. Realizing he was trying to get his trousers off, she hurried to help him, and when they were finally cast aside, she trailed wet kisses over his waist, dipped her tongue into his navel and continued her downward path. She was determined that he would have a hard time forgetting her.

With an oath, he pulled her upright and pushed her down, fitting his body over hers. And then he was plunging into her over and over again, until they were both crying out their release.

Then she lay in his arms as he spoke softly to her. She could hear his love for her in the sound of his voice, could feel it as well as hear it. It reached out to her, surrounding her like the velvety wings of a butterfly, wrapping in soft circles around her body. Tears welled into her eyes, brimming over and rolling softly down her cheeks.

"Why do you weep?" he asked.

She could not answer him. How could she? Would she say the tears were because she could not bear to lose him? She knew as well as he did that the white men would never allow them to live in their world. Neither could they return to his tribe.

If they stayed together, they would be outcasts from the rest of the world, and she could never ask that of him; so she remained silent, and they fell asleep in each other's arms.

The next morning they stood on the hill overlooking her brother's farm. As they watched, a man with dark red hair stepped out the door, a cup in one hand. He sat on the edge of the porch and sipped at the contents. He'd only been there for a moment when he was joined by a toddler with the same red hair. Picking the child up, he cradled it in his arms. A moment later he was joined by a petite blond woman.

Mary Elizabeth knew without a doubt the man was her brother Jeb. Her eyes misted with tears as she watched him cuddle the child in his arms. It was obvious Jeb was content with his life.

"Go!" Chama ordered in a ragged voice. "There is your brother. Go to him."

Mary Elizabeth's eyes darkened with pain. Her throat was dry, her body trembling. "It . . . it wouldn't be right," she said, her heart thudding in her ears. "I owe you."

His face was still, his gaze watchful, waiting. "What do you mean?"

God! It was awful! What did he want from her? Didn't he know she was dying inside? Did he want her to beg? Well, she wouldn't! "What about the horses you paid for me?" Her voice was sharp, her expression strained.

"You need worry no more about the debt."

Her lips tightened; her nostrils flared. "I am honor bound to stay with you until the debt is paid!"

"Your brother does not have a hundred horses," Chama said. "I have seen only two."

She reined her horse around. "Then, we have finished here. We will return to the mountains now."

Something undefinable flickered across his face, and his dark eyes held a strange gleam. Gripping her mount's reins, he pulled her up short. "The horses are a gift."

A rosy blush stained her cheeks. "Are you trying to

318

shame me?" she demanded. "I've done nothing to deserve such a gift." Her eyes glittered as she held his gaze. "I tell you there is nothing left to do except stay with you."

He seemed to focus on her desperation. "What do you want of me?" he asked in a ragged voice.

Surely he knew! *God! Does he want blood?* Gathering together every shred of her self-control, she swallowed hard and whispered, "Please. No more."

He was tense, waiting. "You must tell me."

Mary Elizabeth's pulse hammered violently. She had thought to salvage some of her pride by pretending the bride-price was her reason for staying with him. But he seemed bent on stripping her of every ounce of pride that she possessed. "I was a fool to come here," she whispered unsteadily. "I could never be happy without you. Don't make me stay."

His eyes glittered. "Is it so hard to say the words?"

She swallowed hard and nodded her head.

He sighed. "You would become an outcast."

"I don't care," she said shakily. "I only want to be with you. Please don't make me stay with Jeb. We could go back to the cabin in the Sangre de Cristo Mountains. You said yourself everything we need to have a good life together is there."

Reaching out, he tilted her face toward him. His eyes were dark, loving. "Will you not tell me how you feel?"

"I have!"

"No. Why is it so hard to admit you love me?"

As though a dam had burst, the words came tumbling out. "I do! I do, Chama. I love you. I love you."

"And I love you," he said huskily, pulling her into his arms and kissing her face, her eyes, her nose, her lips. "It has been like ripping the heart from my body to bring

319

you here," he grated. "I was tempted to say your brother was dead. But I couldn't. Your happiness means everything to me."

"Then, take me with you," she said, holding his gaze. "And please, don't ever let me go."

"Never," he promised, his lips covering hers in a wildly exultant kiss. She returned it with fervor. Although the journey was long, they would return to the cabin in the mountains. And they would live out their life together. . . .

Forever.